DEAD FINE

Also by the author:

GUIDED
WASTED
MIDNIGHT SHERBET

DEAD FINE

DEAD FINE

emmasmithbooks.com

for those who fell
victim to first love

wtf is happening???

why are there police
outside your block?

wdy think?

they know, owen

are you okay???

i'm fine

dead fine

THE BEGINNING

I'm in the bath when the police knock on our front door.

I don't know why I jump so much, dropping my bodywash on the floor with a clatter. It's a cheap, lemony kind, and yellow liquid oozes over the floorboards and down the cracks by the skirting board. I don't know why I'm surprised at all. It's not like I wasn't *expecting* them to call; just not now, not this soon.

I still shiver when Mum calls up the stairs. A loud, "Lilz! Lily! Get down here!"

"I'm in the bath!"

She knows that, of course. But it doesn't matter.

I take my time getting dried, listening to the drone of voices drifting upstairs. Mum, increasingly panicked, and the police, calm, collected. Two men, I think, different to the community officers who led the programme for troubled kids Owen was part of in year eight or nine. Proper officers, serious ones. The kind you call when someone has gone missing, when a child commits suicide… or when a dead body is found in the woods, an adult female, probably already starting to decompose.

I check my phone, still patting my hair. There are three new messages. One from Loz, my best friend, asking if she should buy the white Nike Air Force she saw on Depop, or the pink Jordans she spotted down the market in Nottingham a few weeks ago. I don't know why she ever bothers asking me. It's not as if I have experience in making such choices…

I'm lucky if Primark has decent dupes.

The other two are from Owen.

Owen, whose name still has a pink heart emoji beside it – and an aubergine.

Owen, my boyfriend of five years, almost. Owen, who's so much a part of my soul that he rarely ever messages me, only ever calls, and even then, only in a crisis.

wtf is happening???
why are there police outside your block?

My flat – flat being a very loose term – is a two-floor "apartment" on an estate at the edge of Vibbington, near the secondary school. Owen lives in a proper block of flats, five storeys high with mould crawling on the walls and wood rot in the cupboards. His front door faces mine, just a stretch of tarmac separating the two.

I swallow, fingering my phone. My nails skim the keyboard, but I don't press send. I painted them green at the start of this week, because green is supposed to relieve stress, help with nerves. Over the last month or so, my room has slowly filled up with all shades of the colour. Even my walls are green – English sage, it said on the tin.

"Lilz!" Mum calls again, more urgent this time. "Get your bum down here!"

"I'm coming, gimme a sec!"

My pyjamas are on the floor, next to the clothes I wore to work… when I last went in, that is. A black hoodie, as required, and a pair of Mum's old flares which didn't fit her when she last cleared out her wardrobe. I pull the hoodie back on, a pair of flares, stick my feet into flip-flops. My clothes reek of sweat, of burger fat and cheese-on-toast.

"*Lilz!*"

I brush my hair – not for any reason. Ten strokes, five on each side. My hair is long and straight and blonde, the kind of pale yellow which will eventually fade to white. There's still crusty mascara on my lashes.

They're in the living room. I can hear them as I open the bathroom door, make my way down the stairs. Mum hasn't made them tea, probably because we're out of teabags, and Dizzy, my little sister (actually Daisy, but no one ever calls her that), has left her dirty socks on the bottom step for somebody else to clear up. I kick them out of the way, crunching my knuckles. The door is ajar. I can see a fluorescent vest, vibrant yellow, big, black shoes.

The officers look up as I enter, standing to greet me, giving semi-friendly nods. They introduce themselves as Puck and Barker. Both Puck and Barker look too young to be doing this kind of work, clutching their walkie-talkies and gesturing for me to sit. I go to the sofa, where Mum is perched, face creased with anger – or worry.

"Lily Dart?" Puck – or maybe Barker – asks, trying to smile but resorting to a grimace. "We have some questions for you."

I nod, trying to act calm, collected, like I don't know what they're talking about and don't really care.

"Okay?" I say. "Okay."

"We found a body in the woods this morning, on the other side of Vibbington," Barker tells me, but the words, the *specifics* of them, fall on deaf ears. I already know what he's going to say, what he's trying to tell me. "An adult female, presumed to be in her early forties. We're still trying to identify her, but given the state of the body and how long it's been there, it might take some time."

Wait.

The body hasn't yet been identified?

I freeze, trying to keep my expression neutral, but my heart's racing and my mind is whirring.

If the body hasn't been identified, why are they here?

Why have they come to speak to *me*?

This wasn't part of the plan. The plan was that the police would come to me *after* they identified the body, after speaking to those close to her. That's how it works, right? I thought they'd figure out my connection to the deceased and call on our flat on the off-chance I might have information, that they could call me a *suspect*.

Puck takes over, frowning. "The reason we're here, Lily, is because a jumper was left tied round her body. A school jumper, with a Vibbington Secondary School and Sixth Form logo. Your name was written in the label. Lily Dart."

My name was written in the label.

Of *course*.

I glance at Mum, face turning more and more crimson by the moment. She's staring back, eyes wide.

Every school year, since I first started at Vibbington Secondary almost six years ago, Mum has written my name in the label of all our school jumpers. There are a whole pile in Dizzy's drawer. She wears mine now – they're too expensive to buy new. I grabbed one that night because I assumed a school jumper would be impossible to identify, as all the kids in Vibbington wear the same. I completely forgot they were *labelled*.

"Do you have any way to explain this?"

I turn back to the officers, mouth gaping.

"I…"

"I think we need to continue this conversation down the station," Puck says, turning to Mum. "Ms Dart, if you could find someone to supervise your youngest daughter while you both –"

"No."

Puck and Barker turn to stare at me, startled. Barker stands first, taking a step towards me.

"If you're refusing to cooperate…"

"No, I'm not refusing to cooperate." I glance at Mum. She still looks bewildered, frown lines on her forehead more evident than ever. "I know who the body is. And I know who killed her, and how."

Puck and Barker are serious now, poised to grab me – do *something* to me, should I be having them on – and stand, hands on their belts, as I stare back.

"It was Owen Sharpley." My voice is cool, level.

I don't feel cool, or level.

I want to cry, to crumble, but I can't. I *won't*.

"Owen Sharpley?" Barker echoes. "Is that someone you know?"

"He's my boyfriend." I take a deep breath. "The body you found is… is his mum's."

@thereallilzdart

one day, we'll
all be... dust

THE BODY

The body. Owen's mum. My boyfriend, a body, and *his dead mum*.

You're probably wondering how we ended up here. How we got to September third, a few days before heading back to sixth form, about to start year thirteen. The police in my living room, telling me they've found a body, that my old school jumper was wrapped around it, Lily Dart in the label. Me grassing up Owen, my boyfriend of five years, the love of my life. Grassing up Owen Sharpley, *who killed his own mum*.

You're probably wondering whether that's true. Was it Owen? Was it somebody else?

Was it *me*?

You don't know me. You don't know if you can trust what I say, or what I don't say. You don't know how much I lie.

Not yet, anyway.

Before you do, there's a whole tale to it, a fairy-tale, one of flip-flops and fried eggs and disgrace. One final summer's worth of scandal to sift through before we uncover the truth, before we're back to September, the beginning and the end. Only three months passed between things being okay and everything turning on its head, the police knock-knock-knocking on my door after finding the body.

The body. Saying that still feels surreal.

Is this making much sense to you? It shouldn't. It shouldn't to *me*, and yet it does.

Let's take it back three months ago, to June. Back then,

you could say my life was normal; it wouldn't be a lie. I was just Lilz Dart, Lily to my teachers, Lilz to anyone who mattered, seventeen-and-a-half, an ordinary teenager, the kind to partake in underage drinking and terrible parties and discos on the beach at midnight. Three months ago, I liked poppy trash from the early noughties, grungier stuff found in the darkest depths of the internet, black clothes, lip gloss, so much eyeliner I could've drowned in it. I was happy, confident, totally not failing my A-levels (just one, but who cares about psychology?).

Three months ago, I used to paint for fun. Not many people know that about me. Dark stuff, canvases covered in black splatters and scratch marks, the kind of artwork teens create when they've never experienced *real* hardship in their life and therefore create one through paint.

Three months ago, I liked playing Call of Duty on Owen's computer, dancing in the rain, skinny dipping in the sea. Three months ago, I could've sat in Loz's room for hours on end, chatting shit and painting her nails her favourite shade of purple. She'd just moved to Nottingham and was in the process of breaking up with her boyfriend, and that was the biggest drama in my life, the only shred of instability tipping the balance.

Three months ago, I had a sweet tooth.

Now, too much sugar makes me sick.

Three months ago, I was so deep in love with my boyfriend, whatever definition of "love" I thought was real. I thought Owen was a part of me, that I needed him to survive. We were so comfortable with each other that his presence was just a given, his support inevitable. I loved him; he loved me. And now?

You'll find out, I guess.

But back to the body.

It's not really as dramatic as it sounds. It *seemed* it at the time, though. The body, a lump of flesh, a murdered clump of cells. Blood, and bleach, and body bags – or bin bags, should I say, the black kind Mum keeps in the top drawer, by the microwave. And the bath. It's still stained red, fading to orange. Owen only showers here now. Who wouldn't?

Owen Sharpley. Brown hair, dark eyes, a permanent frown etched onto his pale face. Soft curves, freckled arms, white skin. Not good at maths or science, only failing slightly more than me in psychology. Owen Sharpley, notorious around the estate and at school for being untouchable, invincible. He wasn't popular, not really *liked*, but half the girls were in love with him, the boys all in awe.

He could've had his pick of anyone in school, even Loz. I remember Chloe Alize, our year's "It Girl" before she dropped out after year eleven, asking him out when we were on a year seven residential. He never told anyone but me. All the pretty girls liked him, the popular ones… and the nerds, the alternative kids, the K-pop fangirls.

But he chose me, Lilz, on a rainy day in October, at the start of year eight. Me, Lilz, who'd been best friends with him since we were four or five, when Owen and his mum were housed in the block opposite ours by the council. Me, Lilz, tomboy and self-proclaimed chav, heavily dyslexic and – not as a consequence but as an unfortunate coincidence – unintelligent. He chose me for reasons I'll never understand, for reasons which will always seem *novel*.

I used to think I'd do anything for Owen.

And when that was tested, I really did do anything, *everything*.

Young love is stupid. Crazy. Dumb. It's heavy, hot, like a

disposable barbecue that lingers and simmers, under the surface, long after it's burnt out. Back then, it was having sex in Owen's bedroom while his mum was at bingo, snogging by the school gates day in, day out, thinking we were invincible, that we'd last forever. Feeling his bare skin against mine and wanting the feeling to go on and on and on, spending so many years getting to know each crevice of a person that you become sure they're made for you, that their body is yours to keep.

Top tip: don't get a boyfriend when you're twelve. And if you do, make sure you don't still have that same boyfriend when you're seventeen.

Even if it lasts, it'll only end in tears.

I sound like a psycho. Bitter, regretful. Like all my memories with Owen were terrible, a mistake.

They weren't. If it wasn't for Owen, Lilz wouldn't exist today. Owen *made* me. He shaped me, twisted me from the meek blonde girl at the back of the classroom into someone sharper, tougher. The kind of girl who could stand up for herself, who was strong, snarky, mean, who didn't care what people thought, who held respect for her. Still a good person, at heart – with a solid moral compass, great incentive – but a hardened version, a nice girl with a not-so-lovely shell.

He melded me into the girl I was that day when the police came, September third. The girl who could tell them, quietly, calmly, that it was Owen, that it was *all* Owen, that it was all her boyfriend Owen.

I'm still not making sense, am I? It's okay – I'm confused, too.

To summarise, it was June, three months ago, when everything started to go wrong. It was June, and everything was perfect. The sun was shining, Loz was back from

Nottingham for a few weeks to stay with family, and us and the rest of our friends were spending every other day at the beach, lounging about and playing games and swimming under the cool sun.

Then there was me, and a phonecall, and Owen, and his bathtub.

His bathtub, and the body laid in it.

THE PROMISE

We went to the beach on June first. Owen, Loz, Kara, Gethin and I.

Owen drove. He'd just passed his test, days after we finished year twelve "officially" for the summer. We still had to go in for classes but our mocks were behind us, and the summer stretched ahead in a cool line of beach days and ice lollies and parties, sun beaming as far as the forecast could predict. Global warming was at its peak, and we couldn't have happier about it.

We parked on the front, then wandered all the way up the beach with our blankets and the remainder of our McDonald's breakfast to the stretch of sand and rocks and endless blue sea at Maythorpe beach. Owen held the umbrella. We always used that umbrella, the one Kara's mum had on her patio until she bought a fancy integrated table-and-canopy set. Loz and I carried the picnic between us.

It's funny how I remember that morning so well. After that, the first few days of June are a haze. A hot, bubble-wrapped haze, one of laughter and love and salty chips on the sand, a template for every day to follow. Looking back is like trying to see into a dream, to pick apart why the events just don't add up, make sense. How they could be so perfect, in contrast to what happened *after*?

Maybe that's why June first is so clear. It laid out the rules, teased us with a promise of what summer could look like, should we be good.

Spoiler: we weren't good. None of us were "good" at all.

Spoiler: I'm going to give you a *lot* of spoilers.

I remember Loz lying down on her towel, first, Gethin just beside her, his arm a little too close to her bikini-clad bum. Kara had a fag in her mouth and was frowning into her phone, tip-tapping at the screen. Owen and I shared a blanket, placed it on the sand just close enough to the sea that we could dip our toes in. It was still technically spring, but the whole coast was scorching. The BBC had painted the countryside a stark shade of red.

"Can you rub sun cream on my back?"

That was Kara, tapping Owen on the shoulder and artfully speaking through her ciggie, the conniving bitch. Owen just shrugged and nodded, reaching over to grab the bottle. He pulled a face at me as though to say, "Could she be more obvious?"

I smiled, smoothing white lotion over my own pale arms and legs. For all Kara fake-tanned, she burnt just as badly as me in the sun. She had the same complexion as me, only with darker, longer hair, legs and arms just as spindly and mottled… not that you could tell.

Leaning back, I felt Loz's hand absent-mindedly stroke my hair, a smile no doubt on her face. I could hear her eyes rolling without looking at her.

Loz never burnt, ever. She still doesn't, obviously. Even when we were kids and would go swimming in the baths just outside Vibbington, Loz would turn a pearly shade of brown within the first half hour, even *without* sun cream. Loz is like that. Effortless, easy. Everything comes naturally to her.

"Pass me a Venom, Lilz."

Chucking her our favourite brand of energy drink from the cool box, I watched as she opened it with her pinky-purple talons and took a long, cold sip.

Loz's perfect tan was only the beginning of ways in which we were opposite. Looks, grades, personality, her endless list of hobbies… People at school always wondered why we were friends, but Loz let it go over her head, ignored the snide remarks and stood up for me when her hockey mates started slagging me off. It was easier for her. She was cool enough, pretty enough that she could *pick* to be friends with the kids from the council estate, with me, didn't have to rely on her middle class parents or one million after school clubs to be liked. Being friends with Lilz Dart made her look *better*. And if I cared what other people thought of me, I'd have said that being friends with Loz did the same for me.

So there we were. Owen, Loz, Kara, Gethin and I. Owen still rubbing sun cream into Kara's back; Loz sunbathing and trying very hard not to look at her phone; Kara stubbing her fag out and giving me triumphant looks as I rubbed in my cream alone; Gethin trying his best not to look at Loz, but failing to stop his eyes trailing her bikini… or lack thereof. When she noticed, she smiled sweetly and unclipped the back of her top, saying, "I don't want to get a tan line, do I?"

And then there was me, Lilz Dart, sat on my blanket with my white legs stretched out before me, can of Venom (the pink one, of course) by my side. I had my earphones in, chugging something angry and metal I'd never pick now, wearing a baggy tee over my swimsuit. We'd go in the sea later, no doubt, but there was no point smoothing buckets of factor fifty over my entire body until then.

It was hot. Very hot. The sun was still rising in the sky, on and on and on, higher in the baby blue abyss. Seagulls squawked and the sea before us sparkled deep cerulean as we sat there, the five of us, our group.

That was when I felt a pair of hands on my shoulders, digging into the fabric of my top. Hot breath on my ears, the scent of the hashbrowns we ate on the way here.

Owen. Owen, Owen, Owen. Familiar and comfortable and safe, all at once, hugging me towards him, planting a kiss on the side of my face…

I could've picked that kiss out from a thousand. The shape of Owen's lips were as familiar as the rest of him, as his floppy brown hair and freckles and spongy tummy, pale limbs. Owen was everything to me, an extension of my soul. I smiled and brought my knees up to hug as his kisses continued down the side of my face.

Here are some things you should know about Owen and I, about our relationship. At this point, we'd been together for about four and a half years. That's an *awfully* long time to be dating someone, especially in a place like Vibbington, for a boy like Owen. A boy cool enough, aloof enough, to not need a clingy blonde dragging him down. That was what most people thought, at least.

I smiled, staring out at the sea. We were different to the rest, to the other couples in our year at sixth form. We'd been together longer than Loz and her boyfriend, Ethan. Contrary to common knowledge, they'd started dating about two years previous, though they kept it secret from the other kids at school for a good few months to avoid speculation. Even when you look like Lauren Accorn – maybe *especially* when you look like Lauren Accorn – you're constantly at the end of crude jokes and demeaning remarks. Everyone wants to know about your sex life.

We tried to double date when they first got together, but it didn't really work. Ethan Morgan was lovely, all brown eyes and soft smile and excellent grades, the perfect match for my wildcard best friend – and Owen and I were none of those things. Owen was sharp, dry, didn't let his softer side show all too easily. He thought Ethan was a total wet-wipe, and secretly, I think Ethan was rather scared of him.

Even if Loz and Ethan had been together for as long as us… I don't think it would make a difference to the fact they were currently in the process of breaking up, which they were both in denial about. Since Loz moved to Nottingham, they'd seen each other about four times, all of which lasted an hour or so, no longer. She'd spent more time with the five of us than her boyfriend.

Back to Owen and I…

We'd been together longer than Vibbington's golden couple, Orla Lloyd and Aaron Robinson-Smythe, who got together a year or two after us and still posted selfies together on their Instagram stories to this day, doused in grainy sunset filters and cringey lyrics. That was a *real* accomplishment. Most people accepted that Orla and Aaron were in it for the long haul, but they *knew* that we were, that Lilz and Owen were meant to last.

We never tried to double date them, of course. Orla and Aaron were the definition of suck-ups, practically becoming Vibbington royalty after receiving the best combined grades at GCSE we'd ever seen in our corner of Yorkshire. They went to a fancy college now; they thought they were too good for our crappy sixth form, which was probably true.

Owen and I had even been together longer than my parents, who split up when I was two – and Owen's, whose dad didn't stick around long enough to even tell Judy his surname. Dizzy is technically my half-sister, though you'd never know by looking at us. Spindly, light-blonde hair, big blue eyes, deathly white skin. Mum clearly had a type.

My dad didn't stick around all too long either, but Owen liked to remind me that at least I knew his name, had a photo of him in my purse the size of a 50p coin. Desmond Dart, Dezza to his friends, Desmond to anybody else. Mum kept his surname, Dart, but she didn't know I still had the photo, cut from an old album I found under the TV before she chucked it. I didn't miss him, not really, but the feeling of abandonment isn't something which fades easily.

I leant into Owen, his body soft beneath me. Maybe he was right. At least I knew his name, had some sort of connection to the man who made me.

Owen's father was just that: a father, not a *dad*. His mum, Judy, used to joke about the man she'd brought back from the pub on Friday night, the shock she received a few weeks later when she realised she was pregnant. He wasn't even local. He'd come up to Yorkshire for a stag do, and ended up having more of a… shag do.

He always liked to remind me of that, too. That however much I complained about my family, his would always be worse.

It's true.

For all our faults, I loved my family. I loved our silly little flat with its brightly painted walls, and the sound of the children screaming in the street outside. I loved our cosy living room with the extensive DVD archives going way back into the early 2000s when Mum was a teen, right before she had me, and our collection of boxsets still with the original faded packaging. I loved our dinky kitchen with the succulents on the windowsill and cookbooks we never used lined up on the shelf, photos stuck to the fridge and drawings from mine and Dizzy's primary school days tacked up on a pinboard, before we learnt there wasn't an artistic bone between us.

I loved my mum. My soft, warm mum, who worked too hard and spent all her spare money on nice bubble bath and candles, who liked foot massages and expensive shampoo she couldn't afford but sometimes got from Grandma for Christmas. My mum, who hadn't been on more than five dates since Dizzy was a toddler, who prioritised my sister and I more than any parent should.

Compared to Owen's, my family was a dream. I tried not to complain about Mum's occasional strictness or her nagging about my grades, because for Owen, it would be a luxury for his mum to even... care.

Mum never liked Judy Sharpley. It's known throughout the mum circles that she wasn't a good parent, which used to rile Mum up. They lived across the street from us for most of my life, so she saw more of Judy's behaviour than I ever did. Mum knew how easy it would be for Judy to just switch up, take some responsibility. But she never did.

"What are you thinking?"

The voice startled me, dragging me from my daydream. I glanced up, meeting Owen's gaze.

"Me? Oh, nothing."

Nothing, indeed. Owen didn't know how much I disliked his mum, and it was an unspoken rule that none of us would ever disrespect her.

My boyfriend frowned, lowering his hands to my stomach, where they made circles against my t-shirt. "You looked like you were in another world, Lilz."

I smiled, reaching up to pinch his nose. I loved Owen's nose, once upon a time. Snub and sweet and freckled, like a blob of golden flesh against his long face. And his mouth. Soft, pink lips, the perfect amount of plump to kiss. Not that

I'd ever kissed anyone else, or that I'd ever thought about anyone's lips but Owen's. But still. I imagined that, if given the option, Owen's lips would by far be the most kissable.

"I *am* in another world," I said, settling back into him. "I'm in heaven."

I heard Kara scoff, felt her expression grate against me. "*Cringe.*"

Kara thought everything was "cringe", but especially me. We'd been friends for a few years now, mainly through Loz and Gethin, Owen's best mate, but things had been fraught ever since we realised she had a crush on Owen. She genuinely thought we hadn't caught on, and was always trying to get him to notice her, like he wasn't already in love with *me*.

"If heaven exists," Loz continued, ignoring her, "then it better look like this. Golden sand, blue sky, clear sea…"

"Venom, and a ciggie," Gethin added, rolling over, away from Loz. "Pass us one, Kara!"

She was scowling as she plucked one from the pack, fumbling for her lighter. I moved to grab the rest of the Venoms from the cool box as Owen grumbled, trying to pull me towards him. We had a whole host of other drinks and snacks in there, including doughnuts and chicken strips and Milkybar buttons, perfect for a day by the sea. I wriggled back as the drinks were distributed, twisting to plant a kiss on Owen's lips, lingering for a second too long, his hands in my hair…

"Oh, get a room!" Kara barked. "Are you *trying* to make me vom?"

I let myself lean against Owen again, gazing into the distance, at the waves lapping the horizon, brushing the sky with their foam-tipped fingers. The Venom was cool and sweet and delicious, energy already fizzing through my veins. It felt perfect. *Life* felt perfect, in that moment.

"I'm so excited for the rest of summer to look like this," I said, meeting Loz's eyes, who nodded back and grinned.

"Me too!"

"It's going to be the best summer of our lives," Owen added, breath hot against my ear again. He waited a second for the others to be preoccupied with doling out the doughnuts, before whispering, "I promise."

THE BOYFRIEND

Perfection didn't *just* look like the beach on a sunny day, not back then. I spent the second of June in Owen's bedroom in his crummy flat on our Vibbington estate, the windows shut to stop flies, a whirring fan jammed over the door. Judy Sharpley had a habit of not respecting Owen's privacy, of wandering in unannounced and leaving random post and washing on his desk with a flick of her hand. We were always careful to put something over the door now, or to wait until she was out at bingo to cuddle up close.

Though it was just across the road from our flat, we always hung out at Owen's. I don't know why. Mum was out a lot, working two or three jobs at a time, and Dizzy spent most of her time out with friends, or at the new community centre by the school. But hanging out in my room – my nice, clean room, with its baby blue bedsheets and band posters over the walls and windows – felt like rubbing it in, somehow. Rubbing in how much *nicer* our flat was than his, how lucky we got when the council allocated housing.

Owen's flat was shit. Like, properly shit. The lock on the door was dodgy, and the balcony which overlooked our road was rotting – badly. The walls were covered in mould, so Owen kept his window permanently open to let in fresh air. Unless it was a day like that one, however, when the sun was high and the air was muggy, warm. We were curled together on his bed in our underwear, trying to cool off as the fan whirred.

Judy was in the kitchen, I think. Owen's flat had four rooms. The kitchen/living room, master bedroom, bathroom, and Owen's tiny box room, barely big enough to fit a small double bed and wardrobe and desk. We could hear her over the sound of the fan, shouting down the phone to one of her many girlfriends.

"What is it now?" I asked Owen, teasing. I prodded his belly, one of my favourite things about him. It was soft and squishy and white, like a marshmallow. "Has Sandra cheated on Marcus, or is Julie firing Moira as her maid of honour?"

"Don't," Owen replied, screwing up his face as though in pain. "She kept me up half the night with her nattering."

I rolled my eyes. Not to speak too ill of the woman, but Judy Sharpley was never respectful of Owen's needs, as her child and *teenage son*. She was never the kind of mother to help him with homework or rehearse lines for the year two nativity, to pay for swimming lessons or cricket, football. He still flailed his arms and kicked like a baby when we went swimming in the sea, and had no concept of rules and discipline when it came to schoolwork. Owen was everything to me, but to say he was raised well would be... well. Incorrect.

"Did you not tell her you needed sleep?"

Owen nodded, said nothing else.

I often got the impression, back then, that there was more to Owen's relationship with his mum than he ever let on. Even though my mum drove me crazy, we were closer than close, had that single-parent bond impossible to break. Owen and Judy were different. They kept their distance when I was round, so we mainly stayed in Owen's room, making food in the kitchen and carrying it back to eat on his floor. She was usually out anyway, with her girlfriends or work colleagues, before she lost her job cleaning at a local care home because she couldn't keep up with the early hours.

Whenever they *were* together, Owen seemed… tense. Like he couldn't wait to get out of her company and sweep me away to his bedroom, where she couldn't embarrass him further. That was her favourite thing to do – embarrass Owen. She'd make these demeaning comments about his body, his grades, tell embarrassing stories from when he was a kid in an attempt to make me laugh.

"Did I tell you about the time he told everyone down the freezer aisle he had a sausage between his legs?" she'd say, bending over the breakfast bar and squawking with laughter. "Or the time he tried to propose to his year one teacher, at his old school? He made her a Sellotape ring and everything!"

I'd been best friends with Owen since he'd first moved into the block opposite as a tiny kid, known him inside out for more than ten years. He was my best friend, my person, the only one for me. Nothing she said could change how I felt about him, but she seemed intent on trying anyway. It was like she was confused at what I could possibly find so attractive about her son.

That being said, I don't think Judy liked me much. She was big and bouncy and flouncy, all glittery clothes and tacky makeup and *Gogglebox*, and she thought I was weird, weedy, that my masses of eyeliner and baggy clothes made me look shrunken, depressed. She called me Owen's "little girlfriend" on the phone to her friends.

"Owen's little girlfriend is here, so I can't talk right now!"

Or: "Owen and that little girlfriend of his are ordering pizza, if you want to come round for some?"

Little was my adjective, formed part of my identity in Judy Sharpley's head. Little, as in skinny and undeveloped, shrewd and glaring.

I think she found our relationship *amusing*, more than anything.

We could still hear her now, shouting down the phone. Her voice rose an octave every time she got a reply, feet thudding on the tiles as she careered around the kitchen. Judy was a big woman, all baggy stomach and flabby arms, and had long lost the body she'd had as a teen mum to Owen, the same teen mum who'd got pregnant via a one night stand with a fully-grown man. I think she blamed Owen for that, too.

Did she have to be so *loud*?

"Distract me," Owen murmured, turning so that he was facing me. He smelled of milk and cornflakes, all wrapped up in his Owen-ness like a comforting blanket, and I smiled, nestling further into him. We should've been long past the stage of butterflies, but Owen's bare skin against mine still sent shivers down my spine, made my fingertips tingle, toes curl.

The fan churned cold air around the room, but his body was hot, sticky, beads of sweat dotted across his forehead.

"Distract you?" I whispered back. "Distract you how?"

I knew exactly what he meant.

Leaning forwards, I pressed my lips gently against his. Like I said, Owen's lips were the perfect amount of kissable; plump and pink and perfect, pursed to meet mine. It was only a matter of seconds before I was on top of him, his arms on my back and squeezing my bum, my tongue in his mouth, hands searching down below.

That was just what we were like. A couple, nearly five years on, just as in love as we had been as twelve-year-olds. Perfection was just as much Loz and my friends and the beach as it was lying in Owen's room, wearing the faded underwear I'd had since I was fourteen, kissing him like my life depended on it as the fan whirred and the rest of the world continued without us.

I felt comfortable around Owen, like I didn't have to second-guess myself, our relationship. We could lapse into silence for hours without it feeling awkward, and almost all our spare time was spent together, in my room or his, or down on the beach, in the park. I'd never really had the chance to feel insecure. I went from being a tomboy kid who didn't give a jot about her looks to being someone's *girlfriend*, someone another human found attractive, wanted to kiss, see naked. I'd never had the chance to care what people thought of me, because *Owen* liked me, and Owen liking me was enough.

Maybe that sounds romantic to you. Hashtag relationship goals. The fact we'd gotten to seventeen having only ever liked each other, kissed each other, slept with each other. Is it, though?

Or is it dangerous, toxic?

Does it create expectations you can't maintain, smother plaster over cracks you don't notice?

I'd never been with anyone but Owen. I had no idea whether our relationship was good or bad.

It *was* good, though, right? How could it not be?

I let out a gasp as Owen tugged at my faded underwear, fingers sliding under…

So… yes. June second was perfect, too. The rest of the day is blurry, like a piece of paper held underwater so the ink runs and spills and smudges, creating one huge, blue blob. I left to go home late that evening, where I scribbled some answers onto my homework sheets and sat up with Dizzy in the living room watching *How I Met Your Mother* for the six hundredth time, curtains closed and my little sister's head resting on my lap. Dizzy might have been twelve, now thirteen, but she was still the family baby. That was the way it always would be, I thought.

Our own mum got back from work late, shoved some frozen pizzas in the oven. She made Dizzy's favourite, microwaving instant doughballs and drizzling them in butter and garlic salt, then cuddled down on the sofa with us to watch. Lily and Marshall ~~were~~ were breaking up on the screen before us. Even though we'd seen it half a billion times, there were tears running down all of our faces.

And that was that. I went to bed feeling devastated about Lily and Marshall, yet simultaneously relieved that that could *never* happen to Owen and I, that we were in this together, forever. And anyway... Lily and Marshall got back together in the end. I'd seen the show enough times to know that. They were made for each other, just like we were.

I messaged Owen before sliding under my duvet, forwarding one of those soppy Instagram posts about soulmates and the science behind them being real. It was a bit of a joke between us that we'd send each other typical "couple-y" things in a totally ironic way, though Owen was rubbish when it came to texting, and probably wouldn't reply until tomorrow. He never needed to be on his phone; why would he, when I lived just across the road? The quote was cheesy and the background covered in flowers, and I knew he'd probably like the message with a grimace then forward it to Gethin in exasperation, as if to say, *how cute*.

It was true, though. The Instagram post. I really did think Owen's soul was made for mine, that we were meant to be together.

I settled back against my pillow, a smile on my lips as I closed my eyes.

I didn't get out of bed again.

I didn't.

I didn't.

@laurenaccorn

happy mind
happy soul

THE BEST FRIEND

In some ways, I wish the biggest drama of June third was Loz's text, received in the morning as I was getting ready for school. We only had a month and a half left, but we'd completed our mocks, and all our teachers had made clear it didn't matter much if we missed a lesson here or there. So when Loz messaged me, in all caps, spelling out the inevitable, the obvious thing to do was drop everything and pull off my stupid sixth form lanyard, forgetting all about Owen, yelling goodbye to Dizzy and running out of the door.

I think Loz had been in Nottingham a few months at this point... I can't really remember. Her parents split up when we were in year nine or ten, and her mum, a high-flying solicitor, moved to Notts when we were fifteen to follow her career. Loz stayed with her dad in Vibbington until her GCSEs were done, then started sixth form here too while the logistics of her move were smoothed over – and her fancy new bedroom was being decorated.

She hadn't started college yet, so she'd come back to live with her dad for a few months, spend time with us all before we started summer jobs and she stayed with her mum and aunt in France during August. Loz's dad was just like her... vivacious, fun, sporty. We all – me in particular – wished she'd just stayed here with him, but that wasn't our choice – or hers.

lilz i'm freaking out xx

I paused, stopping to text her back.

i'm on my way xxxx

You might still be wondering why I was friends with Loz…
or, more accurately, why she was friends with me. You might
be thinking, *vivacious, fun, sporty?* That doesn't like you, Lilz.
Because it doesn't… *Lauren* doesn't.

But that's why it worked so well. She was the extrovert to
my introvert, the pink to my blue. She'd paint my nails
crimson while I updated her playlist, and take my Instagram
photos while I edited hers. We were total opposites, but that
was why it *worked*. It was why it always had done.

We met in year five, when Loz was placed next to me in
the seating plan. Our teacher at the time had this thing for
pairing up opposites, and Lauren Accorn was truly my
opposite in every way. Dinky and cute and polite, the kind of
kid to hold doors open for teachers and volunteer to
distribute water bottles on sports day. I was the kind to stamp
on teachers' toes then run away screaming, to hide water
bottles behind the benches then unscrew all the caps, sloshing
them onto the ground one by one (only once, and it was
Owen's idea). I was still a pretty shy child, but one who felt
no need to be *nice*.

I thought she was a right snob, sat next to me all prim and
proper, dark blonde hair neatly parted and pink lips pursed as
though with distaste. Lauren *Accorn*. What kind of
pretentious surname was that?

I'd known her for years before this, obviously. At least, I'd
known *of* her. She was always the lead part in our nativity
plays, the one chosen to present leavers' cards in assembly and

stand at the front to lead hymns. She was in the school choir, the gardening club, on the girl's football team and steel band. She wore these rectangular glasses with little pink frames, and was glancing down at me through them now.

"You like Mary Hooper books?" she asked, eyes wide, staring at the paperback on my desk. And that's how you become best friends when you're nine.

There was more to Loz than her perfection, which was wrong of me to assume. She wasn't as dinky and pink as she acted, had a lot more bite than bark. She could keep her mouth shut, smile through criticism and gossip, but she could've hit the other kids where it hurt most in an instant. Almost as soon as we became best friends, she became my protector. It had been that way ever since.

We moved up to secondary together, stayed close even when Loz was placed in all top sets and I hovered between fourth and fifth. We stayed close through my little emo phase, which gifted me the nickname Depressive Dart, and Loz's first (disastrous) relationship with an older guy called Steven when we were in year seven. We stayed close even when Owen, who'd been my bestie since forever, my number one, started hanging out with us at school, crept from being a "home friend" to a school friend. We stayed close even when he asked me to be his girlfriend, outside Tesco on a rainy day in October, with Gethin, his best mate, and Loz, mine, watching from a distance and giggling into their hands.

Loz and I just worked. I don't have any bigger reason than that. I knew her better than almost anyone, and vice versa. I hoped, back then, that was the way it would always be.

When you have a best friend like that – someone so important to you, more important than most things – there are certain rules. Rules like dropping everything, even school, when they're sick and need something from the pharmacy, or when they can't sleep and need someone to stay up late watching *How I Met Your Mother* with. Rules like dropping everything when they message you to say they think they've fallen out of love with their boyfriend.

I practically careered out of our estate, sending Owen a quick voice note to explain why he couldn't see me today. He fired back another, something about being tired and hungover, to which I couldn't help but frown. If he was hungover, that meant he must've gone out with Gethin and his pals last night... but I left his pretty late, and he said nothing about going out later.

I pushed the thought from my mind, however, focusing on the road.

Loz's dad's new place was a five minute sprint from mine, ten minutes meandering. She used to live a lot further away when her parents were together, but Vibbington is a small place, and all the council owned property and private flats are near enough to one another. My trainers crashed along the pavement as I ran.

It was a tall building, Victorian, with an aggressive black door and a metal knocker. Loz's dad lived on the ground floor, but to get to the other flats you had to use a rickety set of wooden stairs to the right of the building, which Mr Accorn was terrified would fall down and crush his fuchsias.

I waited a few seconds now, listening to a pair of hands fumbling with the lock, jangling keys.

And then the door opened, and Pete Accorn stood before me, beaming and gesturing for me to come in.

"Lilz!" he announced, shutting the door behind me. "Lauren, Lilz is here!" He gave me a once over, shaking his head, and said, "My, haven't you changed since I last saw you.

Shouldn't you be in sixth form today? I hope my daughter isn't incenting you to skive off..."

I just grinned, shaking my head. Pete had always been like a dad to me, kind and affectionate and funny. Truth be told, he was part of the reason I wanted Lauren to stay living in Vibbington so bad. I'd barely seen Pete since she moved, and it felt a little like a hole in my heart, in my life, a hole only a father figure could fill.

"Nope," I lied, winking at him. "School has become... optional, since we finished our mocks."

"That never would've happened in my day..." He shook his head, leaning back to shout down the corridor, "Lauren! Lauren, you're keeping her waiting!"

We heard sheets rustling, a Loz-sounding groan emerge from her bedroom. He turned back to me, sighing.

"Do excuse me, Lilz. I've got a job interview to head out for."

"Good luck! I'm sure you'll smash it."

Pete hadn't worked since the divorce. I'm pretty sure Loz's mum was still paying for his flat, at least partly, but he got some help because of his depression, which had stopped him working as a caretaker at one of the local primary schools. I noticed now how he was wearing one of his best shirts, tucked into grey trousers, and couldn't help but smile.

"At least you think so," he replied, straightening his tie, then stretched his head back up the corridor. "I'm going, Lauren. Have a good day, won't you? I love you!"

That's when a harassed Loz appeared in her bedroom doorway. She'd very clearly been crying, and gave her dad the most forlorn of expressions as he pouted his sympathy. I tried not to feel jealous as she ran towards him and he gave her a squeeze, murmuring, "There's a tenner under the cookie jar.

Get yourself something nice from the Chinese, yeah?"

"I love you, Dad."

"Love you more." Pete smiled at me, raising a hand. "Pray for me, girls!"

Then he was gone, shutting the door behind him with a loud *crack*, leaving us alone in his flat with at least half an inch of drama stored between us.

"Oh, Loz," is what I said, as she cried, "Oh, Lilz!"

The Chinese didn't open until three, so we decided to order pizza instead, a weird breakfast choice but exactly what we needed. Our go-to was Hawaiian with chips and chip spice, two bottles of diet coke, and we placed our order while sat on Loz's bed in her purple bedroom, the curtains closed to block any sunlight and Loz's bottom lip trembling all the while.

"So," I said, once we'd gotten out the nail stuff and placed on some music – mine, of course – on the speakers above her bed. Painting nails was like therapy for us. It was what we did every time there was a drama or scandal, something any level worse than neutral.

"So," Loz agreed, picking up a shade of dark plum. "I need something darker than dark, Lilz. This is serious."

"Explain."

Loz bit her lip, glancing down at the bed. "I'm, like, ninety percent sure I don't love Ethan anymore."

Those were the words which made everything come crashing down.

It's funny, now, that that seemed like such drama. At least to me. June third was going to be all about Loz and Ethan, their relationship, how it was all going wrong. It's funny how I genuinely hoped it was the worst thing to happen all year, that nothing would top this, that Loz needed my support and so I was going to stay by her side all day, perhaps invite Owen, Kara and Gethin over later for more food and a proper chinwag.

Teenagers, eh? We act like it's the end of the world when minor things happen, when our childish relationships fail. We can't cope with anything bigger until the worst is overtaken by worse, when our brains are forced to stretch out and deal with actual tragedy, crime. Until then, we push the bad stuff out. Pretend… pretend it never happened.

At this point, to Loz, her and Ethan's inevitable breakup felt like the worst thing to have happened that month so far, and for the rest of summer, as long as it went on. Sunny skies and tearstained faces, breakup sex and drunken texts… I could see it all now, stretching on ahead. And it was *sad*. It was sad that Ethan would end up heartbroken, that Loz would lose one of her closest friends and first proper boyfriend. It was sad, but it had to happen. I was here to make sure it most definitely *would*.

I made Loz explain everything to me, unpack her feelings one by one, getting to the bottom of how and why she'd fallen out of love with Ethan Morgan, who, in more ways than one, seemed perfect for her. When the pizzas arrived, she bawled into the chip box trying to get her words out. In the end, it came down to time, and age, and experience. She was seventeen. She still felt attracted to other people, people she couldn't speak to, try things out with. Ethan had been great, but he wasn't forever, not for Loz. She needed more than him.

"It's being at Nottingham, too," she told me between sniffs, using the serviette to dry her face. "I'm not a sex addict or anything, but it's hard, being away from him. Facetime isn't the same."

I got the rest of it, I really did. Loz was outgoing, liked meeting new people, found it socially stimulating. But struggling to maintain an otherwise healthy relationship without the physical contact... I tried to understand that, but I couldn't. How could something as simple as mileage cause a person to fall out of love so quickly? Owen and I would stay together if I moved far away, surely? We'd been together too long to let distance come between us.

But then... would we? Owen was terrible at messaging, didn't even really like phonecalls. We saw each other almost every day at my house or his, but so much of our relationship was physical that I don't know how we would've survived being long distance.

That was when I started to panic a little, though I couldn't show Loz that. She and Ethan hadn't seen each other that much when she was still in Vibbington full-time, so surely it shouldn't have mattered so much, going long distance?

If she and Ethan couldn't hack it, what about Owen and me? We were pretty sure we weren't applying to uni, but what if we decided to, or one of us got an apprenticeship down south and had to move a million miles away? Owen could drive, but fuel would be expensive. Paying the phone bill would be expensive. Not being together *every single day* would be expensive.

"I just can't bring myself to tell him." Loz dragged me from my thoughts. "I know he'll be heartbroken, and I ..."

"Loz." I tried to focus on her, calm my breathing. It didn't matter if Owen and I couldn't survive long distance, because *that wasn't going to happen*. He lived opposite me, and always would. He loved me. We were made for each other. "Loz, you need to tell him. He'll figure it out soon anyway, you've hardly seen each other since you got back."

"I know." My best friend bit her lip, stretching a hand out to admire her newly-painted nails. "I know."

"So you're going to tell him?" I checked. "You're going to tell him as soon as you next see him?"

Loz nodded sheepishly as her eyes began to water again, and I pulled her in for a hug over the half-eaten pizza, the chips already going cold.

"I'm proud of you," I whispered, pulling back and trying for a smile, and she nodded.

Beep. Beep. Beep.

"Is that my phone?"

Loz frowned at me as I fumbled around on the bed, trying to find it. It was tucked under the pizza box, screen flashing. I had an incoming phonecall. An incoming phonecall from *Owen*.

"Let me just take this," I said to Loz, frowning, though my heart was thudding. "It's Owen. He probably wants me to pick something up from the shop on my way home. I'll be two minutes."

I took Owen outside into the corridor, perched on the sofa as I swiped to answer. I tried not to worry. I tried not to assume anything was wrong. But I knew Owen needed me, and whenever he wanted to call me, I was there.

"Owen?" I answered, pressing the phone to my ear. "I'm with Loz, did you –"

"Lilz."

That was when I knew something was wrong. When my boyfriend said "Lilz" like that, voice barely a whine, filled with more fear than I'd heard from a human being before.

"Lilz."

"Owen?

owen? i'm with loz, did you -

lilz.

lilz.

owen?

owen, what happened?

lilz.

something happened.

owen, just tell me what happened.

owen...

i can't.

lilz, please just come here, right now.

i need you -

where are you?

home.

okay.

...

THE PHONECALL

"Owen?" I echoed. Instinct cut in and I switched to serious mode, sitting up straighter and speaking clearly down the phone. "Owen, what's happened?"

I'd done this once before – technically twice. Owen had turned up on my doorstep high out of his mind, after spending the night with Gethin and a few others in the park, and was crying his eyes out, properly crying, one of the first times I'd seen him really *cry*. Mum and Dizzy were asleep, so I made him a cup of tea and we cuddled on the sofa as he sobbed, too sleepy and delirious to do anything but hold me.

The second time...

Anyway. This was different. Owen sounded scared. Properly scared. I could practically hear him shaking, feel the tremor of his lips, hands barely grasping the phone.

"Lilz," he repeated, tone the exact same as before, just an octave higher. "Lilz, something happened."

Something happened.

My mind switched to panic mode then. Car accidents, accidents involving Mum and Dizzy. Or a terrorist attack, a shooting, something involving Dizzy, my little sister...

In my heart, I knew what the problem was, but I couldn't help but panic. Maybe that was my brain trying to push out the worry, blind fear, convince myself it wasn't *that*... I don't know. My eyes filled with tears anyway. I felt them rolling down my face as I sat there, Owen clutched to my ear, that frightened, animalistic voice repeating my name.

"Owen, just tell me what happened," I tried to say, but my voice didn't sound right, all worried and squeaky and weird. "Owen…"

"I can't," he told me. "Lilz, please just come here, right now, I need you –"

"Where are you?"

"Home."

Home. He was at *home*.

"Okay," I said, nodding, voice a lot stronger than I felt. "I'll just tell Loz there's been a problem, then I'll come find you…"

"No."

"Sorry?"

"No, you can't tell Loz." Owen sounded terrified.

Actually *terrified*.

"Just tell her your mum needs you, and that you need to go home now."

"But she knows I'm talking to you?"

"Fine. Tell her I'm at school, and they want you to come in and explain why your attendance is so poor. That's not completely unbelievable, is it?"

"Owen. What's going on?" He was scaring me. He was really, really scaring me. "Is it Dizzy? Is she okay?"

"Yes – what? Why would…"

"Because you won't tell me what the fuck is going on!"

Owen paused. I could hear him breathing heavily, trying to control himself. "Just come home."

Then he hung up.

For a moment, I just sat there, staring at the blank TV screen. I could hear my music still playing in Loz's room, the speakers blasting songs which were angry and red-hot and *present*, so much more so than I felt. It was like my hands and feet had unattached themselves from my body and were floating around me, unsure of where to go, what to do. Where even was I?

"Lilz?" Loz appeared in the doorway, frowning at me. My vision was blurry as I stared at her, and she asked, slowly, "Is everything okay?"

I didn't nod straight away, but when I did, I added, "There's been a problem at school, and I need to go in, sort some… coursework stuff."

Loz shrugged, fanning her nails, though I could see she didn't believe me, that she knew there was more to the story. "Okay. But ring me tonight, yeah? I'm not going to do anything about Ethan until I'm sure."

"I will."

We didn't move for a second, room silent all around us.

"Want some pizza to take back with you?"

"Nah. Your dad paid. Let him have it for his lunch."

"Cheers."

It felt awkward, so awkward. Why did it feel awkward? It never felt awkward between Loz and I, ever.

"Are you sure you're okay, Lilz?"

I nodded, smiled.

The walk back to my estate was too long, longer than it felt on the way to Loz's this morning. I thought the Ethan thing was urgent, but this felt… different. Owen had emphasised how quick I needed to be, but I couldn't bring myself to run again. It was like my whole body was made of lead.

The estate was silent, warm. The concrete walls of each block sweltered. Our own balcony was covered in wilting plants and garden accessories, fancy painted pots and metal sheep. Owen's rail was almost ready to snap, the bottom so rotted that it was soft and squishy to touch.

I made my way up the stairs, careful not to lean on the wood. Owen's front door was pale pink and had a heart-shaped knocker, the only modification they were allowed to make to this outstanding piece of British architecture. I knocked, once, twice.

It was Owen who came to the door.

Was Judy still there? Why was he smiling, a little sheepishly, like he'd done something wrong?

"Hi," he said. There was still that terrified gleam in his eyes, one of fear, regret. I put my arms around him immediately, feeling his body, soft and warm beneath me. He was wearing a blue hoodie, a soft shade, and cosy joggers. I pulled back, stopped breathing.

Blood.

Why was there blood splattered over his hoodie?

It's funny how I knew what it was right away, even though there were a multitude of red liquids which could have been splashed across him.

Maybe he'd been painting the living room red.

Maybe…

Or maybe it really was blood, and my worst nightmare was unfolding before me, just like that.

We both realised at the same time. He stepped back, pinching the fabric between his fingers.

He looked horrified.

Horrified, like whatever had happened was only just dawning on him.

"Owen?" I said, though it came out more like a question. "Owen, what's happened? Why is there blood all over you?"

I'll never forget what he said next, how he said it. With such trembling satisfaction, relief…

But with the fear of a little boy caught shoplifting, eyes glassy and enraged.

"She's dead," he said, just like that. "We did it, Lilz. Mum's dead."

lilz is everything okay?

will you message me if you need anything?

bestie i'm worrieddd

is everything okay with owen?

ik you're not at school

i'm here for you xoxo

THE MONSTER

"What?" The word echoed all around us. It was the only thing I could think to say.

Owen's mum couldn't be *dead*. That was... preposterous, crazy. She was Judy Sharpley, so loud and glitzy and alive, and was probably out at bingo right now with her friends, trying to win a shower gel hamper or some kiddie toys she could flog on eBay. She wasn't dead. She just *wasn't*.

"Lilz," Owen repeated, voice shaking. "Lilz, what have I done?"

I barely heard him. All the blood in my body had rushed to my head and I could feel myself panicking, hyperventilating.

What have I done? What *had* Owen done? Surely that didn't mean he'd killed her, that the splatters on his hoodie were...

"Lilz," he said, more urgent this time. "Lilz."

I grabbed his hand, soft and warm in mine, and tugged him into the living room out of the daylight. We closed the door behind us. The middle of the flat was taken up with a huge corner sofa, the kitchen to one side, and the TV was on low, playing some crappy rerun of *Homes Under the Hammer*. I looked at Owen, realised his whole body was vibrating. My brave, I-don't-give-a-shit boyfriend was vibrating so badly his teeth were chattering, eyes couldn't focus.

"Owen," I said, taking charge again. "Owen, sit down, I'll make us some tea."

Judy kept teabags in a jar by the kettle, and I'd carried out the procedure enough times to know what was what, where things were kept. I used two of her charity-shop mugs and filled them with milk and boiling water, sharing a teabag between the two. Owen perched on the edge of the sofa, his beautiful face white, splotchy. He looked like he was going to be sick.

"Owen," I told him, reaching around him to rub his back, squeeze his waist. "What happened? Talk to me, please."

But he couldn't speak, shaking his head and swallowing a gulp of scalding tea.

I knew my boyfriend like the back of my hand, was sure we could get to the bottom of this, somehow. But deep down, fear wouldn't stop curdling inside me like a long, black snake. I'd never seen Owen so scared before. His pupils weren't dilated, face wasn't slack with alcohol, drugs. He was just petrified, haunted, scarred by *something*.

And then there was the blood. Splatters of it, all over his hands and face and neck. I licked my finger, reaching up to wipe a circle from his cheek. It was pinky-orange now, mixed with my saliva, and smelled like a butcher's block.

"Owen," I said. "Why don't you take off your hoodie?"

I had to help him. He still wouldn't speak, lifting his arms so that I could raise it above his head. His body was still the same... the freckle by his nipple I loved so much, and the wiry hairs beneath his armpit, the crescent-shaped mole on his shoulder. But something was different, wrong. He had goosebumps in places no one ever should have goosebumps, and his nails were bright pink, a little too scrubbed to be *Owen's*.

"Talk to me," I murmured, into his ear. He let out an in-pain moan, squeezing his eyes shut. "Owen, talk to me, please. Why do you think your mum's dead?"

My boyfriend paused, froze. I watched as his body turned stiff before me, mouth curled into an ugly grimace.

"Owen?" I prompted.

Then, "I killed her."

Silence. My heart was pounding, pounding so loud I could hear it in my eardrums, about to burst. Those three words, pulsing around us both, surely not true, surely a lie, an exaggeration. Judy couldn't be *dead*. She was alive when I left last night, right? Owen couldn't have killed her. This was all just a joke. A sick, twisted joke.

"You didn't," I told him, but even my voice was uncertain. "You didn't kill your mum, Owen."

I swear he rolled his eyes, then. Pulled a face, as though to say, *How stupid are you, Lilz?* But I couldn't believe it, didn't *want* to believe it. Owen wouldn't do that. Owen wouldn't –

"She's still in the bathroom." His words sliced through my thoughts, scissoring my doubts. "She's still in the bath, Lilz."

"What do you mean?" I asked, though I knew exactly what he meant. Owen was calm, now. He'd stopped vibrating, and was staring at me with placid eyes, brows straight. "What do you mean, Owen? That she's… in the bath?"

"Yes." Owen was looking at me as though I was deliberately acting dumb, and rolled his eyes again, though a little too familiarly, like this was all just a joke. "I killed her. In the bath."

No.

No, no, no.

He was joking, he had to be. The splatters on his hoodie and face were just ketchup, a prank gone too far. Maybe he really had been painting the living room – was he stressed because it was against council rules? Kara and Gethin were probably filming this for YouTube or something, laughing from behind the door to Owen's room, which was ajar.

But the bathroom door... it was closed. Closed, flush to the frame. The light was on. I could see the pinpricks of yellow spilling round the edges.

"Who's in the bathroom, Owen?"

My boyfriend was weirdly steady as he stood up again, still topless, joggers on his bottom half hanging loose. I could see the line of his dark blue boxers, the soft flesh of his lower back flopping over the edges. I wanted to pull him back onto the sofa with me, pretend this was all just some horrible joke, but I couldn't, couldn't bring myself to. The Owen stood before me wasn't the Owen I knew. It was like he was possessed, raising a hand to point at the bathroom door.

"She's in there. I killed her, Lilz. She... she drowned, and then I tried to..."

"You tried to do what?" I repeated, still in disbelief, closing my eyes tight and hoping, praying... "To finish the job? Why, Owen? Why would you do that?"

"Because... I hated her. Because she was a bitch, and I hated her, *hated* her –"

"Owen, Owen!" I rushed to grab his hands, which had formed furious balls by his sides. "Owen, breathe, breathe."

"I've always hated her, Lilz. You know that, right? You've noticed how she treats me, what she does to me? You know how she... how she..."

"How she what?"

Dread.

Dread. That's what I felt, curling inside me.

Dread, like I didn't want to hear what he had to say next.

"How she... how she would call me names, make up stories. You know that, you heard it all. It was even worse when you weren't around. And sometimes she'd... she used to…"

I felt sick. Physically sick, like all the pizza from earlier was about to come hurtling out of my mouth.

"Used to what, Owen?"

Don't push him – you don't need to know this, you don't.

But I wanted to. I wanted to, for my boyfriend's sake. And because I needed to know exactly what was going on, where to turn next.

"She used to… hit me. Slap me, pinch me. Mainly when I was younger, and she knew I couldn't fight back. She never respected my boundaries, ever. She'd come into my room with no warning no matter what time of day it was, no matter what I was doing. I couldn't trust her to give me privacy even when I was in the bathroom, and she had no boundaries for herself, either. She'd tell me such personal things and get me to do the same, and she'd be so degrading when I did, made me feel shit about my feelings all the fucking *time*.

"And when I'd complain, she'd…" He paused. "You know that burn I said I got from Gethin's lighter? It was her. She did it with her straighteners."

He took a deep breath. "But that's not the worst of it.

"When I was fifteen, she broke my arm. Do you remember it, Lilz? I had to go to hospital because my arm was in literal *pieces*, because I told her I wanted her to give me more space and she grabbed me so hard *she broke my arm*.

"And when I was eleven, and missed that week off school because of migraines? Her. She played music so loud for a week because she'd been dumped and felt all depressed, that the police were informed and came to turn it down. And I was so mortified, because you never see this stuff, ever. I think your mum does, but you… I try to shield you from it, because I'm scared that if I tell you, you'll think I'm like that too.

"Social services almost got involved the last time. I was sixteen, and I cracked my head open when she pushed me into the island. Hospitals are told to report it if kids keep getting suspicious injuries. But I couldn't tell. I couldn't, Lilz. I loved her. She was my…"

He was crying now, properly crying.

And

I

wanted

to

be

sick.

I clutched Owen tighter, nails digging into his hands. I didn't know what to do with myself, what to say, apart from how *dare* she? How dare she do that to my boyfriend, to an innocent little boy, her very own *child*?

It was criminal. It was actually *criminal*.

That monster. That monster, psychopath, *witch* –

"Owen," is all I could say, resting my head on his chest, eyes closed. "Owen, I…"

"And then it was just too much. She made me come into the bathroom," he continued, voice steadying again, like he was trying to distance himself from the event again, twist it into a story, a thing of the past. "She was… in the bath, and I kept hearing her screaming my name, over and over and over and over and over and over and over and… and I… and I just lost control, I'd had enough, I didn't want to see her like that, I –"

He was crying louder now, crying like his heart was about to break, like it already had.

And so was I. Tears were leaking out of my eyes, faster, harder, like they wouldn't stop, like they were never going to stop.

"So I killed her. Her head was under water, she was drowned, I'm sure of it, and I – I – I tried to…"

"You tried to what?"

Owen's hands were shaking as he pulled them from mine to wipe his face, dry the tears.

"You'll have to see for yourself."

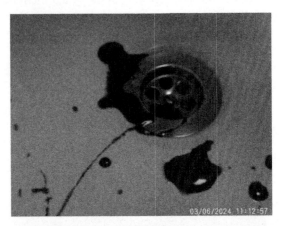

03/06/2024 11:12:57

03/06/2024 11:13:30

THE BATHTUB

I was right behind my boyfriend as his hands found the door handle, pushed it down.

All I was aware of next was the vomit hurling out of my mouth, all over the bathroom floor, every shred of pizza and chips from earlier, splattering the skirting boards and side of the bath.

I'll spare you the details. Partly because I don't think I can, but also because I physically can't describe what I saw that day, the scene in Owen's bathroom. This isn't a horror movie. It's my *reality*, and I can't… I can't…

I don't know what Owen was thinking, how he could do that, even now. All I remember is him sitting me down on the toilet seat, sick pooling at our feet and soaking through our socks, repeating the same sentences over and over again, in some sort of variation.

"It's okay, Lilz, it's okay. You can look at her. She's dead. I tried to cut her up because… because…"

Yes, you read that right.

He tried to *cut her up*.

Only in half, mind. I don't know if that makes it worse. Judy Sharpley was a large woman, and Owen was holding a bread knife to his side. A *bread knife*. As in, a silver knife with a glossy black handle, the blade tip serrated. We'd used it a million times to chop up a frozen pizza or those baguette garlic breads, but it was barely recognisable now.

Globules of something white and pink covered the

serrated edge, streaks of glistening blood staining the metal. Flesh. Chunks of Judy Sharpley's *flesh* stuck to the knife's blade, skin and sinew and...

"Oh my God." I could hardly breathe, about to heave again. Was I hyperventilating? I was hyperventilating –

"It's okay, Lilz. I only tried to do it to make her – her – easier to transport, I don't know, I –" He held my hair, stroking my back, voice trembling as we huddled together on the lid of the toilet. "Lilz, just... look at her. It might help you to process it, realise... that it's not that bad, really."

It seems ludicrous that you'd even have the strength, the courage, to take a look at the body in that state. A drowned, bulbous mess of flesh, sawed down the middle, across her stomach. She was naked, of course; she'd been in the bath. But Judy Sharpley didn't deserve dignity in death, not even a little bit.

Maybe it was anger which propelled me onto my feet, barely aware of the sick seeping through my toes, slish-sloshing as I walked. Owen's bathtub was yellow with age, scalloped at one end, but he'd let out the water already, and the murky liquid gathering around her body was mostly... blood, fluids, I don't know. All I could think as I stared at her, this woman I'd known my whole life so far, a woman I'd never really liked but hadn't suspected of anything so sinister, was how much I hated her. How much I absolutely *hated* her.

And how much she deserved it. As awful as it was, she deserved it all, you can't deny it. For her body to have been mutilated so badly, cheeks swollen with water, lips puffy and slack. And her eyes... her eyes, staring at me, a horrible shade of green turned grey. Her mascara was running, running right down her cheeks. She looked hideous, like the monster she truly was.

It wasn't even because I loved Owen, couldn't believe the torture she'd put him through over the last seventeen years. In that moment, Owen could've been anyone. Anyone unlucky enough to be born to someone like Judy Sharpley, abused, emotionally or physically, unable to get away, manipulated into *complying*. It could've been me. It could've been Dizzy. They were the thoughts which caused me to keel over, knees hitting the bathroom's linoleum floor, gulps coming out thick and fast as I sobbed.

Judy was a bad person. A very bad person. The kind to raise a child just to abuse them beyond recognition, like they were some sort of animal.

The bathroom smelled like meat.

"Lilz…" Owen's hand was soft in my hair, making circles on the top of my head. "It's okay. Let it out, Lilz, then we'll… we'll…"

Neither of us wanted to even think of what to do next, in that moment. There were the obvious choices, but… we didn't want to think about moving the body, *hiding* the body.

I glanced back at Judy, trying to take deep breathes, process her body properly.

And then I looked back at Owen.

"Do you think we should fill the bath up with water again?"

My boyfriend frowned at me. His cheeks were still speckled pink with blood, hands shaking, just a little. "Why?"

"To… get rid of any excess blood. I don't know. It just feels…"

"What about… I don't know, her blood getting into the waterways, or bits of flesh clogging the drainpipes… I don't know what to do, Lilz, I…"

"Let's have another cup of tea."

***

I washed Owen's hands and face in the kitchen sink, with one of Judy's dishcloths. Stained it pink, a shade of pink which reeked – *reeked* – of death. Deadness, dead flesh, dying. Owen's face was scrubbed and sparkling, eyes glassy, staring at me through the weak light. It was overcast now, but humid, stifling. We kept the windows open and a fan circling cool air.

Staying at Owen's tonight. Love you.

The *love you* was necessary. I'd never felt more grateful for my mum's sarky remarks, the way she always fought my corner, had my best interests at heart. She drove me crazy, but she'd raised me with love and care and feelings which were genuine, authentic.

okay, dizzy and i are getting an indian so come over if you want x

I wished I could just say yes. Say yes, and act like everything was fine, like I could go and eat my usual korma with my mum and little sister, and that when I next say Owen his mum would be alive and kicking in her stupid bloody bath.

I'd love to, but we're watching a movie. If you get me a korma I'll heat it up for brekky tomorrow. Extra poppadoms!

I smiled to myself as Owen disappeared into his room for a fresh hoodie. I needed that, a message from my mum, something to ground me. A reminder that things were okay, that life would still go on as normal, no matter how wrong it felt now.

When Owen returned, scrubbed and sprayed liberally in aftershave to mask the blood scent, he smiled and reached out to hug me. A hug turned into a kiss, a kiss into a snog, and soon we were laid on the sofa, Owen atop me, straddling my legs between his joggers. Our sick-soaked socks lay were rolled up in a ball in the corner of the room, and the body of Owen's mutilated mother lay in the bathtub, surrounded by a puddle of lukewarm fluids.

If this doesn't give you an insight as to how close we were, how comfortable, I don't know what will. Owen had just killed his mother, slicing her down the middle with a serrated knife. I had to keep reiterating that in my mind, reinforcing the idea that Owen had drowned his mother, *chopped her up*. Did that worry me? Did it cross my mind for even a moment that holding someone – let alone your parent – underwater as they struggled, kicking up a storm, gasping for air, might suggest a lack of empathy, psychopathic tendencies?

I believed Owen when he told me what his mum had done to him, made him do, how that had scarred him going forwards. I believed him… but not because I loved him. I believed him because he was damaged, traumatised, because I know now from my hours of internet trawling that male victims often aren't taken seriously by authority, that they're too scared to speak out as a consequence. I know that was most likely why Owen didn't say anything, why he continued to live under Judy Sharpley's rules long after he realised they were wrong. In some messed-up way, he believed it was his obligation, that he owed it to her to stay quiet.

I also know what it's like to feel the pressure build up, like a pan of pasta water on the stove. Bubbles, bursting at the surface, thicker and faster, exploding into nothing. The final surge as the water hits boiling point, blowing the top off the pan and soaking the room in suds.

But that doesn't make it *right*.

It's a fine line, I think. Little Lilz of June third didn't understand that. She saw Owen's actions as self-defence, excusable, years of pain growing too much to handle. She held her boyfriend close as he kissed her, didn't care that he was using her to numb it all, to push out the memory of his mother's body behind the bathroom door. She let him pull off her top, like he'd done a million times before, kiss her breasts, her stomach. But she couldn't stop thinking about the serrated knife, covered in flesh. The blood splatters on her boyfriend's face, the bathroom walls.

Maybe that says a lot about me, the person I am, the person I didn't realise I *was*. I couldn't let go, couldn't push it from my mind. I'd seen Judy Sharpley's dead body, her innards, the liquids draining from her limp flesh as she stared up at me through the weak bathroom light. I knew, even then, that the image would haunt me for the rest of my life.

But I loved Owen.

I loved Owen, and so in my head, there was no option but to help him cover this up, the secret which would, of course, cause everything to implode.

What would you do, in that situation? Don't sit there, all high and mighty, and tell me you'd go straight to the police… or across the road to Mum, explain exactly what had happened, what Owen had done. Just *don't*.

When you're in love with a person, it doesn't even cross your mind. You have to protect them; it's your duty, as a girlfriend, their person, their soulmate. Anything they do, you're in it together.

That might sound stupid. It is stupid, really.
But then love is stupid. So, so stupid.
And first love is the most stupid thing of all.

dan's household supplies   54367
22 main street vibbington june 3 2024
east yorkshire ---- ---

item(s)   value

bleach...........................£3.59
rubber gloves....................£0.79
bin bags.........................£1.99

SUBTOTAL.........................£6.37

total amount paid in cash

PLEASE RETAIN FOR YOUR RECORDS

THE PLAN

We lay on the sofa for an hour or so. Does that sound weird? Making out with a dead body just metres away, soaking in its own juices? Owen didn't seem to notice… and if he did, he was too engrossed in me to pay the situation any attention. I was still in shock, I think. I didn't mind being his distraction.

"I love you," he kept saying. In hindsight, maybe that was his worry talking. Like if he didn't reassure me enough, I'd run straight to the police.

"I love you, I love you, I love you."

He clearly didn't trust me as much as I thought he did.

I'd actually seen a dead body once before, I thought, Owen's hands on my bum, in my hair. At a funeral, when I was seven or eight. Mum wasn't close to her parents. We barely even see Grandma now; she never approved of Mum being a "single parent" to children from separate fathers. Grandad died when I was still in primary school, and close family got to see his open casket. They went off biology more than relationships to define *close*.

I remember him looking very white, poised. His skin was waxy and made up, cheeks swiped with rouge, lips almost… pursed. You couldn't see his eyes. I don't even remember what colour they were. Just translucent lids, drooping slightly, and faded lashes, swiping his cheeks. Mum kissed him, out of respect, but I hung back, little Dizzy clutching my hand. She must have been three or four.

Judy Sharpley's death bore no comparison, of course. I

tried to imagine how the embalmer would deal with a body like that, a body sliced in two. Would an open casket be allowed? Would he stitch up the wound, cover it in bandages, dress her in something big and flouncy and floral to hide the incision?

It didn't really matter what I thought, though. Judy Sharpley would never have a funeral, never be embalmed, a fact which was becoming more and more evident as I lay beneath Owen and stared up at the damp living room ceiling.

My boyfriend was a murderer. We couldn't tell anyone about this, about this day.

And we were going to have to try our very best to hide the body.

I made us lunch after a while, maybe just for something to do, I can't remember. Obviously I wasn't hungry. Packet pasta, cheese and broccoli, sprinkled liberally with the pre-grated cheese Judy bought from the supermarket. Her whole fridge was filled with stuff like that... pre-chopped carrots, melon slices, cubes of mango. In the weeks after, teaching Owen to prepare actual meals was like teaching a baby to walk. He could saw his overweight mother in half, but had no idea how to dice or fry an onion. It was almost laughable.

We ate at the island, with more tea. Both of us had bare feet. There were slightly sticky, sicky footprints leading from the bathroom door, reminding me of something else we'd have to do, a task we'd have to perform. Cleaning the bath, the floor, our clothes. I passed Owen extra cheese, wondered, briefly, how he could take such big mouthfuls, not flinch. Was he still trying to ignore the thoughts, forget about what he'd seen, done? Even the thought of that serrated knife ploughing through flesh, crunching bone, muscle, fat... I pushed the plate away, stomach heaving. How was I supposed to eat, thinking about *that*?

"Are we going to make a plan?" I asked, shaking my head. "Like... a plan of what to do next?"

"Can I finish this first?"

So I sat and watched as Owen finished the rest of his pasta, cheese and broccoli stained all round his mouth, then finished mine off, too.

I did the washing up before joining him at the island again, using that same dishcloth to remove the sicky footprints from outside the bathroom door. The living room and kitchen were now pristine, but it still smelled, smelled like decaying flesh, even though the body had only been there for... what, four, five hours? When had he killed her? Had she been in the bathroom the entire night, unconscious? Or...

I didn't want to ask that question.

"Shall we go through to my room?" Owen asked, shuddering. "It won't smell so bad in there."

In his room, his nice, warm room, we sat on the bed, across from each other. Owen was clutching the duvet between his fingers. It was silent, the air outside too hot, humid, sucking up any sound.

"So," I said first, glancing at my boyfriend. "What do we..."

"We move the body. We transport it in my car, dump it far away, in Vibbington Wood, where no one will find it for ages. And then... we wait. We hope nobody finds it, but if they do, I don't know, we deal with the consequences, claim my mum walked out on me months ago and I had nothing to do with it."

I swallowed, staring Owen levelly in the eye. That sounded easy, too easy. Surely it wouldn't happen like that?

In hindsight, he said that all too quickly. He didn't need a minute or two to think of a plan, figure out where to turn next. He'd... *thought* about this, thought about how to hide a body, where. Was that just a coincidence? How was *I* to know?

How was I to know *anything*? I'd never killed anybody before. I'd never hidden a body, never hidden so much as a bottle of perfume stolen from Mum's dressing table. I'd never shoplifted, rarely trespassed, held my friends back because I was too scared to partake in any kind of illicit activity, to stray from the law.

And yet here we were, about to dispose of Judy Sharpley's dead body, like we were part of another world.

The outskirts of Vibbington had recently been nicknamed the Forest of Death by anyone who mattered, who understood the sinister connotations of the bridge over the stream, the dark, winding trees. A girl had committed suicide there almost five years ago, tossing herself over the bridge, after she played a part in the "accidental death" of someone in my year. We still get told about the life and legacy of Lexie McCoy at every event, still donate to the charities set to remember her, give money every term to organisations helping bereaved families cope with the loss of young children like Lexie. It was Loz's cousin who found the older girl involved, lying on the rocks below with a broken neck. There had been countless teenagers to overdose there since, at least two dozen accidentally, left to die after a party gone wrong, drugs exchanged via the wrong hands...

Half the land was owned by a man named Giles, but there was still a vast amount of forest left untrodden, too close-knit to attract dog walkers or rambles, the trees growing side by side and interlocking branches.

It wouldn't be hard to hide a body. I don't know why it

didn't come to me sooner.

We knew the forest well, like most Vibbington kids. We'd spent hours there throughout the years, usually with Gethin and his mates, because it was a prime spot for drinking and smoking and engaging in general anti-social behaviour.

"Okay," I said slowly, nodding. "How do we move the body?"

"Bin bags."

Bin bags.

The very thought turned my stomach.

"We'll take my car," Owen continued. "Clean it out well after, but cover the back seats in more big bags, sliced open, to cover any of the fabric, stuff that'll stain. We'll need to wrap the body, stop it from… leaking. We'll need old clothes, jumpers, something of yours – that way they won't link it to me."

I didn't like the way he said "sliced". There'd been too much slicing already, that day. And… something of mine. Why mine? I know Owen had a distinct style, that his clothes were old and unwashed and that Judy often labelled them with 'Sharpley' to avoid buying new stuff, but…

"Okay. Okay. I'll nip over to Mum's, grab some bits." The plan was taking shape in my mind now, growing wings and a body, fluttering out of my hands and flapping around the room. It was substantial, could stand on its own.

We'd take the body to the woods after nightfall. There was no CCTV there, or around our estate, which had caused no end of drama amongst the residents.

But it didn't matter anyway…

Because they weren't going to find the body, were they?

"No one will even notice she's missing," Owen said, reading my mind. "Mum's flighty, doesn't keep the same group of friends for long because she falls out with them so quickly. She's rubbish at social media, hardly uses her Facebook, just uses eBay to flog stuff now and then. I'll tell her friends she took off down south for a while – she went to college there, did I ever tell you that? – to see an old mate. After a few months, they'll forget all about her."

"What about money?" I queried. "Her benefits? How does she get them?

"I'll sort it all," he continued. "I've seen Mum do it enough times. I can use her benefits until we give up the flat, and... then I'll move into a separate place, a bedsit, I don't know. I'll be fine, Lilz. You overestimate how much the world cares about people like us. If anything, Mum's situation makes it easier for us to just... erase her."

Erase her.

Like she never existed in the first place.

"Are you sure this will work? It just... I don't want you to get found out, Owen. I don't know what I'd do if you... if you..."

It wasn't like me to get scared, to worry. Lilz Dart was bold, brave, didn't voice her doubts.

But this was *Owen*. I loved him, cared about him more than anything else in this world.

The thought of him going to prison made me feel physically nauseous.

"It'll all work out, Lilz, I promise." Owen reached across the bed, clasped my hands tight in his. "Do you trust me?"

And I did. I really, truly did. There was no doubt in my mind that this was the right thing to do, the only option.

"I do trust you," I whispered, as his lips met mine with a kiss. "I just don't want to lose you, Owen."

"You'll never lose me." His voice was soft, barely audible

as he dripped the words right into my mouth.

Liar.

Liar, liar, liar.

THE WOODS

My first big mistake was running back to my flat to get clothes Owen could wrap the body in, stop it from leaking, almost like a bandage, something to hold it together long enough for us to transport her. Mum and Dizzy were in the living room still, Dizzy asleep with her head on her lap, as I stuck my head in and said, "Hey. I'm just picking up some clothes, I'll probably head to school straight from Owen's."

Mum nodded, smiling. This wasn't unusual. I often ran back and forth between the two flats; it was the best thing about living close to Owen, feeling like we basically lived together.

"Have you had a good day?" She looked weary, dark circles under her eyes, and I suddenly felt bad about lying to her. But I pulled a face anyway, shrugged.

"It was fine. Uneventful, you know? Pete has a job interview, and Loz is breaking up with Ethan."

Mum's eyes widened, and she shifted so hard she almost woke Dizzy. "Uneventful? You'll have to catch me up properly tomorrow."

"Are you working?"

Mum nodded. "Two shifts."

Mum worked for the hospital, cleaning, amongst other things. Her working two or three shifts a day wasn't unusual, and was the reason she was always tired, snappy, ordered so many takeaways and bags of frozen doughballs. But... maybe her working tomorrow would work in our favour.

I smiled, feeling the second part of the plan formulate in my mind.

"I'll see you tomorrow, yeah?"

Upstairs, I disappeared into my room first. I didn't really have that many clothes. I worked the occasional Saturday at a diner in town, and was hoping to increase my hours once the summer holidays began, but it was barely enough for a few hoodies and faded, charity shop jeans. I picked through my wardrobe, heart pounding, trying to find something suitable.

Two black hoodies, too small for me now, and a pair of strawberry pyjamas I'd loved as a kid. The black skirt I wore to funerals... because I wouldn't be going to a funeral any time soon, right? A summer dress which was a bit too booby, a gift from Mum, and some scarves which used to belong to Grandma and had been donated my way (gross, old-fashioned and threadbare). But that was it. The rest of my clothes were things I wore, *needed* to wear. I could get rid of maybe one more top, but that was it.

I felt guilty the moment the idea dawned on me... but I had little other choice.

Dizzy was only twelve, still growing, and was already a good few centimetres taller than me. Mum was always complaining about having to buy her new clothes. I tiptoed into my little sister's bedroom, listening to the TV still playing downstairs, droning on.

It was pink and girly, the opposite of mine, makeup and romance novels dotting the shelves, bed covered in cloud-shaped scatter pillows and blankets she'd crocheted in pastel green and blue. There was a Dizzy-shaped hole in the middle of the bed, where she lay most days watching YouTube or reading, painting her nails pink. I swallowed. I'd have to move fast, in case Mum woke Dizzy and she came up here to go to bed…

Her bottom drawer was full of old clothes. Dizzy was sentimental, loved to keep things which no longer fit her but had "memories", but this wasn't the time for sentiment. I grabbed a pair of purple joggers, a pastel pink hoodie with a dog on the front. She probably wouldn't even notice they were gone.

Next, I opened her sock drawer. She had a whole heap of tights she never wore, in all colours of the rainbow. A pair of cycling shorts she hadn't worn since year six were added to the bag. I frowned, scouring the drawer for more.

And then her school uniform. Dizzy had a few new pieces, skirts and jumpers and the like, things she'd picked up at lost property or adopted from her friends. But there were also my old clothes, fuzzy cardigans and tops, the same pairs I'd worn when I was in year eight and nine… only they were already too small for Dizzy.

Perfect.

"Bye, Mum!"

"Love you."

Back at Owen's, I passed him the rucksack of clothes and watched him disappear into the bathroom with them.

That was my part, done.

***

Owen put the body in the bag. Two bags, technically… the body had two halves, after all. I couldn't bear to watch, could barely stand the smell. He came out covered in blood again, another hoodie, ruined. Was that stupid? We'd have to do a whole new wardrobe shop next week – for him too, not just me.

"Hey," he said sheepishly, holding the knife in one hand and a stretch of black plastic in the other. "I've had to double bag it, but I'll… I'll need help carrying. Do you want to put on some of my old clothes?"

I nodded wordlessly as he ducked into his room to get a pair of joggers, returning with the blood-splattered hoodie from earlier. I pulled my jeans and top off, tugged Owen's clothes over the top. I often wore his clothes around the flat, but only to smell him on me, wrapped around me… not so that I wouldn't stain my own clothes with the blood of his murdered mother. The hoodie smelled awful, pungent, but I knew the body would smell worse.

We wore trainers to wade through the bathroom, the sick-covered floor, blood splattered here, there and everywhere. There were too large lumps in the bathtub, wrapped in black bin bags. I was only grateful you couldn't tell the shape of her body, her face, where her head and arms were, swaddled by layers of clothes.

Not yet, anyway.

It had only just turned dark. I didn't know where the hours had gone. It only felt like five minutes ago that I'd turned up at Loz's, ate pizza on her bed, worried about Ethan Morgan and her dad's job interview and how she was moving back to Notts in a few weeks, probably for good. How could things have changed so dramatically since then? *How?*

"You grab that end," Owen said, breaking through my thoughts. "We'll move this half first."

It's funny, looking back, how that was even a sentence he could utter. This half, this half of his *mother's body*. How was that normal? How was holding half of your mum's severed corpse *normal?*

I reached into the bath, avoiding the chunks of flesh and

streaky blood, holding in my breath and trying not to breathe through my nose. The bag was slippery, heavy. I could feel her fatty arms beneath my hands, her shoulders. Owen was clutching part of her stomach. I was suddenly all too aware of the lump protruding from the plastic, a bulbous lump where her nose must be.

"Oh my God," I murmured, shaking my head. "Oh my God."

Our estate had garages at the end of the street, and Owen decided it would be best to carry the bags all the way there rather than park the car outside his block. It might look suspicious, like we were trying to hide something, and we wouldn't want that, would we? And so we opened the front door, carried Judy Sharpley's head and torso down the rickety stairs with the rotting railing, onto the street, down the pavement. The light was on in our living room window still, curtains closed, but the street was dark, silent. The flats here were mostly occupied with older people, or kids our age who'd been placed here with their families when the buildings were bought by the council fifteen, sixteen years ago. There was never anyone around at this time of night.

Judy Sharpley didn't need a garage. Owen had started renting the space from a neighbour when he turned sixteen and got a job at the greengrocers' in town, then bought a second-hand car from some guy Gethin knew. He passed his test pretty quickly, but at this point had only been driving for a few weeks. The car was red, blood red. It felt weirdly fitting.

We had to put the bag down as Owen opened the garage door, rewinding it above our heads. The lights were automatic. We'd used the garage a few times over the last year, for parties and to hang out without getting rained on. There were rainbow LED strip lights zigzagging across the back wall, band posters tacked here and there.

"Wait a minute," Owen said, glancing round at the street, checking nobody was watching. "Drag the bag in here, then wind down the door. I need to put some plastic over the boot."

Was I scared, in that moment? As I wound down the door, flicked a switch so that the lights would stay on? Was I even *thinking* straight? Worrying, even for a second, about what would happen if we were caught, if all this went wrong?

Owen had more bin bags in his pocket. He pulled out the reel and snapped two off, used some sort of car tool he had on the workbench to cut the seals and open the black plastic, creating a sheet. I looked down at the bag, resting by my feet. I remember thinking... *Thank goodness it isn't leaking; we can't stain the concrete.* Like the concrete mattered, not the fact my boyfriend had sawn his mother in half.

It was surprisingly easy to shift Judy Sharpley's body, lift the top half into the boot and settle her amongst the plastic covering. Owen flexed his fingers, staring at the shape of the bag, where her nose protruded from the plastic. Swallowed, slowly and carefully. Then he switched back into serious mode, grabbing my hoodie and gesturing for me to follow.

We made it back to the flat in two minutes, wandered back through the bathroom, the sick-soaked floor. Grabbed the bottom half of the body, two plump feet and huge, fleshy legs. Owen couldn't look at this part. Its human qualities were so much more obvious, felt much more real. We weren't just disposing of rubbish. This was a body. This was *Judy's body*.

Down the stairs we went, onto the street. Down the pavement, walking faster, faster, wanting, needing to get this over with. Judy was heavy, and I could feel something sticky at the top of the bag, oozing from the seal…

We dumped it on top of the first bag, feeling the dull thump, heavy flesh on flesh. The liquid was still oozing, dripping onto the plastic cover below. If I hadn't already sicked up breakfast and lunch, I would've thrown up again, there and then.

"Okay," Owen said, nodding. "This is good. We can wash the knife and dump it elsewhere, but… this is good."

I nodded back, feeling my hand find his. When he squeezed it, it almost hurt. But I said nothing. I understood. Even though this was stupid, even though I wasn't thinking straight at all, we'd done it. I was almost proud of us for that.

We got in the car, garage doors open wide. I got out to close them, lock things up. The street was silent, estate eerily empty. Judy Sharpley's presence alone was enough to change things here, awake corpses from the grave.

Owen drove slowly, steadily. I think he was aware of what precious cargo we were carrying, what would happen if anyone pulled us over to ask why we were speeding through a residential area, or worse. He didn't bother turning the radio off. Kylie screeched through the inside of the car, filling the silence. I pressed my hand on Owen's knee, simply just to feel grounded, remind myself that he was there. His leg tensed at my touch.

The Forest of Death was on the opposite side of Vibbington to the school, where we lived. It took us five minutes to get there, dodging the high street, anywhere we thought might have CCTV. We kept our heads down anyway. Soon we were pulling up to the estate by the forest's entrance, where a path slithered into the trees, the countryside there. It was all council owned, open to the public. It was already midnight, and the dogwalkers and Vibbington chavs had long gone home to bed.

We took the bottom half of the body from the top of the pile, legs and fleshy bottom, big feet. The sticky stuff was drying, like tar. Down the winding path, a breeze rustling the trees, through the field to where the forest began. It was a warm night, the sky black and covered in stars. If we weren't carrying a dead body, I almost would've said the setting was... *romantic*.

Through the trees we went, over the bridge. The other side of the bridge led into Giles' land, and we didn't want to risk him finding it... so we retraced our steps, back over the bridge, hearing the stream trickle below. The body was heavy, but we needed the right spot. That much was integral.

We left the main path, veering through the trees, to where the undergrowth was thick and heavy and the trees grew closer together, so much so that it was hard to break through them, especially in the dark. I had a torch on my phone, but I couldn't whip it out while both hands were occupied.

"This should be fine," Owen said, stopping abruptly. "Just lay the bag down, gently."

The bag.

As though it really was just a *bag*, not a body, a chunk of his mother.

The floor crunched as we laid Judy Sharpley there, in her woodland grave. Owen shuddered, then glanced back up at me through the dark.

"Okay, you wait here. I can probably manage the other bag by myself, but I'll need you to shine the torch through the trees so I can find my way back."

I nodded, flicking on my torch. There were a dozen messages from Loz, but I ignored them, swiping rid of the notification. I could reply to her later.

Owen only took five, six minutes to get there and back, hurrying to lug the bag, face red with effort. But in the meantime, I just... stood there. In the black forest between the densely-packed trees, listening, waiting, wind howling all around me...

Half of Judy Sharpley's dead body at my feet.

THE BLEACH

We didn't speak on the way home. What was there to say? We'd just disposed of a body together, buried it amongst bracken and broken leaves in the forest, beneath the trees. How did we return to normal, now? What even *was* normal?

Judy Sharpley kept her limited cleaning supplies in a cupboard by the front door. Owen locked it behind us. His first port of call was to fill the bath with hot, soapy water, while I found out a mop, bleach, some toilet cleaner. There were new sponges beneath the sink, a bottle of cleaning spray for bathrooms and kitchens.

The bathtub was pink, now. It stayed that way even as I sprayed it with cleaner, bleach, tried to scrub at the speckles of blood. The pink faded to orange, but that was how it settled. A shade of sunset that looked almost peachy in the yellowing bathroom light.

The tiniest hunks of flesh went down the toilet, scooped up with tissue paper. Then came the hairs, fibres, things which would fit down the drain in the bath. I'd buy some unblocker tomorrow, disintegrate all the globs swallowed by the pipes below.

We both went into autopilot as we cleaned, not thinking about the cause of the mess, what the red stains were really from. The room still smelled of meat, and no amount of bleach would change that. I glanced at Owen, swallowing a mouthful of phlegm. It was like we were living some weird, too-realistic dream, unnervingly so. I watched my boyfriend shudder.

Like I said… I'll spare you the details. It's not pretty, not fun. No one should enjoy reading about death, watching true crime videos on YouTube, flicking through missing person stories on Instagram. I'm not going to act like I wasn't one of those people, before… before Judy. I was. I loved serial killer documentaries and angry, dark songs, music with a thumping bass and screaming, murderous lyrics.

I liked to feel something, used tragedy to… I don't know, give me a weird kick, some morbid euphoria. Most teenage girls do. When you haven't experienced something terrible in life, the idea can be fascinating. You want in; we all do. And saying we like true crime, that death fascinates us, makes us feel… different.

I'm not saying it's a bad thing. It's not something we can really *help*.

But there was nothing fascinating or exciting about the cleaning process that night. It was long and dark and vigorous; we were conscious of not waking up the woman next door, or stamping too hard on the floorboards. The squeak, squeak, squeak of my sponge against the linoleum went on long into the night, and the mop continued mopping even after I let go. The whole flat had a life of its own, filled with so much death-scent that the place was buzzing with it, reincarnated. We could've started a butcher's shop there and then from the smell alone, bottling the air, thick with particles of meat. It still haunts me now.

We mopped up the sick, of course, and the footprints we'd led all around the flat. Owen put the washing up bowl on the floor so that we could keep accessing clean, soapy water, filling it up every half hour, like clockwork, but not with so much hot water that we ran out completely. Then he started on the bathroom, using the shower attachment above the bath to give the whole room a proper rinse, even though we'd no doubt cause damp to leak into the flat below.

The bleach was maybe the worst part. Once the blood had dried and disappeared down the drain, we bleached everything. The wooden arms of the sofa, the coffee table, the kitchen island. The bath, its tiles, the toilet seat and skirting boards all had a healthy dose. Even the washing up bowl received its share, scrubbing it so hard that the plastic started to disintegrate.

We were still wearing our bloody clothes, but it didn't matter. We could dispose of them later, somewhere quiet, safe, a lake or the ocean. And the knife. Owen bleached that too, killing every last morsel of blood and flesh and decay. I watched him do so from the island, perched on my stool with my hands latched together and tongue lolling against the roof of my mouth.

It was about four in the morning when we finally finished cleaning. The flat was clean enough that no one would notice how we'd hidden a dead body, used up all the bin bags, scrubbed so heavily at the floor that stains which had been left for years had finally come up with the sponge. We moved mould from the windowsill in the bathroom, mould which had been growing happily enough for as long as I'd known the family, getting thicker and more dense as the years went by and the flat festered in a Judy Sharpley bubble of grime and exhaustion.

We removed alcohol stains from walls, crumbs from the inside of the fridge, even flicked off a speck of blood from when Owen cracked his head on the kitchen island. It was like we were removing layers and layers of history, using up so many supplies we'd have to buy two dozen more to make up for what was lost.

When the deed was done, we both felt the bleach beneath our fingernails, the cleaning supplies crawling on our skin, in our hair. We even smelled of bleach, squeaky clean. We got into bed in just our underwear, leaving the dirty clothes in a pile on the floor.

I could hear Owen's heart beating, sense how tense his hands were, his shoulders. I wanted to reach out and touch him, but I didn't dare. I felt like my hands alone would taint him with fresh blood, the truth of what we'd done.

Neither of us slept for hours, lying there in the dark, listening to one another breathing.

I couldn't get the image of Judy Sharpley's cold, dead eyes from my mind, the state of her naked body in that bath, sawed brutally in half with her very own bread knife…

And the thought of Owen, holding her head under water, listening to her screams as they exploded in bubbles of water. I kept urging myself to think about this, reiterate the fact that *he'd done it*. Imagining her tubby legs and arms kicking, him too strong for her, she didn't stand a chance. My boyfriend, plunging her back under the water for one last time, having the strength and determination to go through with it, to wait until she stopped breathing to leave.

I was astounded, mostly.

Astounded, and not as disturbed as I should have been.

But the events of that night had definitely driven a wedge between us, even if I wasn't aware at the time. For all I still cared for Owen, there was no cuddling, no touching, a gap between us in the bed. I thought it was because he was still in shock, didn't want to push him.

In hindsight, he… changed. After Judy's death, her murder, after we hid her body and thought – truly *thought* –

we'd gotten away with it. He felt powerful. Realised, for the first time in his life, that he had a say in things, in the way his life played out.

Realised, for the first time ever, that he could choose what to do, what to say.

That he was strong… and that he had control.

lily dart

dear best friend of mine who i love very much

hello hello hello

there's a reason i'm trying to get hold of you

what are you doing

lily dart lily dartttt

do you hate me???

reply or i'll think you hate me (˘ ⌒ ˘)

THE AFTERMATH

The next morning, I remember only waking at eleven, twelve, Owen's legs draped over mine…

With somebody knocking on the door.

"Lilz!" came the shout, slightly muffled, under the crack. "Lilz, are you in there?"

"Who is it?" Owen's mumbled reply came from under the duvet, where he was nestled. I rolled my eyes and clambered up, pulling on his dressing gown and rubbing my eyes. They came away pale, squeaky clean, though there was a speck of red on my right hand, just by the nail on my forefinger.

That's when it all came flooding back to me.

The night before, the endless squeaking of the sponge and mop, the red splatters on the bathroom walls, in the bath. Owen, a silent expression, deadened eyes, lugging those two bin bags through the Forest of Death. The blood. So, so much blood, everywhere, all over the flat. And Judy Sharpley's body, grey and pallid, skin exposed, insides spilling out as her sawed-in-half corpse sat stewing in the bathtub.

"Oh my God," I whispered, rushing to check my face in the mirror, my hair. "We can't answer it, Owen. If we stay quiet, they'll just go away."

"Unless you forgot to lock the front door," he replied. A jolt of nerves shot through me as I stared at the lump beneath the sheets. "It sounds like Loz. You better go answer."

I glanced back into the mirror, checked my skin, my blonde head, a bird's nest atop my scalp. I'd thrown it into a bun last night and I was still in my underwear beneath the dressing gown, but I could only see one speck of blood, tiny and round and perfect, watching me like a threat.

I spat onto my other hand, stuck my nail into the glob, moved it around. Waited until all the blood had been rubbed off before swallowing and smoothing down my hair, tying the dressing gown's cord.

The rest of the flat still smelled like bleach. That was the first thing noticed. Bleach, hard and chemical and pungent, thick, like mouthwash or the chemicals we'd use in bottom set science. Bleach kills all germs, doesn't it? At least the flat had that going for it.

The knocking was still going on, interspersed with more and more urgent cries of my name.

I glanced around the living room, giving it the once over. Mop and cleaning supplies, returned to cupboard; sofa, squeaky clean, stained only from pizza and Chinese takeaways; floor, sparkling and stiff to walk on, far too polished for my liking. The bathroom door was shut flush to its frame, closing away the bath and its orangey plastic, the splatters on the tiles which just wouldn't fade.

"Lilz!" came the cry one last time. "Open up, or I'll knock the bloody door down!"

So I pushed down the handle, and sure enough, there was Loz, stood on the balcony, cheeks pink and hair all mussed-up, like she'd been running.

"Hey," I said, after a moment's pause. "Are you…"

"Am I okay?" Loz coughed, scowling at me. "Can I come in, or what?"

"Erm… now isn't a good time." I felt my own cheeks flush then, as Loz raised her eyebrows and gave me the once over, realising I was wearing Owen's dressing gown and making one of *those* noises. "I... yes. Owen's naked. Sorry, it's just not..."

"At eleven o'clock on a Tuesday? Why aren't you at school?"

"I... it must be hormones, or something. Sex drive gone mad."

Loz raised an eyebrow, and I thought, even just for a minute, that she didn't believe me, that she could see straight through me and to the squeaky-clean room beyond. "No judgement, I guess. But... can you go and get dressed, and speak to my outside?"

I paused again. The way my best friend said this was... desperate. Loz never sounded desperate. Stressed, occasionally, of course, and too caught up in gossip to focus on reality. But desperate, never. She was strong and independent and bold, but looking at me now like she really, *really* needed help.

"What's up?" I asked cautiously. "Is it Ethan?"

"I... yeah, it's Ethan. I'm meeting up with him tonight. I just..."

"Tonight? That's good." But I wasn't really listening.

I'd just remembered the knife, sat on the draining board, all alone. It had been washed, of course. But I didn't like the fact that it was just... resting, in plain sight, for Loz and all else to see. There were no plates out, no bread, no butter. Just Judy Sharpley's serrated knife, scrubbed and bleached and drying in the weak sun.

"Yes, tonight. I'm going to break up with him, but I don't know what to –"

And the bin bags. The bin bags were there, too, on the kitchen side. The whole roll of them, waiting to wrap up more bodies, whenever the time was right.

"You're not listening." Loz was looking at me then. Her forehead was creased and her lips were pursed, and I wanted to say that *yes*, yes I was listening, of *course* I was, but no words would come out, and the air between us felt stilted, awkward, like yesterday.

"I am," I said. "You're seeing Ethan tonight to break up with him, and you don't know what to say."

"And I need your help."

"Loz..."

"What? I've never done this before, Lilz, and we've been together *years*. I need some help!"

"Can't it wait?"

"Wait?"

"Until tomorrow."

Loz was looking at me funny. Like she felt... betrayed, in a way. And suspicious. So, so suspicious, suspicious of why I was stood here in my underwear and Owen's dressing gown at eleven o'clock on a Tuesday, and why that was too important for me to support my best friend through her first proper breakup.

"I mean, do you have to see him tonight?"

"What, and delay this for another day?"

Loz looked so *confused*. Confused, and hurt.

"Only because I want to help you do this right, and this isn't... isn't the right time."

"To go and put some clothes on, and talk to me about Ethan?" Loz opened her mouth and closed it for a second, then added, "What's so special about tonight? You spend almost every day with Owen."

She was right.

But she was also so, so wrong.

"Please, Lauren." Lauren. I never called her *Lauren*. "I

just…"

That's when she stopped.

Actually stopped, stopped dead in her tracks.

"What's that smell?" is all she said.

That smell. I paused, too, and for a second went along with it. Sniffed the air, then looked back at her and said, "I can't smell anything."

"It's like… bleachy." She looked past me then. I was too shocked to block her movements, to stop her from arching her neck and breathing in, gazing round the flat, the kitchen and living room and closed bathroom door. "Has Judy just cleaned the place or something?"

"I… yes, yes she has." I was wracking my brains, wracking them hard for something to say. Why would Judy Sharpley clean the flat, when she was possibly one of the grottiest, grimiest women alive? Loz and the others rarely hung out there because she'd let milk and microwave meals go off in the fridge, leave whole tubs of butter to melt on the side. I was used to it, but in Loz's world of luxury, Owen's flat was practically a dump.

"Oh. Okay." Silence. Then, "Why?"

What was it that Owen had said last night? Something about coming up with a plan to tell people, if Judy's friends or anybody else started questioning where she'd gone, why she wasn't going to the pub or to bingo anymore…

"She's gone." My words sounded funny as I said them, pulling a face. "She's gone to visit an old friend for a while, needed a break from… everything. So she cleaned out the flat, then took off without saying goodbye, just sent Owen a quick text to say she'd be back eventually."

Loz raised her eyebrows, mouth open wide. "She's… I can't believe it. I know she was a bitch, but to run off and leave Owen like that, without saying *bye?*"

"He's proper upset about it too," I continued, pulling a face. "So you shouldn't say anything to him about it, or he'll only get sad, you know?"

"Owen, sad?" she said doubtfully. "I mean, obviously. I won't say anything. But... is that why you need to be here with him? He's upset about this whole thing?"

I nodded. "Very. I'm worried he might do something, you know? That he's not in his right frame of mind."

I really, really hoped that Owen couldn't hear us from the bedroom. Even though it was all just an elaborate cover story, I knew he'd hate being made out to look weak, damaged. It was understandable *why*, when all of this was a lie.

"Of course, I get that. You... you really think he'd do that?"

Did I really think Owen would harm himself? No, of course I didn't. But did I think I needed to be here for him today, keep an eye on him, stop him from getting in his head about the whole I-just-committed-murder thing? Yes, yes, I did. He wasn't in his right frame of mind right now, by no fault of his own.

And I needed to help him through that.

"I don't know," I answered, only partially truthfully. "I just want to be here for him today. I'm sorry, Loz. Please don't prolong talking to Ethan if it's playing on your mind..."

"Hey, I'll be okay." My best friend smiled weakly, nodding. "I can do this. I need to *do* it, you know? Ethan isn't right for me anymore. It just doesn't make sense."

I grabbed her hands, squeezed tight. Felt her pulse, limp and anxious, then pulled back, realising all too soon that Judy Sharpley's hands would never pulse again, what that very movement of blood and liquid even *signified* –

"Say hi to Owen for me, won't you?"

I nodded. "Of course. I'll… tell him you popped by."

"Does he want me to tell the others, or would he rather do that himself?"

"We'll tell Kara and Gethin, don't worry. I'll sort it all." Gethin's mum was tight with Judy, and Kara's dad had snogged her once when they were both fifteen (he still had a bit of a crush). If Loz told the others straight away, the news of Judy Sharpley's disappearance would be round Vibbington like wildfire. We needed time to properly clean the flat, remove some of her things, let the bleach smell die down, create a cover story. Those things were important.

"I'll see you tomorrow, yeah?" Loz said hopefully. "And I'll let you know how it goes with Ethan."

"Okay."

I watched as Loz smiled and turned, waving as she made her way down the rickety steps onto the street below.

And I swear the bleach smell followed.

kara faulkner???

please please reply bcs
i'm going mad

loz stfu

i'm busy babe xxx

owen and lilz are being
weird and idk why!!!

bye babe xxx

switching off now xxx

love you too -_-

THE SHOWER

I slipped off my faded pants, bra, swallowed. The hot water was already running, and Owen stood under the stream, white chest glistening, mouth pursed and wet. I wanted to kiss him. I wanted to kiss him all over, lingering on his soft spots... but I also wanted to cry, and run, peel back the skin of his skull and examine the brain within. Figure out why he'd done this, why *we'd* done this, and what the hell was actually happening.

We were at my flat now, across the road. Neither us could've fathomed having a shower – or a bath – in the stained Sharpley tub, staring at the splatters on the tiles, the speckles on our skin. Mum was at work, and Dizzy was at school. It was about half twelve, and the rest of the world was engaged in normal life... except for Owen and I, naked in my bathroom, bodies scattered with sin.

I remember studying *Macbeth* at GCSE, learning about the ways in which Lady Macbeth delt with her guilt. She smelled the blood of her victims long after they'd marked her hands, felt the liquid seep across her hands and under her nails, scrubbed them a thousand times but still couldn't get remove the stains.

I felt like that now. Stained, dirty. A sinner. I looked down at my own body. Pale, flat breasts, skinny stomach, weedy legs. I felt like I could see the blood now, even though I knew there wasn't any *there*, just the odd spot on my nail, behind my ear. My body still felt tainted, imperfect. It had always been, but Judy Sharpley made that so much worse.

"Come here," Owen said, and I let myself sink under the stream. His body was soft, warm, water hot and soapy and delicious. We used Dizzy's strawberry shower gel, washing separately, scrub-scrub-scrubbing every crack and crevice, not looking at one another. The scent was so sweet I felt sick.

We'd showered together before, but only for fun, because we thought it sounded romantic, risqué. Those times, we hadn't actually done much *showering*... or scrubbing.

This was different.

It felt like a ritual, something we had to do, a task we were ordered to perform. I watched Owen when I was done, sure that I'd reached every possible place the blood could have found its way into. He lifted an arm to wash his armpits, a handful of strawberry shower gel in each, rubbing vigorously to remove every lump of blood and flesh. I swallowed as he turned, asked me to do his back. Rubbed it, over and over, his pale skin smooth between my fingers, the scattering of acne like pin-pricks of Judy's bloody sinew.

Maybe this whole thing still sounds strange to you. Not the intimacy of it, but the... closeness. The way the murder didn't tear us apart, but joined us in some sort of weird, pre-death ceremony, scrubbing each other clean of the body we'd only just disposed of. Maybe it is strange, odd. Looking back, I was definitely too blasé about the whole thing... but then who wouldn't be? Judy was dead, and the love of my life, my forever, was going to get the blame unless I helped him, washed the blood from both our hands. There was no point *panicking*.

"Thank you," Owen whispered as I slipped my arms round his waist, his stomach, kissing his shoulders from behind. "I love you, Lilz. I love you so much."

"I know."

We stayed like that for a little while, before Owen twisted round, so he was facing me. I let myself gaze into his face, his eyes, the face I now called mine, mine, mine. His freckles, floppy brown hair, dark blue eyes, pale skin... and that mouth, plump lips, carved into his face – *our* face – like they were meant for me. I had dreams about that mouth. I wanted our children to have it, our grandchildren, for the Sharpley line to carry that soft pair of lips until the end of time.

His kisses were soft now, meaningful, like we were both horribly aware of the reason we were now bound together, even more so than before. The very tip of his tongue, edging into my mouth, exploring, wanting more. And his hands, those gentle hands, pawing at my waist, my skinny body. Owen and Lilz, meant to be. Owen and Lilz, together forever, best friends, partners in crime.

Ha. That's funny. The fact we actually were partners in crime now, not just boyfriend and girlfriend, a sweet sixth form couple.

We'd covered up a murder. We'd scrubbed the blood from each other's bodies, washed the flat in bleach, *so much bleach*. We were bad people. You know that, right? That we were bad people, awful people, at this moment in time. Don't excuse our actions just because we were in love, because Owen had been abused his entire life. It still doesn't make what we did right, not in any way. We should've been punished there and then...

But we weren't.

Instead, Owen continued to kiss me. More and more urgent this time, clawing at my body, fingers venturing where it probably wasn't appropriate at lunchtime in my family's bathroom. But I let him, of course, kissing him back just as hard as we stumbled out of the shower, leaving it running, wasting all the hot water, letting it spray out over the floor.

Into my bedroom we went, dripping wet, still unclothed, curtains closed. I could feel Owen's body pulsing against me, skin hot and sticky and desperate, slotting into mine. I could feel his hands, the soft curves of his nails, brushing my stomach, my hips. And then I could feel him inside me, *really* inside me, and everything was bliss.

Owen Sharpley felt like any first love does. Perfect, hand-made, carved for you and nobody else. That's how I felt as I lay there, Owen atop me, all thoughts evaporating from my mind.

Another spoiler: I still haven't slept with anybody else, even now, in September. Not that I'm dying to or anything. But... even now, three months after we dumped Judy Sharpley's body in those woods, I'm able to look back and reflect on the relationship, on first relationships as a whole. I didn't know my way around love enough to claim for sure whether Owen and I were meant for each other, because I knew nothing else, no better. I thought sleeping with Owen was perfect because I had nothing else to compare it to.

Would...

Will sleeping with someone else eventually feel just as good, just as special?

Probably. That makes sense, right? Because it's not the *person* that matters, or their body, the way it works. It's the situation, how you see the individual. It's the intimacy of letting them see you in such a vulnerable state, acknowledging and loving their mind, respecting their rules.

But I was seventeen. A kid.

I was naïve, and I thought Owen was my soulmate. I thought love couldn't get any better than that. And so there, laid in my bed, Owen's wet skin pressed against mine, I made a vow to myself to protect our relationship, whatever the cost.

If Owen was *really* made for me, I wouldn't have had to try so hard to keep that promise.

If Owen was *really* made for me, nothing would have ever gone wrong.

dear diary

i'm already bored of writing a diary so let's keep this short and sweet

my sister lilz's boyfriend owen said today that his mum has left him, which is literally brutal. imagine running off and leaving your kid like that? lowkey neglect

owen is fit, but if lilz knew i thought that she'd kill me

so if you're reading this, lilz, beware, because i can kill you back harder!!!

anyway. bored again

ttyl

dizzy xoxo

THE FIRST LIE

In hindsight, the first proper lie we told was to Loz. Letting her believe that Judy Sharpley had run away and left Owen all alone in that flat... It wasn't true, of course, but it had an *element* of truth, just a smidge. And for some reason, I didn't feel too bad lying to her. It felt necessary, in a way. Besides, Loz wasn't perfect. She didn't necessarily *deserve* a hand-carved truth, placed right in her hands.

When Dizzy got home from school later that day, she found Owen and I in a tangle on the sofa, wearing pyjamas. Owen usually slept in joggers, but he kept a spare pair of jammies at mine he only really wore in winter. They were tartan and cosy, and he had them on now, matching top and bottoms.

"You skived again," she said, just like that. "You're both going to fail your A-levels."

"Good day to you too."

My little sister pouted, eyeing the takeaway pizza we'd ordered between us. It was meat feast, and the barbecue base had never looked saucier.

"I want in."

We ended up huddled as a three, watching rubbish TV and munching on the pizza and potato wedges. Owen had a habit of picking off the toppings, but I loved the crusts, and Dizzy favoured the barbecue base – and the cheese. The three of us had ordered enough pizzas in our lifetime to know our system, how each of us preferred their takeaway. Dizzy stole two of the cookies at the end, and Owen and I broke the third in half.

"I think Mr O'Flannel wants to shag Miss Marian."

I almost choked on my pizza. Dizzy was still scoffing her face, watching the TV all pert and happy and innocent, barbecue sauce in the corners of her mouth.

"Where did you get that impression?"

"Oh, they have so much chemistry, it's ridiculous." Dizzy glanced at me out of the corner of her eye, smiling and saying, "He gave her *the eyes* today, outside the art block."

Mr O'Flannel was an English teacher at Vibbington Secondary, and Miss Marian was Dizzy's maths teacher. Miss Marian was engaged, I'm pretty sure, and Mr O'Flannel... surely his overenthusiastic analysation of Chaucer was enough to turn off any woman.

"What are *the eyes*?" Owen piped up.

It was the first thing he'd said since Dizzy got back, but that wasn't unusual. Owen was always quiet. He was quieter than I was, quieter than Mum and Dizzy. Our family wasn't like his; I think that's why he liked coming here, to watch movies and cuddle up with a takeaway, some of Mum's occasional cooking. He needed his downtime, liked silence and space, but it made a change to see us from time to time. Us, who were bubbly and chatty and sweet... and the complete opposite of Judy.

"The eyes," Dizzy replied, rolling her own. "You know, the *sexy eyes*. You and Lilz were doing them before I came in."

I actually did choke on my pizza this time, spitting the crust into my hand as Dizzy grinned. "We were *not*."

"You so were," my little sister said smugly, turning her face back to the TV.

Mum always used to say that having an older sister and a

younger mum had made Dizzy wise for her age, older than her years. We'd watched enough racy soaps and scoffed over countless innuendos over the years, all of which made Dizzy incredibly popular with the other girls at school – and the boys.

Having a little sister the exact replica of me had always felt weird. Like people were constantly comparing the two of us, seeing as we looked so alike. Dizzy was a girlier version of me, all pink and pretty, into fashion and romance novels and fluffy things, but she was also snarky, and sharp, and hated school. She was smarter than me – not that it took much trying – but wasted her brains messing about in class, trying to impress boys, getting detentions for silly things like rolling her skirt up too far and going on her phone.

I couldn't really criticise her for that, though. I'd been just as bad when I was her age. I never handed in my homework on time, struggled concentrating in class, wore heavy eye makeup to school and listened to music through my AirPods in maths. But that didn't mean I wanted Dizzy to turn out like me. It's not like I wasn't happy with my life or anything, because I was, I *am*. I wouldn't change meeting Owen, Loz, because it made me who I am today.

But Dizzy…

Dizzy was smart, pretty, funny.

She had – *has* – options.

I met Owen when I was twelve, slept with him at fourteen. My whole teenage years were shaped by that relationship. I'd done so many things I never would have done had I not met Owen, and while I was grateful for the life I had, part of me still wished I'd just been… well, normal. Because my timeline wasn't normal, and neither was Owen's. And while I loved Owen – while I was so thankful for the time we'd spent together – I wanted Dizzy to stay young for as long as possible, enjoy the life I never had.

I watched her for a minute now, heart thudding. I tried to imagine, just for a second, how I'd feel if she was ever placed in a situation like this, concealing a secret she couldn't keep.

"What?" she asked, scowling as she noticed me looking.

"I was just thinking how pretty you are, Diz."

"No, you weren't."

There was a moment of silence before Owen and I burst out laughing, Dizzy sitting wounded and confused between us.

"What's so funny?"

"Never you mind, Dizzy. Never you mind."

***

Mum came back later, finishing work at an obscure time, as usual. She took one look at the empty pizza box and pulled the longest, most hurt expression in the history of hurt expressions, and both Dizzy and I leapt off the sofa to go and hug her. She smelled of bleach, though for the correct reasons, not like us.

"Mmm," she murmured, nestling her own blonde head between ours. "Does this mean my favourite daughters are going to cook me some tea?"

So we did, of course. It was the least we – or I – could do. I was already starting to feel guilty as I boiled the pasta, watching Dizzy spoon pesto into a bowl and chop the tomatoes. Owen's head could be seen above the back of the sofa, expression hidden. I watched him through the gap in the door as the pasta bubbled away, before turning back to help Dizzy uncork the wine.

Mum ate on the sofa as we flicked on *How I Met Your Mother* and curled up around her. Owen had moved to the armchair. For once, he didn't complain about our choice of show. His expression remained impassive as we watched Ted, Robin, Barney, Marshall and Lily do their thing, Mum's fork clinking against the bowl, spearing pasta, tomatoes. The room smelled of stale pizza and pesto.

Then Owen reached onto the coffee table for the remote control, and turned the TV off as the credits rolled.

Mum glanced up from her pasta, frowning, as I did the same. But my heart was thudding, properly thudding. What was he doing? Was he...

"Owen." Dizzy and Mum were both throwing back and forth between my boyfriend and the TV, confused. "What are you..."

"Alice." Owen addressed Mum by her first name. He'd never really called her *anything* before, not to her face, but especially not Alice, so casually, intimate. The word came out of nowhere, splitting the room in half. "I... I'd like to tell you something."

Mum continued to frown, but didn't hesitate as she placed the pasta bowl on the floor, half-full. She was tired and hungry, and didn't look pleased.

I swallowed, glancing back at Owen. What was he doing? Was he about to tell them what happened? What we *did*?

Mum followed the movement of my head.

"Is this about Lilz?" That's when she looked at me, realisation dawning, and asked, "Are you pregnant?"

"Mum!"

Even Dizzy looked outraged as she burst, "Lilz isn't *pregnant*."

Mum narrowed her eyes, like she didn't completely

believe me. She still didn't pick up her pasta bowl. Owen looked nervous, but I didn't know what else to do, how to react. I wasn't even sure what was about to come out of his mouth.

"Fine. Go on, Owen."

"What's going on?" Dizzy was confused, too, sat between Mum and I with a big glass of full-sugar coke in her hands. "What's happening, Owen? Lilz?"

Owen looked at me, letting the room fill with air.

And then he said, "My mum's gone."

Silence.

Both Mum and Dizzy had expressions of shock, staring at Owen like they didn't understand what he was saying.

"Gone?" Mum echoed first. "What do you mean, *gone?*"

"She left me. Last night. Left to go and see her friend down south. She isn't… isn't sure she'll come back."

Mum's mouth opened and closed, eyes wide.

"She didn't want to be here anymore, in Vibbington, with me. She's left me the flat to use until I'm eighteen, when I'll… I'll get a bedsit, or something. The council will cover it for a while as long as they don't know she's gone, but she's hoping to get a new place down in Lincoln eventually, when everything is sorted. I'll figure things out, then try to contact her eventually, let her know that she can apply for housing again and start a new life. I think you'll understand why she's done this, Alice. You know she wasn't cut out to be a mother."

And as I listened to him speak, telling Mum these lies, cold lies, relief flooded through me, selfish relief, stretching out to touch the corners of the room.

He wouldn't tell them about the body.

Of *course* he wouldn't.

112

I was stupid to think that, even for a second.

"A bedsit?" Mum echoed again, shaking her head. "No, Owen, no. If you ever need anything, you know you have a room here, I've always said –"

"You have enough on your plate without getting in trouble with social services, Alice."

Is it odd that I found that weirdly… sexy? The way he was being so mature about this, so matter-of-fact, referring to my mum by her first name. He sounded so old, so adult. So in control.

Stupid Lilz.

Stupid, *stupid* Lilz.

My cheeks were pink, and I wanted nothing more than to stand and entwine my hands through Owen's hair, kiss his perfect white shoulders… Until I realised that we were both lying to Mum, and that she looked heartbroken, so bloody heartbroken for poor abandoned Owen.

"Did she say why she was leaving?" Mum asked.

Dizzy's voice was forlorn as she added, "Yeah, Owen. Did she say why?"

Owen shrugged. "She… was tired, and run-down, and sick of this area. Mum's flighty, you know what she's like. She left a message saying she needed a break, a fresh start. She used to go to college across the Humber, so she has friends down there. That was it. I think she was done trying to pretend she liked being a mother, when all she's ever wanted is her freedom. While she was my carer, she couldn't get that freedom, you know?" He looked shifty for a minute, eyes down.

Then he said, "If you ask me… I think she might have met another man."

My own mouth dropped open.

"Oh, Owen…" Mum's eyes were glistening, filled with tears. *Tears*. The story was so tragic, so sad, that my own mother had been reduced to tears by it. "I'm so sorry. I know Judy wasn't the best mother to you, which is why I've tried to give you the best life possible here, in so many ways. It's not easy, being a mother. Please don't think she didn't love you, because that's not true. But… Judy had problems she needed to work through before letting you in. I think we all saw that."

Mum carried on talking, but my eyes were focused on Owen. He looked *triumphant*, in a way. Like he knew the plan had worked, that we'd gotten her on side.

"Please don't tell anybody yet, Alice. I need to stay living there for a while, just another five months or so, before I turn eighteen and can get my own place."

"But Owen…"

"Please." He really did sound pleading, desperate. Convincingly so.

This time, I didn't think he was lying.

"I… I won't tell." Mum bit her lip, wiped a tear from her eye. "Oh, Owen, come here for a hug! You know you're welcome here any time, don't you? There'll always be food in the fridge, hot water, a bed to sleep in…"

Dizzy joined in the hug too, both her and Mum facing the wall, Owen facing me.

He was smiling.

And winking.

We won! the wink screamed. *We won!*

But had we really won? Hadn't we just… lied?

It was no different than me lying to Loz, I know that now. But the way he lied, the way he showed no remorse, said everything so sadly, so calmly, felt… different. Wrong.

Guilt writhed in my stomach as Mum pulled back, wiped her cheeks again. Even Dizzy was welling up.

This wasn't right. This wasn't right at all.

But was there any other option?

07/06/2024 10:11:17

07/06/2024 10:11:05

THE SKY

I think the whole world knew of our deception, the week after. That's how it felt, anyway. Like the planet was welling up in its effort to conceal the truth, turning the sky a shade of hot green, the earth yellow and dry, coarse. Tuesday night melted into Wednesday morning, warm and hard, like bone, and Wednesday faded to Thursday, which felt the same, so mind-numbingly hot and thick and... easy. Too easy.

The sky stayed that shade of minty green, covered in a haze of misty cloud, as Owen and I drifted in and out of our post-murder trance. It's funny how badly I stored these memories, how poorly they were filed away in my brain. Maybe that was deliberate. Maybe June-Lilz knew this time wasn't one I'd want to remember, so many accounts from that first week are fragmented, stored in the wrong order, confusing to pick at.

The things I do remember aren't exactly... clear-cut. I know we took the week off sixth form, understandably, and that we had to send a letter to explain to Mr Roberts that because of a recent family tragedy, we needed time away from school to grieve. It wasn't a lie. He responded promptly, sending his condolences – and those of the other sixth form staff. Owen crumpled up the letter and threw it into the bin, beside the sponges and mop head we'd used to clean the flat.

That must've come before the bin-job, then. Yes, of course; that makes sense. We didn't get chance to dump the stuff until Friday, around lunch time, when Vibbington had been swallowed by a sweltering haze and nobody noticed a sordid Lilz and Owen traipsing to the car with a big black bin bag, a tea towel concealing the serrated bread knife.

We drove to the coast, of course. Where else? Owen filled up on the outskirts of town as I sat in the passenger seat, watching my boyfriend as he injected fuel into his blood-red car, pushing his floppy hair out of his eyes and panting in the heat, tugging his joggers around his waist before heading in to pay.

I love you, I thought as he disappeared inside the shop, watching the movement of his hips, the sway of his body. *I love you, Owen Sharpley. I'd do anything for you.*

We didn't stop driving again until we were well out of Vibbington and had driven a substantial distance down the Yorkshire coast, away from home. Past the towns, the dog walkers' beaches and flat expanses of sand, tall, chalk cliffs edged upwards away from the landscape, beaming in eery intimidation. Even for June, the land was waiting to become luscious and green, and this heatwave wasn't helping. The clifftops were grassy and sandy, so dry you could've set fire to the whole world up there.

The car park was empty. It wasn't really a car park, anyway, just a scrubby patch the public had commandeered for parking by this particular bay; it wasn't as popular as others up the coast, which had cafés and signs about endangered birds and parking meters.

Owen pulled right up to the edge, as close as he could get.

Then we stopped. The world stretched out ahead of us in a horribly blue, electric blanket. It was the most colour I'd seen all week, since Judy Sharpley's innards had spilt out over the white of the bath. A deep, saturated shade of ocean, sparkling in the sun, the kind you'd only ever spot on holiday in Spain (not that I'd ever been to Spain). For a moment, I couldn't do anything but stare.

It didn't feel right that the world should be this beautiful, this perfect, when we were committing such a crime.

"Come on."

Owen stepped out first, grabbing the bin bag from the boot. I took the knife, still wrapped in his tea towel. Nobody would see us here. I couldn't see another house or car for miles, and the cove below looked bare, white, untouched.

I followed my boyfriend down the clifftop's steep steps, which had been badly carved into the landscape, eroded over the years. I couldn't help but picture a time before ours, for what purpose the steps had been built into the cliffs here, whoever had come before us. Smugglers, taking illegal alcohol and cigarettes to sell to the surrounding villages... or soldiers, invading armies, landing in this cove undetected before their attack. And couples. Couples, riding here on horseback, stopping by the edge to picnic on the cliffs, to kiss in private, away from their public lives.

Owen didn't appear to be thinking much. His face was still, serious, lugging the black bin bag like his life depended on it. In a way, I suppose it did. The serrated knife was heavy in my hand, metallic, cold. The tea towel kept slipping sideways.

"Careful here," he called up to me, reaching the bottom of the steps, which were slippery with seaweed and chunks of green flesh. I swallowed, trying to avoid stepping on the carcass of some white bird, one which looked a whole lot like the breed our local news teams were always raising money to save. The scent of salt was overbearing, the rocks on the beach glistening, sea stretching on in a long, bright blue haze.

"Okay," Owen said, gesturing to me. "Pass me the knife."

The bin bag was bulging, resting beside him on the rocks. I passed him the knife.

Owen's movements were swift, quick. He didn't think too much as he arched his arm and sent the thing flying over his head like a boomerang, slicing clean through the air and landing a good fifty metres away in the sea with a splash.

He couldn't even look at me; it felt wrong to congratulate him, however impressive the move had been. I watched as my boyfriend picked up the bag, moving forwards, Adam's apple grating his throat. His trainers gripped the rocks, eyes trained on the ground. He moved far enough out that he could open the bag and tip the contents into the sea, watching them float away, eyes glassy, the now-red mop head bopping like a seal. The bag went last, floating amid the waves, before falling below the surface and losing itself forever to the ocean.

"We're such litterers," I tried to joke, but Owen was too choked up to reply.

***

The rest of the week, and subsequent weekend, followed similarly. Owen spent most of his days at mine, lounging on my bed or curled up on the sofa with his eyes half-closed and a takeaway resting on his lap. He only showered in our family bathroom, as we didn't have a bath, and ate Mum's meals where possible, until we both offered to cook for her and even drove into town for supplies, venturing into Vibbington's centre for the first time in days. We didn't see anyone we knew. It felt strange knowing the whole town was continuing as normal, despite what we'd done.

You might be wondering if we felt scared, at any point that week. We'd killed someone, hidden a body deep in the forest. Were we nervous, on tenterhooks, convinced that any time someone knocked on the door it would be the police, ready to steal us away to the station and identify Judy Sharpley's decomposing corpse?

But... we weren't. What was done was done, and we couldn't change that, couldn't go back in time to reverse the events of June third. We had to live with the consequences, and worrying that we'd be found out wouldn't help anything, not now. We had to act natural, calm, until Judy's friends and acquaintances started asking questions, knocking on the door, messaging us via Judy's phone, which was dead and hadn't been charged since her death.

Loz didn't break up with Ethan that week. She messaged me to say they were officially taking a break, that they'd meet up in a week or two, before she went back to Notts, to discuss everything after they'd had chance to think things through properly. That was the plan, anyway... until she sent me a follow-up message on Saturday afternoon, out of the blue.

Just rang Ethan and ended it. It was weighing me down and I needed to get it over with. I feel like such a BITCH but it was the right thing to do right Lilz?? I'm stressing the frick out, he sounded like he was going to start BAWLING. Call me soon, okay?

I typed out a response pretty much straight away, eyes wide. Owen was making us both a sandwich in the kitchen – bread, butter, pre-sliced cheese – and Dizzy was out with a friend, Mum at work.

Maybe I should've told Loz to come round and talk about this.

Maybe it would've helped.

But I didn't.

YES IT WAS THE RIGHT THING. the minute you lose feelings it's cruel to still continue the relationship. I do be proud of youuuuuuu x

I was smiling into my phone as Loz sent a similarly gushy message back, as Owen entered, holding the plate of sandwiches and frowning.

"What did I miss?" he asked, placing it down on the coffee table. "You look like someone just offered you a puppy."

"Sort of," I replied, to which he raised an eyebrow. "Nah, Loz just broke up with Ethan. It's been on the horizon for... well, the last six billion years."

"I didn't know they were unhappy," Owen said, slipping onto the sofa beside me. His arm around me was instinctual, his breath on the side of my face. "I thought they were going to be another Orla and Aaron, together till the end of time."

"Not a chance," I said, wrinkling my nose. "Loz is way too fun. She likes change, meeting new people, having experiences. She was never going to stay with him once she moves."

"I guess not..." Owen reached forward for the sandwiches, pulling the plate onto his lap. I watched the hinge of his jaw as he took the first bite, a globule of butter at the corner of his mouth. "Well, good for Loz, then."

"Good for Loz?"

"For getting out the minute she realised she wasn't happy."

I nodded, trying to process this. Was that really the right thing to do, under all circumstances? What if... if Owen started to lose feelings for me? After almost five years of being together, would he view our breakup in the same way? Important to get out the minute he realised he wasn't happy?

"Owen?" I asked, poking the side of his face. "What would you do in that situation? If… if you realised that you weren't happy, and wanted out? Would you break up with me?"

He took a second to think, swallowing his mouthful. "I guess. But it would be complicated, because we've been together for so long. I'd probably take a long time to think about it, and we'd have a lot of very serious conversations." He adopted a goofy smile then, turning to me and rolling his eyes. "But that's never, ever going to happen, you realise that? Me and you really *are* a forever thing."

"I know." My stomach felt all mushy and gooey as I cuddled into him, listening to the chewing of the cheese sandwich. I picked my own from the plate, turning it over in my hands. "And not that this will ever happen, but…"

"But…?"

"What would you want me to do if I realised *I* wasn't happy?"

"With our relationship?"

"With our relationship."

Owen cocked his head, frowning. "Well… it wouldn't matter, would it? We committed a murder together, and I have evidence of that. So you're tied to me. I have the power to frame you, dear Lilz. You can't get out that easy."

I really, really thought he was joking. I burst out laughing, shaking my head and jabbing his side.

"I am tied to you. And you're tied to me, *dear Owen*."

Owen had a small smile on his face as he nodded, eyes fixed on the TV. Oh, *Owen*! How funny you were. We were tied to each other; he had the power to frame me for murder. I couldn't get out that easy, and he knew it.

never trust the
blue eyed boy
.'〈‒.'+'.'

THE SLEEPOVER

Going back to sixth form was surprisingly underwhelming. Nobody knew Owen's mum was dead; Loz had well and truly stuck to her word, so no one even knew she was missing. Ethan Morgan ignored me when I tried to say hi in the common room, and his friend Lucy, a mousy girl with big green eyes, gave the dirtiest of looks as we walked by. Kara was all over Owen, as usual, and Gethin spent the whole day complaining about this girl from Throwsley who'd slept with him then ghosted, muttering all through sociology and into the afternoon.

It was sunny still, even for a Monday, which were known for being dull. We ate crisps on the school field at lunch, watching Nora Baio and Alicia McKnight show off their hockey skills on the AstroTurf nearby while the boys clapped. Loz had been on the team before she left. Nora might be captain now, but Loz could've knocked any of them out with her stick.

Owen and I weren't known for our sporting prowess… which is why I was surprised he had the strength to hack that knife through Judy Sharpley's body, those thick bones, flesh.

The five of us met up in town once our lessons were done, collapsing in front of Tesco with a collection of ice lollies and cool cans of Venom.

Our sixth form didn't have a strict dress code, but Kara and I were still sweltering in our jeans and t-shirts as Loz basked in an itsy bikini top and teeny shorts. She looked incredible as usual, and she'd done her eyeliner so fiercely it could've sliced my skin. That was the thing about my best friend. As incredible as she was, she never failed to terrify me.

I realised then that this was the first time I'd seen her since she'd knocked on Owen's door that morning, and couldn't help but flush every time she looked in my direction, like she could see right through me. She seemed... sad, in a way. Dejected. Breaking up with Ethan might have been the right thing for her to do, but that didn't mean she wouldn't miss him.

"Hey," I said, poking her arm. "You okay?"

She pulled a face back, lifting a hand to shield her eyes from the sun. Fully made-up and boobs popping out of her bikini, she certainly *looked* okay, but I knew my best friend better than that.

"Just sucks, doesn't it?" She sighed as Kara moved a little closer to listen. Gethin and Owen were engrossed in a conversation about Formula 1 and how Gethin's weed supplier had just been busted, and Loz shuffled up to let Kara in. "Did Ethan seem sad today?"

"Crushed," I admitted. Even Kara nodded, sharp face somewhat... sympathetic. Like I said, she was better friends with Loz than was with me; she knew how to be nice to the people she liked, clearly. "Wouldn't even catch my eye."

Loz gave a little grin. "Is it bad that I'm almost *glad* he looked sad?"

"Very," I retorted. "But that just makes you human. And humans are bad."

"Not all humans. Lilz-shaped humans aren't bad."

I smiled, I couldn't help thinking, *Little do you know...*

Kara piped up, twisting her hair around her finger. "Can I... suggest something?" She bit her lip; "I know we haven't had a girly sleepover in a while, so how about it? Tonight, at mine? You two can both sleep on my sofa bed, and me and Lilz will skip period one tomorrow so we can lay in."

Loz looked at me, instantly perkier. I was about to say yes, to nod and agree and go along with Kara's plans, even though I'd really rather not visit her weird little hole of a home on the other side of Vibbington. Then I stopped.

Owen.

I hadn't spent a night away from him since... since Tuesday. And the thought of leaving him to go back to Judy's flat alone made me feel a little ill.

"I don't know, Kara," I said, trying to shrug it off. "Sounds good, but I promised Owen he could stay at mine tonight. He's... going through some stuff. I don't think it would be wise."

Kara narrowed her eyes, glancing between the two of us. "I assumed as much. What's going on, anyway? Dad says Judy wasn't at bingo, and you *did* have a whole week off..."

"Family stuff."

That was when Owen overheard.

Frowning, he slipped an arm around my shoulder, smiling smoothly at Kara. "What's happening here?"

"I invited Lilz and Loz for a girly sleepover tonight," Kara said, teeth on show as she smiled back. "You know, alcohol, making out, pillow fights..."

"All the good stuff," Owen joked. I winced, letting his arm drift away a little. It was clear Kara had said that deliberately to make me uncomfortable, giving me the side eye, smirking.

Owen didn't seem to have noticed.

"Exactly. I mean, you know Lilz..." Kara looked at me pointedly then, and said, "But your girlfriend here is being a spoilsport, and doesn't want to come because she promised you could stay at hers tonight. How pathetic, eh?"

Owen frowned, and not in defence of me, the girlfriend in question. The pinch to my side meant something, I knew it did, fingers digging into my flesh. But I couldn't think of an excuse, lips zipped closed.

"Well... that's certainly true." He pretended to think for a second, then tapped the side of his head, like he'd had an idea. "I know! How about you girls have a girly night first, while the boys get up to some... business." He glanced at Gethin, and I knew it had something to do with weed, whether the supply of such a substance or the sale of something similar. "And then, once we're done, we can all hang out in my garage and camp there tonight? A few drinks, a smoke..."

Kara was the first to nod, always up for any of Owen's suggestions. I opened and closed my mouth, still unsure. The garage...

We'd have to make sure it was completely clear of any blood, any of Judy Sharpley's liquids. And we'd have to get some room spray. Lots and lots of room spray – or a diffuser. The whole place still smelled of blood, of dead bodies. Even asking our friends back to the estate felt unnecessarily risky.

Why couldn't we just go to Gethin's, like we usually did when there was anything worth celebrating? Gethin's house was crappy and covered in a sheen of beer, but at least his parents pretty much let us do what we wanted.

At least we wouldn't find spots of blood on the floor, the skirting boards.

And at least the whole place wouldn't reek of bleach.

"Perfect," Loz nodded. "I'll get Dad to pick us up some drinks at the off-licence later, Kara, to take to yours. Cocktails, pizza, and a movie? Sound good?"

"Sounds good." I replied. "What movie?"

"Scrap the movie! We're getting *deep*," Kara replied. "So you're in, Lilz?"

I nodded, because I didn't really have a choice, did I? "Sure. I'm in."

x3 burgers, chicken
kebab with extra
pickles, garlic mayo, no
lettuce, double pitta

ta x

THE FAIRY HOUSE

I only went home to get a pillow and a spare change of clothes. We'd be coming back to the estate later anyway, but I didn't want to wake Mum or Dizzy by traipsing in and out to collect my things.

> I'm not coming home tonight.
> See you tomorrow. Love you x

I left the note on the kitchen table, where Mum would see it as soon as she got in.

Then I set off to Kara's.

Kara Faulkner lived in a semi on the other side of Vibbington, a horrid little house that always smells of rotting lavender and "good vibes". Although Kara was all long dyed hair, false nails and bright orange tan, her family was the opposite. Her chavvy dad married a hippy back in the 90s, and she filled the house with tat before giving birth to their first and only child, Kara-Jay Faulkner, a spindly thing, pale and skinny as a rake, just like me. The house hadn't changed much, since. It was still filled with dreamcatchers and quotes from fairy books, traps in the garden to try and catch elves, weed brownies in the fridge.

Kara's own room was just as bad. She loved tacky cushions and throws, which she owned in abundance, and collected crystals with different meanings, lined up on her windowsill to "charge". The lighting was all moody and came from lava lamps, those sunset ones you get for selfies, and she had so many clothes the wardrobe door had fallen off.

Loz loved Kara's room. She said it gave her energy, while mine sucked it out of her. The different colours and hope and permanent manifestation... Loz and Kara would spend hours pouring over the meanings of different crystals, their star signs, reading too much into each. I wasn't about that sort of thing. Fanciful nonsense, a waste of any *normal* person's time.

Kara was waiting at the door, staring anxiously out onto the street. Her house was visible from right down the road as I approached; there was a sign by the door reading 'The Fairy House', and the garden was planted out with flowers of all kinds, left to climb the walls and overgrow, in true cottage-garden style. What Kara's mum didn't realise is that half the flowers were actually *weeds*, as I knew from my few weeks in the school gardens as part of my year eleven work experience. Dandelions are only lovely when you've no idea how fast they can spread.

Kara was wearing a teeny pair of silk pyjama shorts, exposing two streaky legs, like bashers of orange bacon. She'd taken off her makeup for the facemasks and dead sea mud later, but still had on a pair of horrific fake-eyelashes, hanging from each corner.

"Lilz!" she said, painting on her best fake smile and waving. "You're here first."

The silence was awkward as I made my way up the garden path, dodging gnomes, funny little wooden fairies. The road was quiet, semi-detached houses with rotting foundations and overgrown front gardens blocking us in. The homes here were only a step up from the buildings on our estate.

I knew this street well, of course; we all did. It was the street Lexie had lived on, a girl who'd died when we were in year eight. I hadn't known her well – she didn't have many friends – but Kara always talked about how they'd walked to school together sometimes, and went to the same primary school for a year in a nearby village. The street had an aura of death about it, forgotten youth and decaying flowers. There was a plaque at its head, below the road name. *Lexie McCoy, always in our hearts*. I wondered whether anyone would put a similar plaque at the head of our estate... or whether Judy Sharpley's life was even worth a wilting rose.

"So..." Kara said, glancing down at her phone. She pretended to tap out a very long message as I stood there, staring hard at one of the little wooden fairies.

It was a relief when Loz arrived, bounding up the path still in her too-small bikini top and shorts, half-zipped hoodie thrown over the top. Her hair was in a high pony and there were snacks piled into the carrier bag by her side, and she just looked so unbelievably Loz that for a second I almost forgot what was happening, that Owen and I had hidden a body, that Loz had broken up with Ethan, *that Owen and I had hidden a body* –

We went straight to Kara's room, bypassing the kitchen, where her mum was giving her dad what she called a "herbal treatment". He was laid flat on the table, unclothed, and his back was covered in herbs.

"It's their anniversary in a few weekends, so they're doing this whole cleansing thing before they go away." Kara cocked her head, an idea only just coming to her. "You should all come round that weekend. We can have a party!"

"I'll be in Notts," Loz said, and Kara pulled a face.

"You could travel back for the weekend?"

"I'll be working." Loz scowled again, adding, "I go back next Friday for good, and I'm doing weekend shifts at this stupid café until I start college in September, except for when I'm in France."

"So… how much will you be able to visit?" I could feel my chest deflating, realisation settling in.

"Probably not that much. A few times in July, less in August, maybe once at the start of September?"

"It's going to be so dead around here without you," Kara said.

I couldn't even be offended by this; I felt the exact same.

We settled on Kara's bed, rearranging the popcorn and cheese puffs as she ordered the food. Burgers all round, and a chicken kebab for her dad, who shouted up the stairs to request extra pickles and garlic mayo, no lettuce, a double pitta. The fairy lights were on, Kara's lava lamp reflecting a funny glow around the room.

It felt weirdly familiar, sat on her quilted eiderdown like that, munching off-brand cheese puffs and staring at the butterfly lightshade on her ceiling. Listening as Kara ranted about the boy she was shagging, flicking through his Instagram to show Loz, talking far too loud and with her mouth open, false nails attacking the screen. Weirdly familiar, and… spooky. Spooky in that so much had changed this past week, yet here I was, laid on Kara's bed, acting like nothing had ever happened, like this was all normal.

Kara and Loz had no idea, of course. All of this was normal to them. Loz knew Owen and I were going through it, but she still thought her breakup with Ethan was a worthy rival to our drama – and so it was, in a way. Focusing on something so minor helped make the murder seem redundant, insignificant. It only took a few minutes for the pair to tire of talking about Kara's boy, and the conversation soon turned to Ethan Morgan, to the breakup which shook the nation. Loz stopped nattering and fell silent, staring at her phone, face a funny shade of green.

"What?" Kara said, frowning. "It's not Ethan, is it?"

Loz nodded, face still very, very green.

Hey. I know you said this was for the best, but I still miss you so much, and I want to talk about this properly, in person. You can't just dump me on the phone and call it quits, Loz. We need to talk about this, make sure it's for the best.

"Don't reply," I said immediately. "He's trying to guilt you."

"I second that," Kara piped up, to my surprise. "He knows you'd never break up in person 'cause you'd be too busy trying not to suck him off."

"Piss off," Loz said weakly, still staring at her phone. "What do I do?"

"Ignore him," I repeated. "You did the right thing, getting out when you weren't happy. And in a week you'll be back in Notts, with a million other options."

"But…"

"No buts." Kara snatched the phone away, pushing it under her leg. Loz inhaled sharply. "You're not replying, okay? And we're not going to spend the whole night talking about him, because you're clearly not ready and it'll only get you down. Agreed?"

"Agreed," I said. "This is an Ethan-free zone, yes, Loz?"

"Fine." Loz pouted, but I could tell she agreed, that she knew this was for the best. "Is it alcohol time yet?"

***

By the time the takeaway man knocked on the door to Kara's fairy house, we were three considerably tipsy girls, struggling to get down the stairs without bursting into peels of giggles. The man couldn't stop ogling Loz in her skimpy bikini top, until Kara made some quip about objectifying women and he flushed bright red.

"Men," Kara said, rolling her eyes. "I don't know why you settle for Owen, Lilz, when you could just pull a girl instead."

I blushed almost as much as the takeaway man at that. "That's not how it works."

"Then how *does* it work?" Kara dropped off the kebab in the kitchen, then turned back to lead us up the stairs. She almost tripped on the top step, letting out a snort of laughter and shaking her head. "I've never met any other bisexuals before. Especially not bisexuals with long-term boyfriends."

"*Bisexuals*," I echoed, though the expression on my face was far from amused. "We're not a breed you know. Us "bisexuals" come in various shapes and sizes."

"Really?" Kara raised two eyebrows and pretended to looked shocked. The burgers smelled meaty and bloody, like sawed-apart flesh. Suddenly, I wasn't so hungry.

"What's with the sudden obsession over bisexuals, Kara?" Loz intercepted. "Are *you* bisexual? Is that why you can't stop staring at my tits?"

"I'm allowed girl crushes, *Lauren*." Kara glanced at me slyly as she pulled out one of the burgers, layered it with fries. "As are you, Lilz."

"What's that supposed to mean?"

I knew exactly what she meant.

"I mean, you're not bisexual just because you find girls hot. I've said it before and I'll say it again, but you and Owen have been together for too long, and it's causing your desire to come out in funny ways –"

"Funny ways? Like liking girls?"

"– like claiming to love Owen, but still wanting to shag other girls."

"That's not what bisexuality is. You *know* it's not."

Kara smiled smugly, taking another bite of her burger-and-fries. I didn't want mine anymore. The patty was rare, blood seeping out of the sides and onto its cardboard box. The cheese looked orange, like plastic, and the whole thing smelled horrific, exactly like the flat that night, Judy Sharpley's body decaying in the bath.

"Girls, girls. Let's not bicker like children." Loz gave me a warning look then, and for a moment I wanted to smack her. To smack her, simply for taking Kara's side over mine, as though *I* was the one aggravating *her*, just for defending myself. "Do you not want your burger, Lilz? I'm famished."

I passed it over, taking a handful of her fries. They were soft and buttery and hot against my tongue, but I didn't want them, couldn't eat them. I was still bubbling with anger at Kara, but also with unease, distress. I wanted tonight to be a distraction, to remind me of how things could continue on as normal, even after we'd hidden Judy's body. Instead, it served as a warning. A warning that things weren't okay.

Kara is a bitch, out to steal my boyfriend. Loz has just broken up with Ethan and is moving to Nottingham for good. I recited it to myself, over and over.

Owen, my boyfriend, drowned his mother then sawed her in half with that bloody serrated bread knife.

And I helped hide the body.

🔍 **how to tell your friends**

... you don't like them

... you're bisexual

... you're pregnant

... you're broke

THE COMING OUT

I came out as bisexual in year ten, two years after I got with Owen. It wasn't a big deal. I mean, it was, and it *is*, but I didn't try to make it any bigger than it already felt.

I started slipping it into conversations in the canteen, sharing jokey bi TikToks and memes to the group chat. Kara had only just joined our group, but the others were more surprised, though they tried not to show it. Loz was unfazed, of course, though the jokes were unrelentless at first – until I told her to stop being so insensitive, that I'd rather she just asked me how I felt outright.

Because I wanted to talk about it, I really did. I wanted to explain. I didn't want bi to just be a label I adopted, but a living, breathing part of my personality, something I'd pretty much always been aware of. And I wanted my friends to understand. I didn't want them to doubt me or succumb to believing stereotypes, just because I had a steady boyfriend. I wanted them to *believe* me.

I saw a TikTok once that claimed everyone is bisexual, just a little. That each human has the capacity to explore their sexuality, to try it on with both genders; that years of living inside the heterosexual norm have conditioned us to be straight, straight, straight.

I don't think that's the case.

If it was, gay people wouldn't struggle so hard to come out as gay, and I'd just call myself a *straight* girl, not a bi one.

The thing is, I knew I was bisexual long before Owen.

Whatever Kara says, being in a long-term relationship didn't "turn" me bi, didn't awaken desires I never knew existed, purely out of desperation and boredom. I think that says more about *Kara* than anything, the fact she can't imagine loving one person for that long, being satisfied by them after all those years.

I liked boys and girls before I even knew it was an option, before I understood how it even worked. My playground crushes were equally straight and gay, swung from side to side like a pendulum. I thought Chloe Alize was hot long before she asked out Owen, considered Kev Jones was fit until he stopped growing at just an inch shorter than me. And then there was Owen, and Owen, and Owen. I never stopped being attracted to Owen.

Apparently that's hard for girls like Kara to understand. How can you know you still like boys and girls if you've only ever had one boyfriend? Weren't you too young to know before you met Owen? What if Owen has turned you *straight*?

I'm not saying figuring out my sexuality has been easy, smooth sailing, not even just a little bit. It's been confusing, and painful, and downright annoying. I didn't have to come out as bi. I had a steady boyfriend, and no one cared about my sexuality, really. I wasn't looking to get with a girl any time soon, so what did it matter if I stayed in the closet or not? Was I just looking for attention? Did I want to be different, to pick up a label I could call my own?

But the struggle with my sexuality hasn't come from my own desire to shag girls, or to mess around with anyone other than Owen. It came from the struggle to be myself, comfortably, around my friends and boyfriend, knowing deep down that they didn't really know me.

That's why I came out as bi. Not because I wanted

attention, or a label, or to do something radical for once.

I came out as bi in order to be me, so that my friends and family could understand me better, so that I didn't feel like was hiding a part of myself from anyone who loved me.

I came out as bi for *me*, not for anybody else.

I told Owen before I dropped hints to the group, of course. About a year and a half after we'd been together, but still hadn't slept together – that came a few months later. We were lounging in the park, sharing a stolen cigarette (and Judy Sharpley's long "lost" lighter) when I turned to him, poking his face with my fourteen-year-old hand, puffing out my cheeks.

"Owen?"

"Lilz?"

I smiled, rolling my eyes. "Owen?"

"Lilz?"

"Dear boyfriend?"

"Gorgeous girlfriend?"

"What would you do if I told you I was bisexual?"

Owen paused, taking the cigarette from his lips. He stubbed it out on the grass before throwing it away, into the bushes, and turned to face me.

"I'd ask how you *know* you're bisexual, when you only have eyes for me."

I swallowed, suddenly nervous. "What if I told you I've known for a while – like, since before we got together – but I never had the words to express it?"

Owen cocked his head for a moment, frowning, before saying, "Then I'd say okay, that's fine. And thank you for telling me."

"Okay." I nodded, glancing down. "I'm bisexual."

There was a silence, broken only by two screaming

children careering down the path before us. Owen's eyes were wide, but not too wide, not enough that he looked shocked, and I had to resist the urge to poke him again.

"Owen?" I said hesitantly. "Owen, talk to me."

"You're bisexual?" His voice was curious as he turned to me, dark eyes snagging mine. I swallowed again, throat suddenly full of tears, and nodded. "As in... you're attracted to men and women?"

"That's one definition."

Owen snorted as my vision went turned blurry, eyes wet, and slipped an arm around my back. He felt warm and safe and lovely as I cuddled into him, breathing in his Owen-scent and probably snotting all over his t-shirt, but he didn't seem to care, hugged me back with so much strength everything else disappeared for a moment. It was just me and him, alone in the park, the only people left on earth.

Until he pulled away a little and said, "I actually find that super, super hot."

I sniffed through my tears, finding a smile from somewhere. But the smile was... confused. Forced, even though I didn't have the knowledge to understand *why* his words felt so wrong.

"And who knows, maybe it gives us more options in the future..."

I laughed and nodded, hoping he was joking, assuming for sure that he was – not that it would have been funny either way. We were fourteen, and he was ignorant, and a boy. That excused it, right?

I don't want to paint Owen in the worst light, not when you already know what he's capable of, what he did. But... Owen Sharpley isn't perfect, not in the slightest. He wasn't always the best boyfriend, the most loyal. He found it sexy that I was into girls, and always tried to engage with that side of me in ways I won't go into, ways which made me feel uncomfortable, exposed. I liked girls, but I was in love with *Owen*. He was enough for me.

Fetishising bisexuality is a real problem, but Owen... Owen was just Owen, and I don't think he could help how he felt. Maybe that made him a natural sleazeball, I don't know. I don't want to look back on all of our relationship and think it was bad, bad, bad, because he gave me some of the best years of my life, a first love so sacred, so special, that I'll always look back on it through rose-tinted spectacles.

He wasn't a saint. Sorry to disappoint you, but no boy really is. I was Owen's girlfriend and I knew he loved me as a *person*, but towards the end, there was much more to our relationship than love and affection, attachment. And I don't mean that in a good way.

Looking back, maybe I should've realised what he was really like, how he viewed me. But there's no point dwelling on that now. It's over. The police are in my front room, questioning me about the body in the woods, and I just grassed up my boyfriend, my best friend.

Anyway...

Let's resume the story.

Where were we?

THE HIGH

We left Kara's fairy house for the garage late that night, all of us now in hoodies and trackies to stay warm. There was a chill descending, even for June, and a wind whipped round the estate as we arrived and knocked on the garage's big doors.

"Hello, ladies," Owen said, opening the door with a grin. It rose above our heads, his blood-red car moved onto the street outside and its usual resting place spread with blankets and cushions, a crusty tarpaulin. The garage smelled fresh, like it had been recently scrubbed, and the concrete floor was clear, empty. I swallowed, smiling at my boyfriend, as he extended his arm for me to sink into.

"Have you got the goods?" Kara asked, eyes narrowed.

Owen nodded as she grinned.

The goods? I felt my heart sink to my stomach. *The goods* sounded anything but good. We were only doing this to cover our tracks, surely, to act normal by hanging out with friends and partaking in regular social engagements? "Goods" hadn't even entered my mind.

Gethin was sat on a beanbag in the corner, a cigarette poised at his lips and a bottle of beer squashed between his legs. He was eyeing Loz and Kara up already. We'd been best friends for years, meaning Loz had snogged Gethin on several occasions without it amounting to much, but he'd fancied Kara way more since she started hanging out with us. Gethin was that kind of guy. Loz's big boobs were more interesting than her brains or talent for sports, fashion, and Kara had that icky, fake-tanned, false-eyelashed complexion which drove him mad.

Kara knew that, of course, but sat a fair distance away from him, closer to where Owen had set up camp with his plastic freezer bag of what looked like... well, you can guess. I swallowed again, suddenly feeling my mouth fill with far too much saliva. Not *drugs*. Not so close to my flat...

Contrary to popular belief, I'd only ever tried weed once, at some party this guy Oli in our year once tried to throw. It was kind of lame, but the stragglers all ended up in the garden after with a collection of earthy cigarettes we passed round in a circle. I choked so much Owen had to go and get me water, and spent the rest of the night terrified out of my mind by the fire, the dark trees towering overhead. If just one puff had affected me so much, I dreaded to think what more could do.

Unlike Owen and Gethin, I didn't really understand drugs. Alcohol once a week or so, sure, but drugs... drugs were stupid, dangerous. They were unpredictable, addictive. I knew my boundaries when it came to drinking a beer once in a while, a few shots of Sourz. But drugs weren't so safe. You don't always know what you're smoking, and that scared me. You hear horror stories of accidental overdoses, drug-induced deaths, fatal heart attacks, crippling addiction. Horror stories which sound rare, sure, but are people's *actual* realities.

I continued thinking about this as I watched my friends pass around the bag, taking one each, even Loz. Owen didn't even offer it to me. I would have declined, but him passing me by made me feel... childish, infantile. I took a can of cider instead, staring down at the floor.

I knew how tonight was going to end.

I'd seen Owen high before, of course. So high he could barely walk in a straight line, tumbling through my front door and letting me hold him, stroke his hair. He was reduced to a child, in that state. A little boy who needed cuddling and patting and reassuring. It wasn't just paranoia, delusion. It was genuine, bone-deep fear.

I touched Owen's arm gently as he lit the tip, breathing in. His lips already looked less appealing suctioned against the rolled-up paper, and I could only imagine how bad his breath would smell.

"Are you sure this is a good idea?" I asked quietly, but Kara overheard from where she was sat to his other side, rolling her eyes.

"Oh, lighten up, Lilz! It's just a bit of weed. It's not as if we're doing anything hardcore."

Not yet they weren't.

I sat back and watched as the rest of them lit theirs, laughing and puffing in and out, filling the room with a sour, earthy stench. I wanted to go home. I wanted nothing more than to be in the living room right now with Mum and Dizzy, watching TV with a big bowl of microwave popcorn, but I had no choice other than to sit and examine the scene before me as they chatted lazily and scrolled through their phones, my best friends, hand on Owen's knees to stop him getting any closer to Kara.

It sucked. But I didn't know why it sucked. I'd always hung out with my friends before while they smoked and drank and did things I didn't want to necessarily partake in, like that time they dared each other they could finish off a whole bottle of vodka in one night for no apparent reason. But this felt... worthless. Tired. There were much bigger things at stake, like... like...

And there it was. The inevitable question which sent me down a spiral, which led me to where I am now, sat in the living room opposite those two officers. The question you should maybe ask yourself if you're feeling lonely, lost, like you've made a trillion huge mistakes and this is only the beginning of them all.

What else was there?

What else was there, besides Owen and Loz and Gethin and Kara, drinking and smoking and laughing far too loud, even though the weed couldn't have had an effect yet, surely. That was the question I asked myself, sat in Owen's garage on the concrete floor, the very spot we'd carted a dead body to just a week previous. What else was there for me, Lilz, in this crazy world? Was this… it?

Because in that moment, I felt terrified. Trapped. Realisation was sinking in and I was drowning, drowning so hard I could barely keep my eyes open in that smoky room, heart thudding fit to burst. Was this it? Owen and I, doing drugs and having sex and hanging around with people I only half-liked, in our bloody murder cavern? Was this what the rest of my life was set out like?

Even Loz was moving on, leaving Vibbington, moving to Notts and starting a new college, where she'd eventually apply to university, get a degree, spend three years partying and making new friends and having *experiences*. What about me? Was I destined to be like Owen and Gethin and Kara, sat around in a dirty garage getting high while the real world moved on around us?

It hit me, then. All of it. The things Mum had jokily tried to get through to me my whole life so far, things she knew I had no interest in hearing. That Vibbington wasn't the be all and end all. That one day, I might wish I'd tried harder in school, applied to university, travelled somewhere new and exciting, met new people, found new opportunities. Maybe... maybe find a new boyfriend, or girlfriend. She never said this out loud – she loved Owen, obviously – but she meant that maybe, just maybe, Owen wasn't all there was for me. That maybe, one day, I'd discover something outside of the Sharpley bubble, something *really* worth living for.

I think that moment was the first time I ever truly realised the gravity of the situation, what I'd signed up for. I loved Owen, but we were now tied together by some stupid murder pact, one which said, *If you go down for this, we go down together.*

I was stuck in Vibbington, didn't have the grades to go elsewhere, and Loz was moving to Nottingham to have a whole new life without me. I wouldn't have my best friend anymore, just Kara, who hated me, who was biphobic and ignorant, and Gethin, druggie Gethin, who only ever thought about weed and sex.

And Owen, of course. Owen, the boy I loved, the boy of my dreams, the boy who had the power to change everything for me.

Owen, the boy who'd drowned his mother in the bath, and chopped her body in the bath with a serrated knife.

Oh.

My.

God.

***

They got very, very high.

Higher, in fact, than I ever thought was possible.

I was sat in the middle of the circle now, and it was two in the morning. Gethin was flat out on his side, snoring, and Loz was cuddled into his chest, giggling absently as I remembered to take a photo; she always liked to be reminded of how she'd acted the next day, so she knew not to drink or smoke too much again. Owen was still puffing away, eyes half-closed, and Kara was burning up; she only had on her trackies and bra now, leaning towards Owen in the hopes that he'd notice her.

I wasn't worried. My boyfriend was loyal, even when high out of his mind. He didn't need *babysitting*.

That was when Loz let out a high-pitched squeal, and I turned to her with a frown. Her eyes are wet and she looked like she was about to start crying, sitting up straight and moving away from Gethin.

"Lilz," she said, dead serious. "Lilz, I broke up with Ethan."

"I know you did," I told her, grabbing her flailing arms and trying to pull her into a hug. "Loz, I –"

But she was already running towards the door.

It opened too easily as Loz raced out onto the street, tears streaming down her face, gazing round frantically. In her drug-addled state she couldn't figure out which way to turn in order to get out of the street, so she tried her best to follow her nose, but it kept leading her left, right, left, right, until she was dizzy. I grabbed her, held her arms down until she was calm, whispering her name over and over and over, into her ear.

"I broke up with Ethan," she repeated, tears falling freely now, shaking her head. "We've been together two years, Lilz. Two years. What… what did I…"

"It was for the best, okay? You're going to be fine."

I pulled Loz into another hug, and we just stood there for

a minute, in the street, so close that I could feel the heat prickling on her skin, radiating off her.

I hated drugs. I hated that this was the effect they had on you, that they made you this... confused, sad, lonely, fearful. I knew this was just a part of the grieving stage in a breakup, but it felt so messed-up. My best friend was broken, and the weed had only shattered her into more fragments. That wasn't okay. That wasn't okay at all.

When she pulled away, she didn't look like Loz. Her pupils were dilated and her skin was clammy, and her messy bun was halfway down her forehead. She looked at me carefully, and said, "Does cuddling Gethin count as cheating?"

"Loz..." I grabbed her hands, squeezed them tight. "You're single. You can't cheat."

Her eyes filled with tears, breath hitching. I wanted to cry, too. The expression on her face was so raw, realisation stark, that it was almost enough to split my own heart in two.

"I'm single," she echoed, voice tiny against the silence of the street. "I'm... single..."

And then I held her, stroking her hair, as she cried.

THE BETRAYAL

It took a while for Loz to calm down, for her brain to right itself and expression to turn back to normal. She'd been wailing so loud I was worried we'd attract attention from one of the blocks, but all were silent, Owen's flat and my own still in darkness at the other end of the estate. I held my best friend tight and let her bawl into me, because she was my best friend, and that's what you do when you have a best friend, especially if they're upset.

"You okay now?" I asked, squeezing her shoulders. "I'm here for you, you know that, right? This sucks, but... at least you've got me, and Kara, and even Owen and Gethin."

Loz nodded, giving a little sniff. It was true enough. No matter how much she was hurt, it was all for the best, and she still had our amazing friendship group to keep her happy, sane. Besides... she was moving to Nottingham, starting a new college, a new life. I couldn't say this to her now, but I knew she'd meet someone new there, a musician with a six pack and huge pecs, some boy she could tell us all about on her weekends back, the kind of fit, dreamy guy who was ten times more suited to her than the lovely-but-drab Ethan Morgan.

We made our way back to the garage with its big garage doors, Loz still sniffing a bit. We opened it halfway and ducked under, unspeaking, the room still thick with smoke, so much so that you could barely see a few feet in front of you. I made my way back to where Owen had been sat.

I stopped moving.

And stared.

Owen was kissing Kara.

Kissing *Kara*.

At least, that was what I registered two minutes later, after I'd let myself process the scene.

Kara was straddling him, bra now off and strewn across the floor beside us. Owen had one hand on a perfect boob and the other pressed against the side of her face, and they were snogging like their lives depended on it, her trackies-covered crotch moving in and out of his as she groaned and moaned and giggled.

They were high out of their minds, but it didn't *matter*.

He was kissing Kara, my Kara, my *friend* Kara. He was kissing another girl, another girl who wasn't me.

He was touching another girl who *wasn't me.*

Loz wasn't really aware of what was happening, but stood next to me and frowned as I marched towards them and pulled Kara away, onto her backside on the floor beside Owen.

And I slapped him.

I slapped one of his freckled white cheeks, slapped it so hard I left a bright red handprint, and stood back to watch the two scramble to collect themselves.

Maybe I should have been more mad at Owen in that moment, but really, I just wanted to hurt Kara. Hurt her like she'd never been hurt before, make her realise how wrong that was, how much she'd completely betrayed me.

"Lilz, I…" Kara was still sprawled on the floor, topless, hand grappling for her bra.

I hated her, in that moment. I hated her so, so *much*.

I hated her for her perfect body, curvier than mine and

fake-tanned, glistening, with boobs like two perfect cherries sat atop a smooth chest. I hated her snarky expression as she stared back at me, challenging, knowing exactly what she'd done and yet almost finding it... *funny*.

"Lilz." That was Owen, tugging on my hand and gesturing desperately for me to listen to him.

I didn't want to.

I really, really didn't want to.

But I turned, and once I turned, I felt something tug on my heart and my eyes fill with tears.

"It was just a mistake, Lilz," Owen said, eyes wide and apologetic, pleading with me. "Honestly, I've no idea how that even happened. We were just messing around, and..."

"Then tell her to go." My voice was barely audible. Owen stared at me, trying to register what I'd said, as I repeated, "Tell her to go, Owen!"

"Fine, fine!" He turned to Kara, who was pulling on her bra and hoodie, helped by Loz, who still looked vaguely confused. Gethin was out for the count still, on his side with his jaw gaping and drool forming a puddle on the concrete. "Kara, you better..."

"Go, go, I heard." Kara stood, unsteady on her feet, Loz clutching . "We'll just..."

They passed us on their way to the door, as Kara leaned closer and hissed, "You *bitch*."

My mouth was still open in shock as she disappeared out of the garage, and her footsteps were heard with Loz's on the pavement outside as they made their way back to Kara's.

I didn't move for a second; I didn't have to. Owen stood on shaky legs to face me, just as I managed to bark out a tired, broken, "How could you?"

Because that's when it hit me, properly hit me.

After five years together, of only ever being with each other, he'd kissed another girl.

He'd kissed her, touched her, felt his skin beneath hers, her tongue in his mouth. I could feel the tears on my cheeks, wet with shock and hurt and sadness, as Owen reached to wipe my face, to move them away with his hands, his fingers. It wouldn't make it any better, him doing this, acting like this. It couldn't, not ever.

"We were just messing around, Lilz. I didn't even know what was happening, I…"

That wasn't an excuse, but I was too choked to do anything but nod.

Because more than anything, I was… surprised. Surprised that Owen, the love of my life, would even *think* to do a thing like that. That the thought of kissing Kara would even make sense in his head.

"I made a huge mistake, Lilz, I'm sorry."

A huge mistake.

A *catastrophic* mistake.

I nodded again. "Just… don't let it happen again, okay?"

Owen was high. He'd had a lot to drink. I didn't want to believe he'd ever cheat on me if such circumstances weren't in play, but they were, and I had to trust him. I *had* to.

"Oh my God, Lilz, I wouldn't, of course I wouldn't!" Owen slipped his arms around me, wrapped me in his warm, cosy Owen-ness, giggled into my hair, kissed my forehead. "God, I'm so sorry. I was so stupid. I love you, yeah? You know I love you, I love you more than anyone *ever*."

I let him kiss me.

I let him kiss me, knowing his lips had been pressed against Kara's only minutes earlier.

I let him kiss me, because I was Lilz, and Lilz of June was

stupid.

    Very, very stupid.

    Maybe the most stupid of them all.

Judy Sharpley

judy sharpley
gyus im selling tv and radio gud price, link to
my ebay in comrents

karen myers
dropped you an inbox judy x

judy sharpley
any boddy know whos making rakett down
street. comrent if u do becos it is lloud wtf

judy sharpley
dont use the app much but wanted to let u
gyus no ive gone to stay with a college friend
in need over the next few months

THE MEMORY

When I woke up, light was streaming through the cracks around the garage door and Gethin was groaning, picking himself up and dusting off bits of dirt, cigarette butts. I was nestled in the crook of Owen's arms as he slept, watching Gethin making his way around the room, collecting his stuff, gathering the blunts back into the plastic bag. He saw me staring and didn't smile, expression flat. Gethin and I weren't that close, but I felt alienated in that moment, the reality of last night flooding back...

Kara and Owen, kissing in the smoky room, Kara's bra off and his hand on her chest ~

I shuffled away from my boyfriend, heart thudding. He was still in his hoodie and joggers and his mouth was open wide as he breathed in and out, eyes sleep encrusted. He kissed Kara. Owen kissed *Kara*.

How was I supposed to feel about that, in the cold light of day? Kara was going to rub it in, no doubt. Even though she'd been high, even though *he'd* been high, even though none of their actions were exactly their fault, I still wasn't sure if maybe, just maybe, this had been brewing for a while. If maybe this had been Kara's intention all along, and Owen had been stupid and naïve enough to fall for it.

I couldn't blame him, I told myself as I started picking up the blankets and cushions, Gethin sneaking under the garage door and skulking back to his own house. I couldn't blame him at all. He was probably traumatised from the events of the last week, and I'd left him alone, even though I knew he wasn't in his right frame of mind. He'd been apologetic, right? That was all that really mattered.

And so I cleared up the garage, putting everything into a pile by the door, before giving Owen a shake by the shoulders. He grumbled and made a noise that sounded like a hoover, before opening his eyes and smiling at me. Light fell over his face in a thin, gold slither.

"Morning," he said, pulling me into him. "I feel like shit."

It took a good half hour or so for him to be in a position enough to help me carry the blankets and things back to the flat – his, not mine – where we let ourselves in and locked the door behind us. The meaty, bloody smell was long gone, as was the bleach, but the place was damp and bare and sad now, as it had been for the last week.

We were missing sixth form again, I thought with a pang. This wasn't exactly going to have a positive effect on my grades. I'd ring Mr Roberts later, explain the situation, maybe ask for some catch-up work from my teachers. Because this was important. After last night – after the realisation that I'd be stuck in Vibbington forever – I needed something *more* to aim for. Even if I just applied to a few local universities, did an apprenticeship in retail or something, at least it would be… different. It would have an end goal, and rewards I wouldn't have that if I continued working at Sally's Diner forever.

I'd started at Sally's Diner about a year ago, soon after I turned sixteen. It was an American-style diner on the outskirts of Vibbington, and I usually just did weekends, working nine to five in the kitchen flipping burgers, sometimes waitressing after school if we were low on staff. I'd called in sick last week to help Owen clean up the mess we'd both made, but I was due back there on Saturday, ready to pick up more shifts once the summer holidays began.

I decided to cook us a proper breakfast now, as Owen stowed away the stuff and said something about going over to mine for a shower. There wasn't much food in – we'd been eating with Mum and Dizzy all week – but I found some bread in the freezer, a manky tub of margarine in the fridge door. Judy Sharpley had left crunchy peanut butter in the cupboard above the microwave, so we made toast, eating at the island, staring at the closed bathroom door.

I wanted to say something about Kara. Maybe that was stupid… or maybe it was more sensible than anything. Getting it out of the way now, while we were eating toast in the kitchen and Owen was unarmed, still coming down from his high.

But I didn't. I just sat there, munching on toast, gazing around Judy Sharpley's flat as sun streamed through the window and the scent of charred bread wafted around us, crunch-crunching the crunchy peanut butter.

Until I noticed a slim black phone plugged in by the toaster, attached to a white cord. A phone which didn't have Owen's trademark blue case, or the zombie pop socket he'd had since he was fifteen.

"You're charging Judy's phone?"

Owen glanced up, let his eyes fall on the charger. He nodded. "Thought it was about time. People are gonna get suspicious if she maintains complete radio silence."

"You know the password?"

"Mum didn't even know how to *set* a password."

I watched as Owen stood to grab it, frowning. It was true that Judy Sharpley wasn't exactly a tech god, which only made it easier to access her phone, her messages, her

Facebook. I don't know why this is where I felt funny, why hiding her sawed-up body in the woods was less scary than disappearing into the depths of her private history.

Owen was shaking as he picked it up, so I put out a hand to steady him. There were tears in his eyes.

Why were there tears in his eyes?

"Okay," he murmured, switching it on. I abandoned my toast to join him on the sofa, sliding under his arm and staring at the screen over his shoulder. There were a good few notifications, mostly from people we didn't know, checking to see if she was okay and why she'd missed bingo and whether she was coming round to the pub on Saturday night, *we're sorry we missed you.*

"At least none of them came looking for her here," Owen said with a grimace, and I nodded. But weirdly, that felt rather... sad. That Judy Sharpley had all these people who could message her and act like they cared, but none had come to visit her at the flat when they realised something was wrong.

We clicked onto Facebook first, where Owen decided it was best to update her status. I didn't know if I would have agreed, but it wouldn't do us any harm. Judy had shocking spelling and no concept of grammar, so it was easy enough to concoct a statement that sounded like it could've been her.

dont use the app much but wanted to let u gyus no ive gone to stay with a college friend in need over the next few months

"It sounds crazy," I said, shaking my head. "Why would she feel the need to tell that to the whole of Facebook?"

"Because she's Mum. And because this way, we're covering all bases. No one will come looking for her once they hear she's gone to stay with a college friend for the rest of summer…"

"And after summer?"

"They'll forget about her. Like I said, it's Mum. Her friends don't usually last that long, anyway."

I shrugged, nodded. It was true, I supposed. But this all still felt very risky, and if I didn't trust Owen as much as I did, I would've been shaking out of my mind by now, convinced that this would be our downfall.

We went onto her messages next, skipping through them to find the important ones. The few family members she was still in touch with, and Kara's dad, Gethin's mum. It was easier than breaking the news to them ourselves. Judy Sharpley was gone, disappearing south to start a new life, leaving Owen by himself. We tried to make it sound more temporary for the sake of them calling social services on the almost-eighteen-but-not-quite-yet Owen Sharpley, and our plan seemed to be going swimmingly, each message more convincing than the last.

"I'm going to keep her phone here, charge it up still, so I can keep replying if I need to."

"Smart." I didn't mean for that to sound so patronising, but Owen frowned at me, shaking his head.

"It is smart, Lilz. This is… this is important. All of this is. You do realise what would happen if the police found out that Mum's missing, that no one knows where she is?"

I felt myself flush. I didn't like it when Owen talked to me like this, like I was a child. But we hadn't properly discussed this yet, shed light on the severity of the situation. It *was* serious. I knew that, and he knew that, and that fact was terrifying.

"I know."

"We'd go to prison, Lilz." He hadn't said this out loud yet, and the words cut through my belly. I nodded, feeling all the blood rush to my head, suddenly faint.

We'd go to prison, Lilz.

We'd go to prison.

"That's not going to happen," I said, pushing my arms around him. "I promise, that's not going to happen. I love you."

"But you understand it's a possibility, if you don't do as I say?"

Do as I say. What did he mean by that?

"I know. I know, but my lips are sealed, and –"

"So this means keeping quiet about certain… things. Things I might need to do, which you don't necessarily agree with. Because I could take you down in a minute, you know. Frame you for the murder. And your mum, even Dizzy. There's no evidence in my car, and you have a key for my flat; you could've killed Mum in the bath, gotten your mum and Dizzy to help cover it up. Or blackmailed me into doing so."

I was spinning, spinning, trying to stay focused on what Owen was saying. Why would he frame me for the murder? Why would he need to?

"Like Kara, last night." Owen read my mind. His hand was on my knee, rubbing circles, but my stomach hurt and my brain ached and I didn't understand what he was saying. "Sometimes I might make mistakes like that, do things you don't want me to do. But… you know we're in this together, right? So you can't punish me, or tell anyone."

"Owen…"

"I mean it, Lilz."

I had to swallow hard to stop the tears from flooding my eyes, my mouth, nodding at him as though I understood. But

I didn't. I couldn't. What was he trying to say? That he was allowed to kiss Kara, that it was justified, simply because he had the power to ruin my life? How did that make any *sense*?

I didn't want him to know what a wimp I was, but my eyes glazed over anyway and I had to fight to stay calm.

"We're in this together," I echoed, nodding. "But that means you can't go round kissing other girls, or... touching them, not like that. It hurts, Owen. It really hurts."

Owen nodded. And then he looked at me, dark eyes stone cold, and I swear, in that moment, I didn't know him at all.

"Do you really have a choice, Lilz?"

@zoeeforlani

love is love

THE DINER

You'd assume that, after something as grounding as a *murder* occurs, after you've hidden a body in the woods, swaddled in clothes and wrapped in black bin bags... something would change. Or, in most capacities, that *everything* would change. Prison. Punishment. A reputation, judgement, life never the same again.

But in our case, that wasn't the reality.

Everything was so... normal.

Too normal.

Casual, placid, the calm before the storm.

Sixth form was fine, those weeks after. Mr Roberts harped on about our grades and revision and summer classes, drumming into us that in a few months' time, we'd be applying to universities and doing our mocks and there'd be pressure, pressure, pressure. We had sessions once a week now to browse university courses and ask questions to former students now at local unis, though Owen deliberately came in late each day to miss them.

Kara didn't say anything about the kiss, weirdly enough. She'd give me nasty looks across the table in the common room, but carried on flirting and joking with Owen and Gethin as usual as I stayed quiet, catching up on the work we'd missed, scouring apprenticeships and opportunities on my phone, just for something to do. It gave me some hope, in the weeks after, even though I was still struggling to up my grades and wasn't sure I'd actually *qualify* for anything outside of Vibbington.

Loz moved to Notts for good that next weekend. Carted most of her stuff out of her dad's flat and into her mum's waiting car as I sat on her bed, painting my fingernails (and most of my fingers) sparkly black, the room spinning. I cried. I don't know why I cried, but I cried. Loz cried too, and we stood outside her building hugging until her mum beeped the horn and they shot off down the road without a look back.

I stood there for a while, unsure of what to do, until her dad pulled me in for another hug and offered to get us both a pizza.

He understood. He understood what we'd both lost, knew as well as I did that once Loz started her fancy new life in the city, she wouldn't want to come back to crummy Vibbington any time soon. I didn't want to believe it, but I won't pretend our friendship was fairy-tale perfect, that Loz didn't change the minute she moved to Notts and started hanging out with all these quirky girls in denim skirts and crop-tops... She came back to us, but, like anyone, leaving Vibbington altered something in her brain, showed her what city life had the possibility to look like.

Was that inspiring? Maybe.

Did I hate her for it? Almost definitely.

And Owen... Owen reverted back to being Owen, in most ways. At least, that's how I remember him being, those first few weeks. Maybe there were signs, and I was too blinded by him to see them.

I felt different. That's all that changed. I still loved Owen more than life, but there was an edge that had never existed before, an extra consciousness that put me on edge each time I thought about him, about our relationship. I didn't trust him, not in the same way. You can't trust someone you're not sure you even *know*.

Who was Owen Sharpley? Because the person who'd looked me dead in the eye, asked if I even had a choice over whether he kissed other girls… he wasn't my boyfriend. He wasn't the Owen Sharpley who hugged me tight when I was anxious, who bought me a big bar of Dairy Milk every Valentine's day, our tradition, who insisted I was the most beautiful girl in the world even though I wasn't, even though I never was.

Owen Sharpley was soft, mellow, though he acted calm and collected on the outside, would never show if he was nervous, unsure of himself – apart from with me.

Owen Sharpley was my best friend.

But he didn't feel like that, now. He felt like a stranger. A cute boy I liked, but would never truly *know*.

Kissing him had an edge; touching his tainted body felt wrong, stilted. I couldn't stop thinking that I was no longer the only girl to feel the muscles in his back, his soft belly, to kiss those plump, pillow-like lips. That I would never be the only girl again. The feeling sucked.

I spent the day at the diner on Saturday, walking there early in the morning, when most of Vibbington was still locked in an early morning haze. Wearing my black polo and old school trousers which were a significant chunk too short for me, I felt like my old self. The person I was before Judy Sharpley, the night in the woods. It felt strange. I pulled the waist of the trousers down as far as they'd go without breaking my non-existent hips, tying my hair into a low pony.

I liked working at Sally's Diner, far more than I'd expected when I first started at sixteen. Pulling on the uniform with its scratchy logo and weirdly long "short" sleeves, pushing my feet into trainers and frowning at the face staring back at me. I had a collection of spots on my forehead, no doubt caused by stress, and a particularly gunky one on my chin. I didn't usually care about things like that, and today, I cared even less. What did it matter if I looked like a greasy mess? This was part of *my* normal, my routine. Working at the diner on a weekend, seeing Owen later, getting a takeaway and crashing in front of the TV with Dizzy. Wandering through Vibbington's streets felt peaceful, hopeful. I could almost forget that Judy Sharpley was dead, that Loz had moved to Nottingham, that Owen had kissed Kara, in that moment.

Almost.

The diner was a grim building. It didn't have the best rep in Vibbington, an old-school Yorkshire town where most residents would rather buy a sausage roll with a hunk of cheese than burgers and fries. Most of the customers were regulars, who sat at the bar and supped beer all day rather than ordered food, but they hosted an abundance of kids' parties throughout the years I worked there... and leavers' days for primary schools, staff meals, that sort of thing.

Sally was the previous owner, but her son Cal had taken over after she died, and was a real stickler for punctuality. He was tapping his watch as I wandered through the back entrance, and frowned at me.

"Lilz, you're two minutes late!"

I flushed and apologised, peering past him. The place was pretty empty; the breakfast rush only started at ten on weekends, and the kitchen smelled of frying bacon and pancakes, maple syrup.

"How was your weekend off?" I blinked as Cal snapped the air in front of me, grabbing my attention. "Lilz? How was your weekend off?"

"Fine, fine. I mean, it was good. Good."

Cal nodded, rolling his eyes. "Sounds it. You're out front this morning, okay? We've taken on a new waitress, so you'll be showing her the ropes…"

Walking through the kitchen and pulling on my red apron was all part of my routine. I sanitised my hands, made sure my hair was pulled back away from my face, grimaced in the reflection of the oven. Daphne cooked breakfast most days, then went home at lunch to prepare for her second job, helping out in a primary school with their home economics lessons. She waved a wrinkled hand at me now as I flapped mine back.

Behind the counter, there was a girl stood by the till. The new girl, a year below me in school, Cal explained. She had long black hair and a face full of freckles, and stuck her tongue out as she tried to work out the change. There was a man stood opposite, rolling his eyes.

"Need some help?" I asked the girl, feeling my cheeks turn pink. I didn't mean to sound patronising, making it clear she couldn't figure out the tills, but the man was getting impatient, tapping his fingers on the counter. And I wanted to get stuck in again, back to work as normal.

"I'm good." The girl jammed the key forward and the till shot open, coins rattling. She was quick to point out the right amount, then scooped them into one hand and passed them to the man. "Do come again."

Interesting.

I always forgot to be polite to the customers – I was nice, but not *too* nice – but she seemed to have it down to a fine art.

"You're new?"

"Zoe. Just finished my GCSEs."

Even *more* interesting. I knew Cal would start hiring new staff for the summer, and I was Zoe's age when I first started, but it felt nice to be older, more experienced, nodding wisely as Zoe held out a hand to me. She was slender and had incredibly long, pointy nails – natural – which dug into my skin as we shook. It was strange, knowing we'd spend most of the summer together, working here at Sally's.

Little did we know how close we'd grow, how instrumental she'd become in crafting September third... I remember looking at her, this pretty girl, with her brown arms and long eyelashes and wide smile, and wondering how on earth I was going to cope with such a bloody ray of sunshine.

The girl I'd worked alongside last year had been nice enough. She was quiet, had pink hair and arms covered in stick-and-poke tattoos she'd given herself. She didn't speak to me much, but when she did, it was mostly just to compare song recs or gush about a new show on Netflix. It was nice knowing I wasn't obliged to talk for a whole eight hours, that I could eat my lunch alone and didn't feel like I had to attend staff nights out.

This girl was different, I could tell. She'd turned back to make another customer a milkshake, already a pro at using the handheld blender, and her whole aura was bubbly and fun, like Loz. I *hated* bubbly and fun, usually, unless it was coming from my best friend. Looking at Zoe felt like going to the hairdressers', envisioning a torturous appointment filled with constant chatter and unnecessary conversation.

She served the milkshake with more whipped cream and pink powder than I'd ever use at breakfast time, then turned back to me with a beam as the man slid away from the counter.

"How do you resist all the food here?" she asked, in one of those artificially sweet voices girls use when they want to make friends. "Like, my mouth was watering just looking at that drink."

"You get used to it. And after a while, you even get a bit sick of milkshakes and maple syrup."

Zoe cocked her head to one side, an amused smile on her face. "You clearly have no idea how much I love food."

"Obviously not."

So Zoe was one of *those* girls. A Nora-Baio-and-Alicia-McKnight kind of girl. She had a Barbie-doll figure, even in the icky Sally's uniform, and clearer skin than any girl eating Sally's food for breakfast, lunch and tea could ever maintain.

She smiled at me again, brighter this time. "So… you go to sixth form here? What's it like? I start in September, and I'm pissing myself. That is, if I get the grades…"

Like she wouldn't get the grades for Vibbington's crappy sixth form.

I gave her a strained smile and pretended to think for a while, finally settling with, "It's good. I mean, it's a bit rubbish, but it's Vibbington, so what would you expect?"

"What subjects do you do?"

I flushed. "Sociology, criminology and psych."

There you go, Lilz. Admit to your new little friend that you're super thick and picked the subjects everyone takes the piss out of, and that you're struggling to even pass them.

But Zoe nodded at me, eyes still bright.

"Wow! That's pretty hardcore. I was considering psych, but I decided it might look a bit odd on my uni applications, seeing as I'm going to be doing astrophysics and they're *very* different. I'm pretty sure I've settled on maths, further maths, physics and chemistry." She chuckled when she noticed my expression, and added, "Hey, like I said, I might not even get the grades. But I want to go to Edinburgh, hopefully, and the requirements are so high…"

I'll bet.

"What about you? Where are you applying to?"

I shrug. "I don't know if I'm going to uni yet. I've not thought about it much."

"But… don't you have to apply in a few months?"

It was June. The deadline didn't fall until mid-January.

I was not stressed.

"Yes, but I'm not worried. We get heaps of time to research where we want to go and figure stuff out. No one really has a clue yet."

Zoe was gobsmacked, shaking her head as though appalled, and I decided, in that moment, that I didn't like her much at all. The Lilz of June found her annoying and pretentious, and so up herself it would've taken both Owen and I a good few hours to pull her head out from up her arse.

"Gosh, I can't imagine being so unprepared. Like, I started looking at university places in year *nine*."

"Let's hope you get the grades then."

"I know, I'm keeping my –" Zoe looked at me then, flushing, as she realised I was being sarcastic. "I mean, I'm sure I'll be fine. I've never flunked a test before, and my mock results would have been enough to get me in."

That was when another customer appeared at the counter, asking for American-style pancakes with scrambled egg, bacon and syrup, and I disappeared into the kitchen to give Daphne the order as Zoe laughed and simpered and took the payment, managing the till with ease this time.

That was my first impression of Zoe Forlani, with her gorgeous clear skin and long black hair and freckled cheeks, slender wrists and long nails.

I didn't much like the girl, but no one could deny she was gorgeous.

Dear year twelve,

It's the end of another academic year, and you're now officially halfway through your time at Vibbington Sixth Form. It's been a wonderful year, and all of you truly are a credit to the school and community.

As we do every year, I'd like to take the time remember Lexie McCoy, who would have been turning seventeen this year. My condolences go out to those still affected by the tragedy, and my door is always open if you ever want to talk.

Moving on, I'd like to give my warmest congratulations to Kevin Jones and Eva Stewart, our new head boy and girl. Going into the new school year, these two will be in firm control of the sixth form council and any matters you'd like addressing. The budget for the next year will be announced on August 15th, and if there is anything in particular you think this should be spent on, I do encourage you to contact your new representatives.

As the new school magazine flourishes, I'd also like to congratulate Renee Wilson on her position as editor. If you'd like to get involved, it will look wonderful on your UCAS applications, and reporting is a great skill to have.

I wish you all a wonderful summer filled with sunshine and laughter - and revision!

Enjoy,
Mr Roberts
Head of Vibbington Sixth Form

THE LAST WEEK

When Loz left, time stopped for a day or two. Then it kickstarted. Suddenly, the rest of term was flying by at a rate of knots, June fading into July, July slipping away in a haze of cloudless days and a drought which sent the whole town doolally, bringing a hosepipe ban which started before the last week of term. The whole of our estate was in a state of disarray, made worse by the untimely death of Mrs Carlos's geraniums.

I was just relieved that sixth form was almost over, that soon I could put the stress of my failing A-levels behind me and focus on working at the diner four days a week, earning some cash and saving up properly for the future, whatever it may hold. I was excited to see Owen, for things to get back to normal. It hadn't been the same since he kissed Kara that night, and I couldn't blame him. We were both traumatised by Judy's death. Owen still woke up in the middle of the night moaning and whimpering, like bubbles were flying from his nose and he couldn't breathe, couldn't see –

I asked him about it once, cuddling him close to me as the sun rose outside and Owen Sharpley groaned, still coming out of the nightmare. He told me he was drowning, that his head was underwater and no matter how hard he tried, he couldn't get back up to the surface. I held him and kissed him and told him everything was going to be fine, but he just started crying. Owen hardly ever cried. It was a lonely, desolate sound, and a painful one, the sound of a cat being scraped against a brick wall, over and over and over.

"I'm dying," he told me, to which I tried to laugh, stroking his hair and kissing his forehead and insisting that he wasn't dying, that it was just a bad dream, that he was absolutely fine. But when he opened his eyes properly, they were round and dark and full of fear. Even when I switched on the light, it was like he was high again. My boyfriend twitched and made more horrid, animalistic noises while the sun rose over Vibbington and his mother's body continued to rot in the woods.

At least things with Kara settled down as we entered our last week of year twelve. She still couldn't stop flirting with Owen, but she seemed to have accepted that my boyfriend was out of bounds, that she needed to find someone else to entertain. It was a difficult pill for her to swallow. Now that there were just four of us, it felt more like we were double dating than ever.

Owen told me on Monday night that Gethin and Kara had shagged over the weekend. Kara had gone round during the day while Gethin's mum was at work and they'd done it on the sofa. I hated that Gethin and Owen told each other things like that, though I knew Owen was much more discreet.

When he noticed my unamused expression, he frowned and said, "What?"

"Oh, I don't know. It's just *very* obvious that they're both desperate and using each other, and I don't want it to make things awkward between us all."

Owen cocked his head, not understanding. "Why would it? And what's wrong with that?"

"What's wrong with the fact they're desperate and using each other?"

"Yeah. It's not really your place to judge. They're just

having fun, right?"

"But… it's not very healthy."

Owen rolled his eyes, like I was being dense. Maybe I was. I didn't understand how a friends-with-benefits situation could ever *actually* become beneficial in this situation. Gethin had apparent feelings for Kara but would never want anything serious, and God knows how Kara truly felt.

Call me boring, whatever, but I stand by the fact it was my place to judge. They were my friends, and I could see what was unfolding right before my eyes. It was only going to end in tears, and we'd end up even more disjointed than we had been when Loz first left.

As the week continued, Mr Roberts started rolling out the end of term activities, like voting for head boy and head girl, setting up a slip'n'slide on the school field, arming us with water guns and balloons to prank the sixth form's secretary on Thursday morning, during form time. Some girl with ginger hair got head girl – Eva, I think her name was – and head boy went to Kev Jones, of course, who was mega brainy, did five A-levels and everything.

The former year elevens came back for a day to test out sixth form life, worst luck. I spotted Zoe Forlani walking through the double doors with a band of equally slender, gorgeous girls with long eyelashes and nice clothes and folders tucked under their arms, even though it was just a taster day and they weren't going to be doing any work. She waved at me as Mr Roberts started speaking, and I gave a self-conscious wave back. Her band of merry men watched me for a second, sussing me out, before raising identical hands at the exact same time.

It was more than just creepy.

Zoe and I had been getting on surprisingly well, though I

still didn't like her. She was everything I opposed, like Loz in every way… apart from the good parts. She was smart, and there was no doubt in my mind that she'd leave her GCSEs with a handful of eights and nines; she was pretty, her Instagram full of #nofilter selfies, with a pretentious wardrobe to match; she was an animal lover, owned two horses (which told me everything I needed to know) and a dog called Dasher. She liked old music and movies, second-hand clothes shopping in Hull on her days off with those annoyingly beautiful friends of hers.

She was also a lesbian, which came out of nowhere. Lesbian and very out, in the sense that she had the rainbow flag in her Insta bio and used rainbow emojis in every other caption. She was the kind of brave I could only ever aspire to be. Her Jamaican mum and half-Nigerian, half-Italian dad were pretty traditional and hadn't understood at first, but, Zoe being Zoe, she'd made a slideshow on the history of homosexuality, how it wasn't something she could help. They now donated heaps to charities helping decriminalise homosexuality in countries around the world, and watched gay dramas with her to try and "educate" themselves.

Now, don't get the wrong idea here. Bisexual Lilz with a toxic, murderous boyfriend meets a gorgeous girl who just so happens to be gay and realises she doesn't need her boyfriend after all… I'd love to say that's how the story goes, but that would be a lie. It would also be far, *far* too easy.

The last day came and went in a hurried blur of bad movies and laughter and an assembly wishing us all an incredible summer and a healthy, productive break before the hardest year of our lives. Mr Roberts was smiling and clapping as we marched out of the hall towards our final lessons of the year, with just one more hour to get through…

and when the final bell rang, I felt a flood of relief like I'd felt experienced before. It was over. I now had six weeks off to relax and enjoy the sun and get things back on track with Owen, and a weekend away in a caravan in Dorset with Owen, Mum and Dizzy to look forward to...

The four of us made our way out of school together, to where Owen's car was waiting to drive us to the beach. I was grinning as I clambered over Kara onto the back seat. This was it. This was hope, this was adventure, this was...

I saw Ethan Morgan walking out of school with that mousy girl Lucy as we drove away, a big smile on his face, and couldn't help but smile to myself. Things were changing. Changing for the better, no doubt, but changing all the same.

"Ready?" Owen asked, as I nodded.

Things truly were looking up.

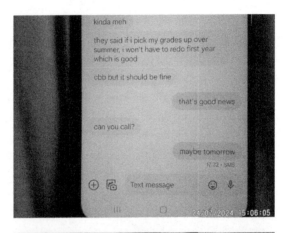

kinda meh

they said if i pick my grades up over summer, i won't have to redo first year which is good

cbb but it should be fine

that's good news

can you call?

maybe tomorrow

17:32 · SMS

Text message

24/07/2024 15:06:05

Incoming call

Loz

United Kingdom

24/07/2024 15:06:57

THE SCARE

Loz had a pregnancy scare just a month or so after moving to Notts. That's how fast she changed, morphing from my best friend into someone I barely recognised.

Initially after the move, we rang each other every few days, just to check in. We'd usually just natter about nothing, dissecting the kiss (Loz agreed that Kara was entirely to blame) and picking apart Ethan's Snapchat location and ever-rising snap score. She briefly mentioned the college induction day she went on, where they told her that if she picked up her grades from last year, she could carry her A-levels on and start in September as a second year, rather than going right back to the beginning. She told me this in an ecstatic voice, and I replied with equal vigour, delighted for my best friend.

She didn't tell me about Marcus, however, some guy she'd met in one of her sessions. He'd also just transferred colleges and had a body like Dwayne Johnson, and he'd apparently taken her out for a drink, which turned into a second drink, and a third, and a fourth.

They did it behind a building in the city centre, and he hadn't used a condom. She'd been blanking him ever since she noticed her breasts swelling up and that she'd missed a period. It was now two days into the summer holidays and she was crying down the phone to me, insisting that she'd screwed up and her life was over.

"Have you taken a test?" I asked, moving to sit on the end of my bed. Owen was out with Gethin and I could hear Dizzy listening to music across the hall, and it was raining, just a little. We were supposed to have these catastrophic downpours over the next few days before it all wore off and the sun shone endlessly for the rest of July, into August. I liked rain, liked rain way more than sunshine. But it was that horrid, muggy rain, the kind that drags on and on and doesn't seem to stop.

"No, not yet."

So I sat there, talking to my best friend, as she scurried out of her new home in Nottingham to the pharmacist down the road, where I heard her purchase a pregnancy test, the expensive kind, and walk it all the way home tucked safely under her arm. Then (TMI, I know) I listened to her wee on the stick, squatting on the toilet with her phone on speaker mode as she left the test for the correct amount of time, all the while breathing heavily and fretting and panting hard as she tried not to panic.

It was negative. Of course it was negative. The universe must have sensed that it wasn't the right time for Loz to be dealing with a decision like that, trying to figure out how to get rid of the thing growing inside of her. There was no *thing*. She'd probably missed her period because she was stressed, and her breasts getting bigger could only be a good thing, right?

"Not when I already pop out of most tops," Loz huffed. "But that's what Sofia said. She missed three or four periods when she went through her last breakup."

Sofia, I was discovering, was this rich girl who lived down Loz's new street. She was Spanish and had an extensive wardrobe of funky, Loz-like clothes, and sixteen pairs of Nikes, which she kept on a display in her *walk-in wardrobe*. Loz's new room was pretty fancy, but when she and Sofia took selfies for Instagram in Sofia's mansion, Owen and I had never seen anything like it.

"You'd love Sofia," Loz was saying now, for the umpteenth time. "She's just so down to earth, so… groovy."

Groovy. Was that a normal term used to describe a new friend? A vintage top, maybe, or a patterned scatter cushion… but not Sofia, who looked about as basic as you could get. Like Zoe, she was the kind of girl who thought buying second-hand clothing or pieces from Instagram boutiques made you *unique*, when really, every other teenager and their dog was doing the same – or at least wanted to. I was getting sick of girls like that.

"Anyway," Loz said, sensing that I was tiring of Sofia and going to change the subject. "How's Owen?"

"Um…"

I hate that I didn't know how to respond to that.

Everything was fine with Owen; it should've been easy. We were still together, he hadn't mentioned Kara's kiss since the day after when we'd discussed it, and he was still sleeping round at mine each night, aside from the few nights we'd decided we needed some alone time and crept out of the front door and into his flat to sleep together on the sofa in peace. Everything was good, apart from the slight unease I still felt about everything that had happened in the garage that weekend. Everything was very good.

"Lilz?"

"Owen's good," I said, after a pause. "I mean, he's still cut up about his mum leaving, but…"

"Has he heard from her since?"

I shook my head, then realised Loz couldn't see me. "No."

"Not at all?"

"I guess she must just really want a fresh start."

"Jeez." Loz sounded so sorry for Owen that I almost felt guilty, changing the subject to get her off the scent.

"Anyway… are you going to contact Marcus again, now that you're sure you're not pregnant?"

Loz fell silent.

"No?"

"I don't know." She sounded uncertain, conflicted. "I think… maybe, but when the time is right. You know, I don't want to rush into anything here straight away, not so soon after Ethan… and…"

"No, I get that." I paused again. "You must really miss him."

"I do."

I was thinking about Owen in that moment, of course. About Owen, and how devastated I'd be if we ever broke up. How much it would change everything, ruin my life for good. Owen was a part of me. I wasn't sure if I could exist without him by my side.

That was the first time it really hit me that losing Owen was a possibility. I'd taken his company for granted my entire life, sure that he'd never leave me, but now, watching Loz and Ethan split up, I could see how two people could grow and change, morphing from a couple into a couple of strangers.

It was a hideous thought.

"But… I'm starting to see that it was for the best, now that I'm here in Notts." This was the most Loz-like she'd been since I first answered the phone two hours ago, and I smiled into mine, nodding. "Like, I became so used to being Ethan's girlfriend. I *loved* being Ethan's girlfriend. But I'm not at that stage in my life yet. I think… I think being here, in a new city, with a boyfriend back home, it would've held me back. Do you know what I mean?"

I did.

I hated that I did, but I did.

"I mean, if we all stayed with the same boyfriend our entire life, we'd never experience anything new. We'd never want to move away, or test the waters, see if he's even *right* for us. We'd never... know. Not for sure. I love the idea of first love lasting, but I think humans are designed to meet new people, sleep around a bit, figure out what we really want."

"I've got to go."

"Lilz? Lilz, I wasn't talking about you and Owen, I know that's different, but –"

"I'll message you later, yeah?"

I hung up before I could think about it any more.

the 12k gc :p

---

ethan @everyone
hey guys! who's up for an end of term bash to
end all bashes?

oli @ethanmorgzie
sounds sick bro
hey how about we hit maythorpe beach later
its meant to be proper stormy

lish @bigmanoli
erm
oli
do you know how dangerous that sounds

oli @aliciamcknightxo
you scared, lish?
how about everyone else? you up for the
bash to end all bashes?

owen @everyone
yeah man, we'll be there. we've got an extra
seat in the car if anyone needs a lift.
shall we say four o'clock?

THE STORM

There was a proper storm the next night, which was only to be expected. Like I said, life felt good, too good, and this, the rain tumbling from the sky and dark grey clouds hanging above us, felt necessary, a cleanser.

I remember feeling glad as the rain fell and Owen hugged me from behind, staring out of the window on the landing as our concrete estate was battered pewter.

"The 12k group chat is planning something," he murmured in my ear. "You up for some fun?"

The 12k group chat was a Snapchat group for all the kids in our year, or at least those who used social media and actually *liked* the majority of us. We'd no doubt morph into the 13k group chat now we were leaving year twelve behind, but Ethan's group had been planning a little end-of-year blow-out for weeks. Everyone had been waiting patiently for the call.

The plan was to hit Maythorpe beach in the middle of the storm, as the waves were high and thunder rumbled overhead, to park in the car park now that the ticket man would be out of the way and run into the sea, screaming at the tops of our lungs. Going to the beach during a storm was a bit of a tradition around here; it was only a fifteen minute drive, and now that half the year had passed their test, we could go way more often than ever before.

"You ready?" I asked Owen as he pulled on his trainers and grabbed a change of shorts. I was wearing one of his baggy shirts over my swimming costume and had no intention of pulling it off, but I packed a spare black hoodie and some leggings to change into afterwards. I couldn't help but feel a pang of guilt as I thought about how much Loz would've loved this, would've loved diving into the ocean while great black clouds raced above, laughing and shouting along with the rest of our year.

But I couldn't dwell on that.

We picked up Kara and Gethin on the way, both in their swimming things, talking over each other in their excitement. The energy was feverish, ecstatic, Kara practically bouncing up and down as we made it out of Vibbington and onto the coastal road, music blaring.

The car park at Maythorpe was empty, rain lashing down and the sky above us such an intense shade you could barely see the sun. There was no lightning, thank goodness, and Ethan Morgan was already instructing us of the dangers of swimming in a storm, boring and sensible as ever. If the weather got too bad and lightning struck anywhere in our eyeline, we had to get out. Owen rolled his eyes, and Kara caught his gaze for long enough to shake her head. I thought Ethan was being a party pooper too, but maybe it wasn't terrible that at least one person wanted to be safe.

It was a stupid plan, of course. I don't recommend going swimming during a storm, even just in a pool. It's like when those people in movies get electrified in hotels when the wires from a set of speakers accidentally fall close to the water's edge, or the current picks up and whisks you out, out, out to sea.

But we were seventeen and reckless, and that was enough to make the whole thing sound appealing.

I watched as Ethan made his way onto the beach with Oli

and Kev, his cronies, wearing a tight-fitting white t-shirt and comical Hawaiian shorts. I wasn't sure what Loz had ever seen in him. Lucy, Nora and Alicia were next, in identical bikinis, covering just the right amount of skin. Our year's nerdy group was close behind – Samantha, Liz, Boner-boy and Tommy – and Owen, Kara, Gethin and I brought up the rear.

Eva, the new head girl, and her friends Renee and Juliette, drove here in Juliette's fancy white Mini, which was pristine aside from the mud splatters they must've created driving here. Juliette wasn't the kind of girl to *deliberately* drive through mud. Her crippling anxiety had caused her to miss a lot of school over the last few years, and she always looked neat and pristine, squeaky clean.

The few stragglers were still arriving in the car park, when a blue car pulled up, blasting Taylor Swift out into the storm, and some bratty girl from the year above hopped out. She was called Mira, I think, and had dated Oli for a short while before Christmas.

Then I noticed who was with her.

Zoe, smiling and waving at me, and her friends, all in bikinis and cropped hoodies, running onto the beach after us.

Of course… Mira was Zoe's older sister. Both horrifically enthusiastic and smiley, with their long dark hair and big smiles, the similarities were glaringly obvious. But *Mira Forlani*, last year's head girl, who was going off to study medicine this year somewhere down south? One of her friends got into heaps of trouble shagging an English teacher last year, which is partly the reason her group were so infamous. Mira Forlani. *Zoe* Forlani.

Everyone had gathered on the beach now, the rain still beating down. Owen's hair was plastered to his forehead, mouth open wide to catch the cool drops. It was weirdly humid, and you could definitely tell it was July.

"Lilz!" I spun to find Zoe approaching, waving a slender hand. She had green acrylics today – expensive, properly done in a salon and everything – and I wanted to hate her for that, too. "Hi! I wasn't expecting to see you here!"

"Hello." I tried to smile politely, but even that sentence annoyed me. She wasn't expecting to see me here? This was *my* year group, our end-of-year-twelve celebration. She wasn't even in our year, and neither was her sister.

"Do you know Mira?" Zoe pointed at Mira Forlani, who was talking to someone I didn't know in the most irritating, animated way, waving her hands around a lot and beaming. "She got wind that you guys were doing something today, so we thought we'd come and crash it!"

"That's... nice." I didn't know what else to say, so I jabbed Owen on the arm, to kill the awkwardness. "Owen? Owen, this is Zoe, she works at Sally's now. And Zoe, this is my boyfriend Owen."

"Howdy!"

Owen narrowed his eyes at her excitable greeting, and said, "All right?"

"God, your boyfriend is fit, Lilz!" Zoe exclaimed. Then she pulled a face, shaking her head. "Not that I notice that sort of thing, of course. I'm a lesbian, if you weren't aware."

Owen arched an eyebrow. "Do you want a medal or something?"

I kind of wanted to die, in that moment.

"Honestly? Yes." Zoe laughed way too loudly, though it wasn't really funny, and my cheeks flushed pink. Kara and Gethin were looking at her too now, wrinkling their noses.

"Who's this?" Kara asked, scoffing. "Your little girlfriend?"

"She works with me at the diner." I tried to stop my cheeks from turning pink and failed miserably. Trust Kara to make a bi joke the minute she knew I was friends with a lesbian. If Zoe had been a boy, she never would've have said anything.

Zoe looked at me curiously then, as though trying to figure out what Kara meant, so I quickly flapped my hands and gestured to the crowds, saying, "Erm, I think your friends are calling you, Zoe…"

"Are they?"

"Yes, yes, look!"

As soon as Zoe turned her back to go and investigate, I grabbed Owen's hand, looked him dead in the eye and grinned.

"You ready for this?"

"Ready as I'll ever be."

**

Pandemonium.

Forty, fifty bodies, crashing into the water, shouting at the tops of our lungs, feeling the cold liquid lap around our ankles and waists and curl up to our chests. We were running, clambering over each other to get deeper, deeper, falling over and feeling the waves crash over our heads in our hurry to dive deeper under the water and further towards the horizon.

Owen looked gorgeous, like I'd never seen a boy look. He'd taken his shirt off and his white chest was gleaming with bits of seaweed and sand, dark eyes gazing at me levelly through the waves, the spray tossing over our heads. I wanted to grab him, but the water was pushing us further and further apart, under and over. My hair was wet, plastered to my forehead, just like his. I could feel the goosebumps on my arms and legs and yet in that moment, I didn't care. The thunder felt far away, and the rain was so intense I could've drowned in it.

In a way, I think that day in the ocean was kind of like therapy. Feeling the seawater blind me, sting my eyes, take my mind off of everything that had happened. Though I could hear Zoe's irritating screeching and her sister Mira showing off in the shallows, all I was thinking was how alive I felt right now, how beautiful a moment this was, all of us running around being silly in the rain, not caring how we looked, how others would perceive us.

It was freeing.

It was so, so freeing, like nothing I'd ever experienced.

Ethan Morgan was dancing up and down holding hands with that girl Lucy, and Alicia and Nora were jumping the waves deeper than anyone else dared venture, to the point it almost looked dangerous. Oli was flirting with a girl who wasn't Mira, and Kev, our new head boy, was watching Nora Baio with a wistful smile on his face. Samantha and Liz were cautious, not wanting to get their shorts wet, and Boner-boy (I still don't know his real name) was chasing Tommy with a stick he'd found somewhere.

And then there was Zoe. She and her friends looked to be having fun, a little way off from everyone else, splashing each other and using their long nails to cut through the water, which was at chest-height. I caught Zoe's eye, and this time, I gave a proper smile back. She was just enjoying herself, like everyone else. Maybe her positivity could sometimes be misconstrued as annoying, but I never should have begrudged her that.

Owen grabbed me then, under the water. I felt his hands

go around my waist, and suddenly I was kissing him, until an extra large wave dislodged both of our footing and we were submerged completely. I was laughing as we resurfaced, soaked and shivering, Kara and Gethin howling at us, but I just *didn't* care. This was the happiest I'd felt in weeks, months. The most like myself.

The most like *Lilz*.

searching for
silver linings

THE GREEN

Kara and Gethin caught a lift back with some kids they sometimes smoked weed with, and Owen and I drove off in his blood-coloured car, the same car we'd used to dispose of a body with just a month and a half earlier.

I was shaking with cold, wearing my baggy black hoodie, but we'd forgotten towels and my legs were too wet to pull on my leggings. Owen had changed into his fresh shorts in the back of the car, and we were sat at the front now, leaving Maythorpe via the long, winding road which led down to the coast. Ethan Morgan and his friends were in front, Nora Baio driving separately behind, and the nerds all left in Boner-boy's car.

The storm had subsided when we were in the ocean, leaving behind a wave of blue sky drifting through the fluffy remaining clouds. It was warm and muggy and the beach was soaked through with rainwater and salt spray, and we'd all gathered on the sand to run around and chat and enjoy the afternoon, which was nice, but missing Loz. Someone brought a whole load of snacks, but we were on our way to pick up chips now, still starving.

Only I couldn't stop staring out of the window.

As you might have guessed, I'm not much of a nature person. At least, I wasn't back then, in July, when the air was too hot and I couldn't ever get cool and I hated being covered in a permanent sheen of sweat. I lived in a horrid grey concrete block and worked in a tacky American diner; I wasn't exactly a tree-hugger.

But this was different.

The sky was a gorgeous shade, almost teal, absorbing the colours of the countryside around it. Soft white clouds drifted overhead, and a rainbow, the brightest, shiniest of rainbows, formed a perfect arch going from one luscious field to another.

It was more vibrant than I'd ever seen over the drab buildings of Vibbington, such an unbelievable mix of colours, like it had been painted across the sky with some of Dizzy's old crayons.

I swallowed, staring at the thing, wondering when I'd got so pathetic and soppy to have moist eyes at the sight of a *rainbow*.

The countryside was even more unbelievable. A rich shade of gorgeous green, almost yellow in the golden light, saturated from the rain and so thick you could've cut the scene with a knife, like it was playdough. Nothing looked real. The perfectly formed trees with their broccoli-floret branches and leaves, puffy and a dark shade of intense forest; the grassy fields, dotted with cows and wind turbines, spinning, spinning, though not spinning fast enough after the storm before; hedgerows filled with life, even after the drought, coming back to life after craving rainfall for so long.

I wanted to paint the scene, take a photo, a video, though my crappy phone camera couldn't have done it justice. Even Owen had his eyes half on the countryside and half on the peaceful roads, watching the sweeping landscape as it came to life around us, like a movie.

"We don't go on enough drives," he said, like he was only just realising this. "It's so…"

But at that moment, he turned the radio on, completely

ruining the peace.

We pulled over after a few minutes, into a wet little layby with a view over the surrounding East Yorkshire countryside. And for a moment, we just sat there. Sat there, thinking. Thinking about the scenery, about life, what had just happened in the ocean out there... and no doubt about Judy Sharpley, about the contrast between her dead, leaking corpse and the beautiful world we lived in. It seemed barmy that someone so evil could've ever lived here, in such a wonderful place full of life and colour and nature, that someone so *unnatural* could have been a part of the natural world. And that she still was, in a way. That her body was now at one with Vibbington's Forest of Death, seeping its juices through the creases of the bin bag into the leaves and twigs of the ground below.

I put a hand on Owen's leg, let him feel my presence. When I looked over, there were tears in his eyes, on his cheeks.

"Lilz," he said, voice all choked up, uncertain. "Lilz, I did the right thing, didn't I? I did the right thing?"

"Of course you did," I told him, though even I sounded unsure. "She was awful to you, Owen. You didn't have a *choice*."

Owen nodded, wiping his nose on the back of his hand. I hated seeing him like this. My strong, I-don't-care-about-anything boyfriend, crying in the car, reduced to a snivelling child.

But things had changed.

This was Owen, now. Unpredictable, unstable. Upset.

A murderer.

"She hated me, Lilz. She really, really hated me."

"I don't think she hated you."

Owen looked at me pointedly through glassy eyes. "She wanted to make me miserable. She liked seeing me traumatised. She found pleasure in making me cry then… laughing, like it was funny. My sadness was like fuel for her."

"She just shouldn't have been a mother," I reasoned. "She still loved you, because you were her child."

You might be wondering why I was trying so hard to defend Judy Sharpley, given how she'd treated Owen as a child, torturing him like that.

But… I knew how it felt to live in a single-parent family, to only have one person in the world, aside from your partner, who's supposed to love you unconditionally, no matter what. And making Judy Sharpley out to be a terrible person who'd never cared for Owen was even more cruel than anything. Owen didn't need that. Owen didn't *deserve* that, no matter what you might think of him.

"I… I don't know."

"Trust me, Owen."

Owen looked at me, dark eyes meeting mine.

Then he nodded.

His cheeks were pale and his eyelids were blotchy, and he let me clamber over the gearstick to sit on his lap. He pulled back the chair, leaving a gap between the steering wheel and our bodies, and just sat there, unresponsive, as I hugged him, planted kisses on his face and neck, letting him know I was there, that I loved him, that he had me, no matter what.

The greenery from the layby outside was dancing through the windows, leaving lime residue across our skin. Everything was a greeny yellow, calming.

I planted a kiss on Owen's lips this time, like it was the most natural thing in the world.

But he still didn't respond. At all.

And there, kissing my boyfriend in his blood-red car in the middle of the beautiful, rain-soaked countryside, I realised just how *un*natural this whole thing was.

sally's diner   34567890
3 industry rd. vibbington   july 27 2024
east yorkshire ---- ---

item(s)   value

strawb. milkshake.................£2.50
bacon whopper....................£11.10
onion rings.......................£3.20

SUBTOTAL.........................£16.80

total amount paid in cash

PLEASE RETAIN FOR YOUR RECORDS

THE WAITRESS

I think Loz felt a little put out when she saw the photos and stories from our day on the beach. She flicked through them as I sat on the phone to her, making non-committal noises, then changed the subject to tell me about all the fun she and Sofia had had shopping in the city centre.

"Great," I said, hardly enthused, as Loz went on and on and on, natter natter natter. Because I really wasn't enthused. Sofia sounded like a horrid little brat who had too much of her daddy's money and no common sense. Loz wouldn't stop going on about shoes and bags and that walk-in wardrobe, how Sofia's parents had bought her tickets to go and see a West End show for her birthday and she'd offered to take Loz.

"She's great at taking Instagram photos," my best friend continued. "Way better than Kara."

Unlike most normal seventeen-year-olds, Loz took Instagram *seriously*. It was one of the only things Ethan didn't like about her. He couldn't see why she felt the need to show herself off to the randoms who followed her, or why she cared what anybody else thought. I knew Loz was secretly hoping to open her own online boutique one day, that she took the app to heart because it could kickstart her career. She found admitting that embarrassing, so I never brought it up.

I was awful at taking photos. The ones on my account were mainly grungy mirror selfies with my mood lights on and big, baggy clothes, maybe the odd selfie or two taken on my webcam with Owen, but Loz's were… well, very Loz. Lots of outfit pics, selfies with no filter and perfect makeup, a few booby ones taken on the beach. Kara could take decent photos, though she always got too much body and not enough head in. Apparently Sofia was a photo-taking *God*.

"You got the link I sent you, right?" Loz asked, desperately eager. "To the modelling she did for New Look?"

By the time I set down the phone, I was so sick of Loz and Sofia's new friendship that I could've screamed. But I didn't. Because compared to everything else going on in my life, the thought of my lifelong best friend preferring some rich brat to me was hardly worth thinking about.

Owen still occupied ninety-seven percent of my mind.

Owen, and how strange things still felt between us. Owen, and the way he kissed me in the car that day after the storm – or didn't kiss me, I should say, instead just *sitting* there, like a broken doll. Owen, and how... wrong things felt. How stilted. Owen, and how I had no idea what was happening anymore, or what I should do.

He was still practically living with us, and hadn't taken a shower or bath in Judy Sharpley's flat since he'd sliced up her body there. And things were fine. He was physical with me, emotionally there, but he was also drifting, drifting in a way I couldn't describe. I'd been with Owen since I was twelve, and he was still as cuddly and lovely now as he ever had been, chatting lazily about our days at work we prepared breakfast or I did my hair and makeup for a night in the park with Kara and Gethin, drinks with a few kids from sixth form.

But something had changed.

Maybe it was me, not him. Because everything was still the same, but I felt like I'd been swallowed by a pack of tigers and chewed up, then spat out again. My life hadn't altered at all, and neither had our relationship. But I had. I'd been torn up inside, left for dead. I wasn't the same person who'd gone along with Judy's murder because I had no other option, because loving and supporting Owen was the only thing that made sense. I was more paranoid than that girl, a shell of my former self. I was no longer Lilz, but... Lily. That was who I was becoming.

Fearful and fragile, and so terrified of losing my boyfriend that I clung onto him more than ever.

I was working at the diner Wednesday through to Saturday now, the same as Owen at his job, and the four day week took it out of both of us. Kara and Gethin had started something casual, it seemed, and so weekends were spent either "double dating" or hanging with Mum and Dizzy, who hadn't sensed that anything was off.

Maybe nothing was off. Maybe I was being paranoid.

Except for the nights Owen didn't spend with me.

The nights he'd go sneaking off after Mum had gone to bed, claiming either two things. That he was hot and couldn't sleep and needed a walk, or that he was going to meet Gethin, let off some steam. A few months ago, I might've complained about this, but I felt I couldn't now. He'd been through enough, and I had to let him satisfy his needs.

I had a suspicion he was going to see Judy's body, at first. I don't know why. It's morbid, I know, but... I couldn't believe he'd just leave her there, rotting, in a bin bag in the forest. Part of me almost *hoped* that was what he was doing, that the Owen I thought I knew and loved really was that person, deep inside.

He'd come back in the early hours and have a shower in the downstairs bathroom, washing off whatever smell clung to his skin. I still don't know for sure where he went during those nights, though I have a pretty good idea...

But I'll save that for later.

Work, as July came to a close, was my sanctuary. Turning up early in the morning to take orders and deliver food to plastic-topped tables, smiling and adopting my happy-Lilz persona, waving around a menu and instructing the other waitress what to do. The other waitress being Zoe Forlani, still as pretty and perky as ever, who turned up to work each day with the widest smile on her face and an annoyingly positive attitude to everything.

I didn't actually mind her, I was coming to realise. Zoe Forlani was unique – that's an understatement – but she was also a genuinely decent person, and never judged anybody. She got on well with Daphne in the kitchen, was always kind to the guy who washed the dishes and definitely had a crush on her. She was funny, sometimes, in a dry, sarcastic way, and she wasn't nearly as high-maintenance as she made out. The fake nails and permanent full-face were just a part of who she was, who she liked to be.

She was actually one of the most down-to-earth people I'd ever met.

We got on weirdly well, actually, for two such different people. Our conversations would usually go something like this, only interrupted by a whole load more customers and annoying little rat-like children running here and there:

"You like rap music?" she'd ask in disbelief, one eyebrow raised as she went to wipe the counter. "You look too pure and innocent for rap."

"I don't *just* like rap," I'd reason. "I like all sorts. Grunge, a bit of rock, a dash of Billie Eilish…"

Because yes, I was that basic. I was a self-proclaimed chav; what can I say?

"I much prefer pop," Zoe would tell me, before going off

into a spiel about her favourite pop artists, why the industry was looking up for the first time in years, how LGBTQ+ and BAME artists were finally getting the recognition they deserved. It was nice to just listen to her, sometimes, as we wiped down the tables at the end of the day and used the big industrial mop to clean the floor and the lino around each booth.

She still didn't know I was bi, but I kind of liked that. I liked that we got on fine without having our sexuality to connect us, that we could get on just because we were two cool individuals with nothing in common but a whole lot to debate.

I soon learnt that Zoe Forlani was a lot like Mira Forlani, in more ways than one. She had it in her to be head girl, with her preppy, bossy personality, good grades and intense desire to do good for the world; she championed recycling and eating less meat, and tried to be vegetarian at least three days each week; she was popular, and talkative, and likeable, all things which would usually make me hate a girl like Zoe. But I didn't hate Zoe. I didn't have the energy to hate Zoe.

She was too stimulating, sometimes. She really made you *think*. Zoe was much more into politics than I was, knew more about the economy, and would just come out with these mind-blowing statements and queries that almost made me stand back and blink in disbelief.

You see, without sounding too basic, I have to admit that before Zoe, I didn't really have… *opinions*. I mean, I did, but I never really thought about them, not like that. Zoe would bring up things that I'd never even *considered*. I liked that about her.

She was deeper than my other friends. Not in a bad way – I liked gossiping with Loz about boys and nail polish, listening to Kara about whatever boy she was shagging – but in a different way. Different can be good, I was starting to realise. Since I'd been with Owen, I'd never bothered with *different*.

Zoe cared about a lot of things. She thought climate change was the biggest issue we as humanity had faced, ever, and we debated on and off about the matter, but not in an argument kind of way. She hated plastic straws with a passion, whereas I despised going to the cinema and having to ask for two straws because you just *knew* one would go soggy halfway through the film. She was pro-choice, and hated certain political parties. She liked clothes, but thought it was cool that I didn't, that it made her reevaluate her own priorities and the importance she placed on her appearance, on her hair and makeup.

It was like having a cousin, I imagined, who didn't think the same as you and yet somehow looked up to you, thought you were interesting, someone worth knowing.

It was nice, feeling like Zoe enjoyed talking to me. It was nice, and it made a change from talking to Owen day in and day out – much as I hated to admit that.

And then one day, towards the very end of July, Zoe turned to me and said, "Would you like to do something tomorrow?"

Tomorrow being Sunday, one of our three days off.

I narrowed my eyes at her, unsure what she was really asking.

"Erm…"

"I mean, like, go shopping. In Leeds. The train changes at Hull, but they have some really cute shops there, and I thought… maybe, since we get on pretty well, it might be nice to do something outside of work?"

I just stared at her. Get the train to Leeds, go through the hassle of switching at Hull? That had to be a… what, hour and a half journey at least? Wasn't that a lot of effort to go through just to spend the day *shopping*?

"I mean, only if you want to." Zoe's cheeks were pink. "I know you probably have plans with your friends and stuff, so if you can't make it, that's fine…"

I don't know what snapped inside of me then. What caused me to shake my head, smile, and say to Zoe, "No, I'd love to. What time shall I meet you?"

Because I needed this. I *deserved* this. Owen had Gethin and Loz had Sofia and I was just floating, losing my mind with paranoia. I think Lilz of July knew that before she even admitted it to herself.

"Great!" Zoe said, beaming. "Meet you at the station at nine?"

STD SINGLE   TWO ADULTS
28 JULY 2024   no. 3212589
From. Vibbington → Leeds

£11.47   valid all day

STD SINGLE   TWO ADULTS
28 JULY 2024   no. 3212590
From. Leeds → Vibbington

£11.47   valid all day

THE BURRITO

I don't want any of this to come off as condescending towards anyone who lives in a small town, or even just somewhere that doesn't sell burritos.

But when you're someone like me – quietly angry, into takeaway pizzas and crappy American TV – the idea of going to an outdoor food court and sitting amongst a load of twenty-something-year-olds in expensive North Face jackets and Levi's isn't so appealing.

Zoe and I got the train at nine, arriving in Leeds just after half ten. I'd never been to Leeds; all I knew about it was that it was in Yorkshire, and not too far from Vibbington compared to Notts, but far enough that I considered it a trek. The station was huge, like a whole underground cavern, only it wasn't *technically* underground, but the towering buildings and high-rise blocks made it feel that way, and I was felt so overwhelmed as we made our way off the platform that Zoe practically had to drag me into the nearest loos.

We'd spent most of the journey chatting, but I felt so out of place with her, so… common. I'd thrown on a faded band t-shirt and baggy black jeans that morning in an attempt to look semi-cool and casual, but Zoe was wearing a green plaid skirt and this tiny white top which showed off her dark skin and looked amazing. When I left Owen in bed with a kiss, he mumbled something about not becoming a posh city tart and "forgetting my roots".

Leaving the station, it hit me suddenly how far we were

from Vibbington, how different this all was. You might be thinking, *Lilz, get a grip, Leeds is nothing compared to London or Paris or New York. It's just a rubbish city with a ton of shops and some mediocre old architecture, nothing special.* But I hadn't been to any of those places. The only city I'd ever visited in my life was Hull, which was small and flat and full of coarse accents and tumble-down buildings. Mum could never afford the lavish school trips to Cambridge or Shakespeare's house in Stratford, and so the extent of my travelling was a weekend in Cleethorpes when I was fifteen.

When she'd booked for Owen, Dizzy and I to go stay with her in Dorset in mid-August, I'd been ecstatic. That would be my first proper holiday in… well, ever. And this, walking down the street from the station into the city centre, felt just as intense, if a bit scary. I didn't belong here, in my cheap graphic t-shirt I'd found in a charity shop and my Primark jeans, the kind of outfit which had felt almost cool when we'd left Vibbington. It just wasn't *me*.

Zoe was confident, leading the way, chatting about how she came here all the time with Mira and her friends to do shopping trips and the likes, and had even attended pride here, waving a big lesbian flag and shouting at the top of her voice. I could barely get a word in edgeways as we walked, trying not to step into people or out into the road, which was teeming with huge buses and fancy cars. How did people in cities not get flattened every other second?

"Where shall we go first?" Zoe asked, eyes bright. "We could go for food, an early lunch, or I could show you the architecture of the Corn Exchange. What do you think?"

We ended up in the Corn Exchange, a huge city centre building filled with tiny shops and independent trade, the architecture of which was surprisingly beautiful, if you like that sort of thing. We got overpriced coffees each (which were way too strong) and sat on a rickety table to drink, Zoe filling me in on her life as she went, chattering non-stop.

"So," she said, placing down her cup. "First impressions of Leeds?"

"It's big. And loud."

"Not much of a city person, then?"

"I… I guess not."

"You prefer the countryside?"

Did I? Not really. The drive back from the beach had been beautiful, of course, but only because of the rainbow and all of the luscious green, the fluffy clouds and saturated earth. I hated autumn, when everything was starting to die and the world was cold and miserable. Snow annoyed me; it was just too cold and icky and grim, and we never got it properly near the coast. I didn't mind January. Cold but not too cold, and not too wet, just the right amount of frosty and crisp and damp. Then spring came again, and it got hot, too hot. I hated hot.

"What about university?" Zoe pressed. "You'll have to live in a city then…"

I knew she meant well, I really did. But the way she was talking right now just felt condescending, so I shrugged and downed my coffee like a shot.

Zoe Forlani loved shopping, I soon found out, as she bought two halter neck tops from one of the tiny Corn Exchange shops, dragging me into a little room selling artwork in fancy frames and insisting that I pick a miniature for my room, her treat. I wasn't going to complain, even when I saw the price, and picked the darkest, grungiest piece I could find, hoping it would go with the depressing insistence of my bedroom. A girl, with pale arms and legs, staring at the moon, wearing nothing but a slip of fabric. It was weirdly… sensual.

Next was a postcard shop, where we both bought postcards of Leeds, of the city centre reflected over the waterfront. We really *were* that touristy and basic.

Then Zoe took my hand, winking, and led me into a fourth.

"Good morning, girls," the woman behind the desk said. I was too in awe to respond.

The room was full of plants.

Houseplants, hundreds of them, though not the crusty kind they sell in supermarkets on rusting metal trolleys. Beautiful, billowing plants, plants hanging from the ceiling in baskets and jars, lit up by fairy lights which travelled all around the shop. I stared around, mouth wide, as Zoe's hands trailed the leaves.

They were gorgeous, wonderful. The green was so intense it felt overwhelming, and, for the first time since the day of the storm, I felt such a sense of calm take over me, fill my lungs. I was pretty sure from my GCSE biology lessons that plants gave us oxygen, but that green also relieved stress, that it was used in hospital wards to calm patients struggling with their mental health.

I could see why.

There were all kinds of species, ones I'd never seen before, entwined with those I'd spotted dangling over balconies on our estate or getting all manky on Judy Sharpley's window ledge before she got bored and chucked them. Cacti, in all shapes and sizes, some with flowers and some without, and a yucca with a wide stem and huge leaves, in a brown pot. There were succulents in glass jars, and a bonsai (I think) on a little blue tray, the tiny tree stretching towards the light.

I was in love with them all.

"You like plants?" Zoe asked, surprised, coming up behind me. "I thought you were too dark and moody to be a I-need-to-get-home-and-water-my-succulents kind of girl…"

Did I like plants? No more than the next person, I didn't think. But I found myself nodding, much to Zoe's surprise.

"Interesting," she said. "So… are you going to buy one?"

I made my way around the shop properly, feeling the leaves, the different varieties, the spiky cacti and the softer, furry bushes, the succulents with their alien-like offspring. Surely I couldn't keep a plant alive… I was Lilz Dart, known for sucking the life out of any creature. But I wanted to try. I *really* wanted to try.

"Do you need help deciding?" the woman behind the counter asked. I looked up to meet a pair of blue eyes, surrounded by kohl, and nodded, cheeks pink. The lady stood and made her way over to us, where she grabbed my chin and held it in her hand. "What's your name?"

"Lilz," I said, then corrected myself. "Lily."

A lily was a flower, I knew that, but the kind which grew outside or could be bought from a supermarket, which I also knew. There were water lilies, too, which Mum liked to joke she'd named me after when she'd seen a Monet painting and fallen in love with the things. Dizzy was Daisy because she was conceived in the park on a blanket of daisies – not that she knew that.

"Lily," the woman nodded. She was wearing a flowing black dress and it swished around her ankles as she moved around the shop. "Lily…"

Her hands went to the back of a shelf, where a small green plant was growing out of a black pot. It had a white flower, a flower that hardly even *looked* like a flower. It was spiky, like a dog toy, surrounded by a curl of white flesh.

"This is a peace lily," she said, handing it to me. "Would you like something to put it in?"

A peace lily. I liked that. It was small and neat and apparently didn't need direct sunlight, and should be watered every few days if it was looking dry, once a week if it wasn't. I ended up buying a cream bucket to stop the water from draining out of the pot's holes, and a funny mini watering can she insisted I'd need, too. We left with the lily held between my hands, careful not to drop the bucket or my new watering can, which was sage green and very, very not-Lilz.

"I love it," Zoe said with a grin, stroking the vivid leaves. "She can be your first plant baby."

First. Is it weird to say that the thought almost… excited me? I wasn't a plant person. I liked playing *Call of Duty* with my boyfriend and drinking on the beach, not watering my silly little houseplant. But it wasn't a silly little houseplant, not really. It was a peace lily. It had a flower and everything.

Zoe ended up taking me to the Trinity Kitchen for lunch. It was basically just this indoor food court with a dozen different vendors selling food from carts and trailers and counters, with tables set up everywhere to relax and enjoy the food. I'd never seen so many options before, so many cultures crammed into one space. Vibbington was probably one of the least diverse towns in the north of England, and the extent of our food choices came down to Sally's Diner, a pizza place or two, a rubbish Chinese takeaway, a chippy, and the café on Main Street which did wicked quesadillas.

But it was embarrassing, having all those options, not freeing, or fun, an adventure. I didn't know what most things even were, from buddha bowls to halloumi fries and roghan josh, though I couldn't admit that to Zoe. It was humiliating how little I knew about the world.

"You pick," I said, grinning. "Surprise me."

I grabbed a table by the window, sitting there in waiting as she returned with two carefully-wrapped parcels.

"Burrito," she said, passing one my way. "Vegan, by the way. Jackfruit and guac."

What the hell is a burrito? I remember thinking. *And... a jackfruit? Sounds grim.* But the burrito was hot, and, as I discovered, it was really just a fat wrap filled with rice and something which tasted like pork and a whole load of avocado and slaw, vegan cheese (weird) and little black beans.

But it was good. It was very, very good.

In fact, as we wolfed them down, I decided it was maybe one of the best things I'd ever eaten. That this burrito was a work of art, and that I'd never be satisfied in life unless I ate burritos day and night for the next one hundred years, even when I was old and saggy and Owen was dead and I was sat twiddling my thumbs in an old people's home.

In all honesty, that's what did it for me. The burrito, filled with flavours so foreign to my tongue, in Trinity Kitchen in the centre of this huge, bustling city. It made me decide, decide for real. I wanted more than Vibbington, more than my life there, more than the diner and my estate and how bloody British and shit everything there was. I wanted diversity, culture. People who had different opinions and lifestyles, a world full of colour and laughter and *life*.

I wanted out of East Yorkshire, whether Owen liked it or not.

THE TRAIN

We spent the rest of the afternoon shopping, rushing in and out of the Leeds arcades pretending we were old rich woman with cash to splash and a reputation good enough to step inside the upper class shops, giggling and pulling faces at the posh workers behind their backs. Zoe started laughing so badly I had to haul her out of one before the manager reported us, but we were snorting too much to care.

"I love Leeds," I decided, because I really did. It wasn't *too* far from home, and there were four or five unis there which all did different courses, not all of which had ridiculous grade requirements. Knowing that gave me hope, though I didn't tell any of that to Zoe. She had Edinburgh in her sights, and would probably scoff in my face if I admitted this was as high as my goals were set.

We got the train back late, as the clock ticked to eight and the city settled down around us. It was going to be a long journey back to Vibbington, and I was planning to sleep for most of it; we managed to get a table, and sat either side as the train pulled out of the city, leaving behind its tall buildings and spiky barbed wire fencing and construction, the outskirts with its tumbling houses and dodgy backstreets, red brick and blue-tinted sky. July was drawing to a close, and I was weirdly enjoying the light nights, the warm, muggy air of summer.

Zoe leaned back in the seat opposite me, yawning.

"This is lovely," she said, shaking her head. "All of this. I love trains, and I love the sky right now, and I love travelling through the countryside and seeing it all whirl past the window like that."

It was pretty beautiful, I have to admit. My peace lily was on the seat beside me, and I had a bag of shopping at my feet, clothes I'd bought in the second-hand shops of the city centre, all of which were overpriced. I'd blown way too much money today, but I was excited to show Loz what I'd bought later, to video call her and discuss everything in detail. Bloody Sofia better not come up in conversation; I was sure she owned all the things I'd bought, only new, and had them hung in her wardrobe on pristine matching hangers.

"So," Zoe said, smiling at me. "Tell me about Owen."

Owen. I cocked my head, thinking, trying to figure out what I could say to properly introduce my boyfriend. I didn't get asked this question a lot. Usually, people I met were people I met *through* him, or randoms we met together, either at sixth form or out in Vibbington, Gethin's girlfriends and Kara's various partners.

"He's just Owen," I said. "He's great. He's smart, though he doesn't show it and hates school, and he's dedicated – he saved up ages to buy a car and parking permit, passed his test first time. He likes video games, pizza, and he's funny, and…"

That's where I ran out of things to say. Video games and pizza. Those were my boyfriend's defining features.

"How long have you been together?"

"About five years."

"God, that's *ages*."

"Yeah." That's what everyone always said. If we'd been married or in our thirties, forties, this would have seemed pathetic. But not to Zoe, sixteen and probably still single, staring at me with wide eyes.

"You've never been close to breaking up?"

I frowned. *Way to ask a personal question, Zoe.* But the answer was no. No, we hadn't, not even a little bit. We were rock solid, we always had been. That was why I was so convinced we'd end up together, that we were made for one another. That made sense, right?

"He's my soulmate, if you believe in all that. My person."

"That must be nice." Zoe smiled at me wistfully, nodding. She was right, of course, but I rolled my eyes like she was being soppy.

"You'll find that one day."

"I don't doubt it." She looked thoughtful then, gazing into the distance. "Then... how do you know Owen's right for you? If you've never experienced anything else, how do you know that's the best a relationship can get?"

I stiffened. "You just *know*. It's like... human instinct."

"Only some people think they know, and then break up after twenty years of marriage, only to realise their soulmate was... I don't know, their postman or something, all along."

I let my eyes wander out of the window, heart thudding. The countryside was still passing in a colourful mismatch of blue and green and brown, little buildings popping up here and there, studded with sheep and cows and pigs. The train buzzed, smooth and streamlined as it shot through Yorkshire, barely quaking.

Zoe was wrong, obviously. Of *course* she was.

"That won't happen," I said. "Honestly, I know it won't. Owen and I are in it for the long run."

"If you say so." Zoe smiled, shrugging.

I really, truly meant it. But it didn't stop me from pondering Zoe's words all the way home.

Owen Sharpley, age 10 and a bit.

I have a crush on my best friend. She definitely does not like me back, but I think she's wonderful.

She makes everything feel better when it hurts. We play games and watch TV and it is like my mum does not exist and everything will be okay.

Her name is Lily, but we call her Lilz.

Sometimes I wish I was born into her family instead. Her mum is really nice and her little sister is so sweet and cute. But if because I was not, I am going to marry her instead.

I want a normal life like everybody else.

THE START

When I think about the start of mine and Owen's relationship
– really, truly *think* – it all feels lovely and happy and pure.
Because it was. We were twelve years old, sticky year eights,
and it was autumn, leaves tumbling around us as we stood in
Tesco car park in the cold. I was wearing these annoying
white mittens which kept falling off, because I used to get
terrible eczema and the cold made it worse. Owen was
wearing a black beanie Judy had found in a charity shop, and
there were holes in the rim, like it had been bitten by moths
or something (did moths even bite?).

Owen was my best friend. We'd known each other as far
back as my memories went; everything started with him.
Tottering over to knock on his front door after Mum told me
a little boy my age had moved in there, that he was my age
and going to be in my class at school. Asking him to come
and play with me in the park, and wandering hand in hand,
Mum in front, because he was too scared to walk by the busy
road.

We played together on and off throughout our childhood,
just the two of us, sat together in lessons and at lunch. Owen
struggled with reading and writing – we later found out that *I*
was dyslexic, not him, which took us both by surprise – and
we were usually placed in the bottom group for everything,
even when we were six, seven. I witnessed his first "girlfriend"
in the primary school playground in year four, cried to Mum
for days after because I thought I was losing him. I was only

eight or nine, but I knew that Owen wasn't just a *friend*.

Things changed in year five, when Owen transferred to a smaller primary school because his grades were really bad, and they thought he'd focus better at a village school where the teachers could give him more attention. I cried then, too. But we were still best friends, hanging around the estate each night and watching movies in my living room all day at the weekend, taking it in turns to play with the Wii and its one controller I'd been given for Christmas.

Then I met Loz, of course, the platonic love of my life.

And Owen met Gethin.

We became a pretty tight foursome when we moved to secondary school. Loz was more intelligent than the rest of us, and much more popular, but she kept our group floating the right circles – when we would've otherwise floundered. The cool guys always wanted Owen to hang out with them, but he had no interest in kicking a football round the school field or getting drunk in the park... not then, anyway. As kids, we were pretty happy just to have each other.

I remember realising properly that I liked Owen, and finding the words and terms to vocalise that. I admitted to Loz that I had a crush on him shortly after Chloe Alize asked him out and I almost died of jealousy, and she clapped her hands and squealed so loud I swear she almost popped my little eardrums.

"Lilz!" she said, rushing to give me a hug. "Lilz, that's amazing! You like him? Are you going to ask him out?"

That was all the rage back then. Year eights and nines, back when life was simple, would become "boyfriend and girlfriend", a playground status more than anything; most would never meet up outside of school, or even kiss, the extent of the relationship being an awkward shoulder pat or stilted hug. Loz had a boyfriend like that, an older guy called Steven, who only lasted a short while before he decided she was too young for him, even though he was only in year nine and had the emotional maturity of a five-year-old.

I didn't dare ask Owen out, though. The stakes were too high. What if he said no? What if it ruined our friendship, a friendship as long as life itself, and our group fell apart? I couldn't risk that. Little Lilz didn't have the intelligence to even comprehend the fact that if we did get together and it didn't work, we'd ruin the group anyway. Owen saying no shouldn't have been the scariest outcome.

But Loz had it covered, of course. She asked Owen how he felt, confessed that I had a crush on him. He said he liked me back, of course… which is how we got to be stood in Tesco car park, aged twelve, Owen awkwardly rubbing his ear and staring at me with ruddy cheeks as he asked, "Erm… Lilz. Do you wanna be my girlfriend?"

What followed was a small peck on the lips, two incredibly happy kids beaming at each other as I nodded, like I'd been waiting to do for so long. Loz and Gethin came bursting out from behind the wall, so ridiculously pleased for us both, and we disappeared into Tesco to get supplies for a celebration picnic in the park, even though it was freezing and I had to eat the cocktail sausages and scotch eggs with those bloody mittens on.

So that was it. Our beginning. The day we went from being Lilz and Owen, best friends and neighbours, to *Lilz and Owen*, something more, something special. What followed was inevitable, the kind of relationship normal twelve-year-olds *should* have, innocent and pure and sweet. Gentle kisses on the lips, handholding in the playground, a hug as he said goodnight each night and left me standing outside my front door. This quickly developed into snuggling on the sofa while Judy Sharpley was out at bingo or down the pub, Owen's hands sneaking up my school skirt (long before I refused to wear one and went into town to buy myself some trousers). By the time we were fourteen, I was confident that I loved him, that he was it for me.

Most couples break up young because they grow apart, change, become different people. That's normal. But Owen and I had done all our growing, changing. We'd become the same person, growing *together* instead of apart.

So when Zoe asked whether we'd ever been close to breaking up, the truth was that we really, really hadn't. I was Lilz, and I loved Owen. It was just so simple to me.

We didn't have the typical timeline for teenage couples, taking things slower than most, simply because we were so young. We didn't sleep together for two years, meaning both of us lost our virginities at fourteen, which is still ridiculously premature compared to the average teen. And it was good. It was in Owen's room, and I felt safe and secure and happy in the princess pants I'd had for the last four years and the faded bra I'd never grown into and is *still* too big.

Owen was careful and soft, teasing off my underwear, terrified of hurting me. We kissed and kissed for hours until we couldn't hold it off any longer, and then it was happening, and all I was aware of was how much I loved this boy and wanted him forever.

After, we kissed some more, and he told me he loved me. I said it back, and we did it again. This wasn't really a regular occurrence for the next year or so, but we'd gotten it over with, and that felt... good. It all felt good. Owen and I were tied together now, one flesh. I remembered all that religious stuff from primary school, but it really resonated with me in that moment. I truly believed we'd morphed together, become one.

I have a box under my bed of all my childhood memories, but most of them are just Owen. Photos of the two of us kissing and laughing and dancing in the rain, printed using the machine in Boots; tickets from the cinema, the train to Hull, receipts from meals at the café or the diner, long before I started working there; notes he'd write me in class, getting increasingly dirty as we got older. I have little drawings on post-it notes and logos cut from pizza boxes, and Owen's handprint in red poster paint from when we were both five.

Maybe finding their boyfriend kissing another girl and squeezing her boob would've been enough for most girls to break up with them. I mean, you could even argue that most girls wouldn't let their boyfriend get away with *murder*, no matter how badly said boyfriend's mother had treated them.

But then most girls don't have a box of memories with their boyfriend going back to the age of five. Because that's not normal. Only the really, really lucky girls get that.

I remember looking through the box as July slipped into August and it began to rain again, the kind of warm, heavy rain which cloaks everything in mist and causes steam to rise from the earth like a volcano. I sifted through photos of the face I loved so much, my boyfriend, the notes and evidence of all the love we shared.

And I started to cry.

I don't know why. Did it even make any sense? Things were fine. We were still together, right? I'd have to get a new memory box since this one was getting so full, one we could store the rest of our lives in. Wedding invitations, menus from the restaurant we'd visit on our honeymoon, photos of our kids, grandkids, maybe even great grandkids.

When you love someone, imagining any future without them is hazy, confusing. That's why people in relationships seem so blind to reality. It's impossible to envision an alternative, not when all that you want is that person, your person, and the life they've promised you.

Now, in September, I'm getting into the back of a police car. We're travelling to the station so that I can answer questions, and I'm scared. I'm not scared for myself, or for whatever is going to happen once I arrive… I'm scared for us, for Owen and I. I've made my choice; I'm grassing him up. But… what now? What about the future he promised, the life we've wanted for as long as I can remember.

"I love you," he told me, the night we first slept together, age fourteen. "You're all that I want, Lilz, always. You're it for me, okay?"

I nodded, tears in my eyes, in Owen's warm bed in his crummy room in Judy Sharpley's flat. It was hot, but we were both naked between the sheets, and a fan was blowing my hair in front of my face.

"Two kids," he continued, "with cool names, nothing basic, no more Lily or Owen. Astrid, or… Dominik, Dominik with a K."

I smiled at that, moving his fringe with my hand. "Okay. Astrid and Dominik. And where will we all live, our little family?"

"In a proper house, obviously. Three bedrooms, all the floors are ours, it doesn't and has never, ever belonged to the council. We have a garden, a big one with a pond and flowers and loads of trees, and a dog called Stuart…"

"Stuart?"

"Stuart the dog! And we take him for walks on the beach, and go on all-inclusive family holidays to Spain every year…

leaving Stuart with Dizzy, obviously because I'm pretty sure Dizzy would love to dog-sit."

"Owen?"

"Lilz?"

His bare chest was close to mine, face just inches away from me, nose close enough to nudge with mine.

"I think I'd die if we ever broke up."

The silence around us was heavy with love and anticipation, the whole of the world suddenly weighing on our relationship. Owen just rolled his eyes as he leant in to kiss me, lips on mine softer and warmer than any other kiss, hearts beating in sync.

His voice was raw with emotion as he pulled back and looked at me, properly looked at me.

"Then that must mean you're going to live forever."

how was it???

has zoe forlani replaced
me as your bff???

loz!!!

don't be sillyyy

you need to tell me all
about it pls

it was just nice

i really like her :)

THE EYELASH

I got back from Leeds to find Owen still curled up in bed, where I left him that morning. He hadn't moved a muscle, but the room smelled faintly of perfume and sweat, and I frowned as I nestled under the covers beside him.

"Has Mum been in here?" I asked, pinching his nose. "It stinks of bloody Chanel."

Owen sniffed delicately as I let go, then reached up to hug me. "Mmm, yeah, she came in here earlier to say goodbye. Her and Dizzy have been out all day, at that new garden centre."

"What a life, eh?"

Owen chuckled, then pulled me into a proper bear hug, holding me tight against him. "Good trip? You've been gone hours…"

I nodded, smiling into his armpit. "The best."

Zoe messaged me as I was walking home, saying how much fun she'd had and how she was always down to do something similar in the future. I texted her back immediately to agree, saying I'd see her soon. The diner was always hot and unforgiving at this time of year, but it didn't matter, not if I could see Zoe there. It gave me something to look forward to, an outlet now that Loz was gone.

Because without Loz, our friendship group was falling apart. We'd meet up in the park occasionally for chips and a smoke, but I was an apparent spoilsport and ruined the atmosphere, and I didn't like Kara just as much as she didn't like me. As the holidays rolled on, Owen would head out to meet Gethin and the others to drink and do weed and spray-paint the walls of the old warehouse in town, leaving me at home watching *How I Met Your Mother* with Dizzy. I know Kara would sometimes go too, because I'd see the glow of a dozen cigarette stubs on her Instagram story, a streak of pink as Gethin swiped callous words across crumbling brick.

"They're still shagging," Owen told me one day in August, rubbing my belly with his hand. "Get ready for major awkwardness when we go back to sixth form…"

But I wasn't bothered about Kara and Gethin. If anything, it was nice just knowing that Owen wasn't going to be drunkenly kissing Kara anytime soon, that she was taken and off the scene. She'd been after my boyfriend for long enough now, and I needed to know she wasn't going to take advantage of him again.

We still weren't talking about the kiss, not since Owen last shut it down. I was fine with that. As long as I could push it from my mind, I was happy.

I told Loz about Kara and Gethin when I rang her that week, after she insisted I tell her all about Zoe and Leeds and the infamous burrito. She's seen the photo dump I'd posted on Instagram, the first pictures the internet had seen from me which weren't blurry or dark or deliberately taken in a pitch-black room with the flash on. I kind of liked that she seemed jealous of Zoe, anyway; now she knew how it felt.

"Kara and Gethin?" she repeated for the six hundredth time after I told her, voice incredulous. "No, they wouldn't. Lilz, both of them are one-shag only types. There's no way they're *together*."

"I wouldn't put it that strongly," I said, snorting. "I think it's more of a friends-with-benefits situation."

"Lilz," she said, in *that tone*. "Me and Gethin were friends with benefits, kissing a bit every time we got drunk enough. Sleeping with the same guy week in, week out... that's commitment, especially for those two."

"Do you talk to Kara much?"

"Not a lot. She's not really the facetiming type."

"That's a shame."

"Is it?" Loz knew I didn't like her, and could hear the sarcasm in my voice. "Lilz, I bloody love you, but you don't have to pretend to like the girl."

"I know, I know! But I'll have to get in her good books again by the time sixth form comes round..."

"Will you? You have Zoe now. Tell me about her!"

I paused, trying to think of an accurate way to describe Zoe. She was just... Zoe. Carer of all social issues, drop-dead gorgeous, smart, authoritative, all of which I meant in a weirdly good way.

Instead, I said, "Follow her on Instagram!"

"Hang on, I'm putting you on speaker."

I listened as Loz tapped away from the phonecall and searched for Zoe's account, bringing it up with an appreciative gasp. It was mainly selfies, perfect, unfiltered selfies, and full-colour shots, grain-effect applied, Zoe waving a pride flag, Zoe running across the beach, Zoe beaming at the camera with a can of cider in one hand and a vape in the other. She actually didn't vape, she'd told me the previous week, and had only been holding her friend's while she took the photo for her. She valued her health too much.

"She's hot," Loz said, which was basically Loz-approval. "And she's... a lesbian?"

"So what?" I said that way too quickly.

"So nothing." I could hear the smile in Loz's voice, and I

knew what she was thinking.

But it wasn't like that, not with Zoe. We really were just friends.

"And guess who her sister is?" I continued, changing the subject. "Mira Forlani!"

"No *way*."

When Mira Forlani dated Oli, Ethan's best friend, the four of them had gone on a few disastrous double dates before Oli decided Mira was too highfalutin and broke up with her over the Christmas break. Being with the head girl clearly wasn't for everybody.

"Is she anything like her?" Loz continued. "Pompous, pretentious, likes the sound of her own voice…"

"I mean, she'll definitely be head girl when our year goes." I could hear Loz scoffing as I said, "Zoe's… different, though. She's loud, but for the sake of others, not herself. She has nice friends – I met them when they came into the diner last week – and she's smart, polite, you know, just an ordinary year twelve. I think I'll get on well with her next year."

I wasn't exactly going to be sat on her table in the common room, but still. It would be nice having Zoe around.

"You never take photos like this with me," Loz said after a pause, and I could tell she was looking at Zoe's latest Instagram post. "Whenever I try to take a selfie, you tell me to piss off."

It was a Leeds photo dump, like my own, but my post had completely avoided any sign that Zoe had been with me that day. It was architecture and shots of the market, that delicious burrito, my hand holding the peace lily now sat on top of my bookcase, beaming at me. Zoe's was different. A pic of her I'd taken in the food court, photos of flowers and colourful fruit, the river, skyline reflected on the water, and a pristine selfie, high-quality, the two of us smiling till our jaws ached.

"I couldn't really say no."

"Mmm." Loz was still scrolling. I could hear her long nails dragging across the phone screen. "You look happy, Lilz. Really, really happy. I haven't seen you look like that in a long while."

Silence.

"What do you mean?"

"I just mean…" A sigh, hesitation. "I think it's good for you to have a friend like that, one who pushes you out of your comfort zone. Someone new, you know? If you're going to stay in Vibbington forever, you need to meet different –"

"I'm going to uni."

That shut her up.

"You're going to uni?"

"If I can." I let that sink in, before adding. "I've been looking at courses, and I think – if I properly focus next year, anyway – that I can scrape some Bs, maybe a C in psych, and do a course at one of the smaller unis. I'm thinking Leeds."

"Leeds." Even just through that one word, I could hear Loz smiling. "Leeds, eh? Lilz, that's brilliant. I totally think you should go for it."

"You think?"

"I think."

We were both smiling now, I could tell. Smiling like my mouth was about to split open at my seams, heart thudding in my chest.

"And Lilz?" Loz added. "I think you should get more houseplants, okay? Because your room is really depressing."

I was grinning down the phone as I glanced over at the peace lily, sitting in all its green glory on the shelf, smiling at me. It probably did deserve a friend.

"I miss you."

Loz just laughed. "God, one houseplant and you're already turning soppy on me!" She paused. "I miss you, too."

**

Loz and I stayed on the phone for a little while later, chatting about everything and nothing until Loz had to go meet Sofia and some of her new friends for Starbucks, but she promised she'd ring me later in the week to talk about that boy she'd recently seen again, the one she slept with when she first moved to Notts.

"Give me all the juicy details, 'kay?"

Loz giggled as she hung up.

I sat there for a moment then, staring around the room. I went back to work tomorrow, and I still needed to iron my shirt and find my trousers… and I wanted to make tea for when Owen came in, and take the sheets off my bed and give them a quick sprint in the washing machine.

I started pulling off the duvet, taking off the covers and throwing them onto the floor, when something small and fluttery fell out. I frowned, immediately assuming it to be a dead spider (I wasn't scared of them, but Owen was) or a leaf, maybe even a feather that had flown in from the open window…

But it was a false eyelash.

A full eye of them, not just one, but I don't know what you'd call that. A row of pointy, evil-looking things, attached to a strip of black… stuff. It was coated in mascara and the underside still had the shiny remnants of glue stuck tight. I held it in my hand, turning it over and over, wondering how it had gotten there, in my bed.

I'd never worn false eyelashes. I was a simple eyeliner and mascara gal, barely bothered with foundation or concealer if I could help it. This particular eye of lashes wasn't thick or luscious, more natural looking, but as I held it up to my eye, it didn't look... familiar. I mean, it did a bit, but not belonging to anyone I could *place*.

Mum didn't wear false lashes, either, and Dizzy was twelve, for God's sake. Progressive for a twelve-year-old, certainly, but not really into tacky makeup or dressing up. She had a tiny head, anyway, and little blue eyes with pale lashes, like me. This flappy thing would drown her.

But if it wasn't mine, or Mum's, or Dizzy's... Loz had been gone for weeks, and I'd changed my sheets since then.

I placed it on my bookcase, next to the peace lily. It just looked at me, blinking, like it had a life of its own.

I didn't like it.

I didn't know who it belonged to, but I didn't like it at all.

gethin @everyone
what up lads
party at mine?

owen @gethinthegreat
sounds good lad
i'll bring some lagers, are we doing pizzas
again or what?

gethin @owensharps.ii
me and kara have pizzas covered
everyone else: it's bring your own booze or
you're not coming in

eva | head girl @gethinthegreat
this sounds lovely, gethin, thank you!
rsvp-ing for renee, juliette and i - we'll bring
prosecco, happy to bake brownies too!

owen @evastewartlol
we're good thanks
okay so
we saying nine?

THE PARTY

"Party at Gethin's?"

"When?"

"Tonight."

I blinked at Owen. "Tonight? Short notice, much?"

"I was going to tell you earlier, but it completely slipped my mind. It's not like you have anything better to do, right?" Owen grinned at me. He was sat on my bed, legs crossed in front of him, so I shrugged, unsure of what to say.

"I guess."

"Just wear whatever," he continued. "It's only Gethin's. His parents are proper lax, aren't they? They'll probably just be in the pub as usual, chilling."

Gethin's parents were only lax because they didn't care much about Gethin, but that's a different story.

"What happened to Kara's party, a few weeks ago?"

Owen frowned, clearly having no idea what I was on about.

"Kara," I repeated, rolling my eyes. "Her parents were supposed to be out of town, so she was going to have a party. She was debating doing it or not because Loz said she wouldn't be able to make it, but…"

"I don't know. I… didn't realise her parents went away."

"I just didn't think she'd pass up an opportunity to have an empty house, that's all." I was looking at Owen properly, trying to read his expression, because he looked… shifty. And I didn't like it when my boyfriend looked shifty. It usually meant he was hiding something. "If I wasn't invited, I don't care, if that's what –"

"Lilz, there was no party."

"Okay –"

"Just pick an outfit for tonight, yeah?"

"You said to just wear whatever?"

"Yes, but *whatever* to you usually means a baggy t-shirt and joggers, so…"

I winced, stung, but Owen didn't seem to have noticed. He just carried on scrolling through his phone, eyes narrowed, staring at some random Formula 1 drivers with a look of concentration on his face.

He didn't care.

He really didn't care.

I looked at the false eyelash on my shelf, trying to connect the dots. It couldn't possibly have anything to do with Owen, I knew that. It had probably flown in through the window, carried by the wind… or not. My stomach dropped as I thought back to Judy Sharpley's body, trying to remember whether she'd been wearing false lashes, or ever did, even around the house. Because that was the only thing that made sense to me. That Owen had somehow brought in a Judy-related eyelash from the flat across the road, that that was how it had ended up tangled up in the sheets of my bed.

Very stupid, I know.

***

I ended up wearing one of the only dresses I actually owned. A strappy navy blue thing covered in little silver stars, pretty and flowy and modest, with my shoulders covered and not too much of my chest exposed. I smiled at myself in the mirror. Owen had disappeared across the road to change into a fresh white t-shirt and jeans, and I was here, staring at my reflection, as Dizzy rushed back to her room to grab a doughnut for my hair and a box of hair grips.

"I'm back!" she screeched, running in with the box rattling and the doughnut looped over her forefinger. "You're going to look *gorgeous*."

"I better."

My eyes were surrounded by their trademark black eyeliner panda-rings, lashes saturated in mascara. Dizzy rolled her eyes as she did my hair, looking at my reflection as she went.

"Do you not think you should take off some of the eyeliner?" she asked, wrinkling her nose. "It's a party, not a goth convention."

"It makes my eyes pop," I said, as Dizzy put the finishing touches to my hair. I spun round to give her a hug, to which she tried to wriggle away, squealing. "Thank you, little sister."

"Goth! Goth! There's a goth attacking me!"

I let her go.

Owen was waiting outside my building, on his phone again. He looked good, neat and tidy in his white shirt and black skinny jeans, though he didn't look up as I crossed over to him. His hair almost looked like he'd put effort into it, and it took me a few taps on his wrist for him to spin round and give me a kiss, smiling as he noted the dress, the bun, the way I looked so unlike Lilz and yet still so... me.

"You look like a Lily," he said, to which I slapped him. It was an ongoing joke in our friendship group that the minute I veered away from being tough and angry and donning all black, I became a *Lily* rather than a Lilz. But now didn't feel like the time to joke. It was Owen who'd told me to dress like this, insinuating that my usual party attire wouldn't cut it. I felt like a prize turkey, dressed and stuffed for my debut on the Christmas dinner table. But Owen seemed to like it, and I couldn't help but smile into him as he kissed me harder.

I still needed to ask him something, though.

"Owen…" I started, as we made our way out of the estate and over to Gethin's. It wasn't a long way, but long enough that I could ask Owen what I wanted before we arrived. "I need to talk to you about something, and I want you to be completely honest with me."

Owen frowned, turning to look at me. There was fear in his eyes, and that was when I knew. When I realised that everything I suspected was true.

"What?" he asked. "Is everything okay?"

"Everything's fine." I paused, took a deep breath. And then I said, "Have you been visiting your mum's body?"

Owen's face was blank. Completely blank. Like he couldn't for the life of him figure out where that was coming from, or why I'd said it.

Shit. Was I wrong? I couldn't be. Owen looked so off, so… untrustworthy. And this was the only answer.

"What?" he echoed. "Why would you think that?"

"Because… you keep disappearing on a night, and I don't know where you go. You clearly go somewhere I don't know about, and it can't just be with Gethin. And then you shower before getting into bed, washing… *something* off. And I found an eyelash. Well, a row of eyelashes, false ones. In my bed. And…"

A look of panic had crossed Owen's face and settled there as I was talking. Maybe I was right after all. I didn't say anything else as I looked at him, willing him to speak, to give something away.

"You're right. You're right. I have been visiting the body."

There. He said it.

"I didn't want to tell you because I know it's weird and icky, but… I miss her, and I still think about what happened that night, and…"

"That night?" I interrupted him, blood running cold. "Owen, your mum died in the morning. When she was having a bath, and asked you to come in. The morning on June third. I was at Loz's, remember?"

"I meant… the night we dumped the body."

I watched the Adam's apple moving up and down in his throat, and suddenly I didn't know what to think.

"I find it therapeutic, and reassuring," he continued. "Because she's there all alone, Lilz, in the woods. And that… that isn't okay."

"I know, Owen." I pulled him closer as his voice broke, but there were no tears, not a single drop. Maybe he was all cried out, my darling boyfriend. Maybe there wasn't a shred of moisture left in his body. "I know."

We arrived at the party ten minutes later, dawdling as Owen composed himself and I tried to process everything that was in my head. It was already in full swing. Gethin's grim little terrace house was pumping music – the neighbours weren't going to be too pleased – and there were kids already throwing up outside in a bush. Eva, our spotless head girl, was being sick so violently that Renee and Juliette had to hold her back with wide, shocked eyes and pinched noses. Who knew goody-two-shoes Eva Stewart could have such fun?

"Owen!" Gethin announced from the door, where he was stood with his arm round Kara's shoulders in a very we're-mates-but-not-a-couple kind of way. I squinted at them, but there genuinely didn't seem to be a romantic connection there, even though they were very, very drunk. Gethin was hugging Owen, and Kara was hugging me, but it felt superficial and weird and I didn't like it at all.

"Nice dress," Kara said, in a voice which screamed the opposite. "Where's it from?"

Kara herself was wearing the shortest, tightest piece of fabric imaginable, face full of makeup and so much fake tan she looked like she'd been fried. It was patchy and mottled, especially on her legs, with patches so dark on her arms they were almost burnt sienna.

"Erm... I can't remember. You look nice, too," I said, to which she gave me the most horrific glare.

The bulk of our year was in the kitchen, where all the alcohol was piled onto the counter. There were a few year thirteens kicking about before they moved off to uni, but most of the kids were ones we knew, Ethan and Oli and Kev stood by the sink, eating Chinese food from cartons, as Lucy, Nora and Alicia chatted to the local nerds, Boner-boy and Tommy, Samantha and Liz.

Boner-boy was called that because of a little problem he'd had on stage in the school's production of Grease, playing one of Danny's cronies opposite Summer Clay, who was drop-dead gorgeous. I felt a bit sorry for him, to be honest. It had become such a big part of his identity that he'd recently made his Instagram username @thatonebonerboy, trying to get in on the joke.

"What you staring at them for?" came a voice to my ear, and I turned to find Owen, holding out a beer to me. I didn't mind beer, but much preferred coke, which he knew. Clearly we were both meant to be getting drunk tonight.

"Nothing," I said, grinning. "I only have eyes for you..."

I was about to lean up and kiss him when a hand slapped

my arse, and I turned, outraged, to find Gethin grinning at me with a mouthful of sour breath and a horrid look in those green eyes of his.

"What the hell?"

"What?" Gethin played innocent, holding his hands up in surrender. "It's not every day you wear something like that, Lilz."

I glanced at Owen for backup, but Gethin got there first.

"What? Owen agrees with me!"

I waited for my boyfriend to deny it, but he was smirking. *Smirking*.

"Owen!" I said, gripping his arm with my nails, but his attention was elsewhere, eyes wandering. I turned to see Kara, who'd just entered the room, in that ridiculously tight dress with her boobs spilling out of the top and hair extensions covering her shoulders, long, fake-tanned legs attached to spiky blue heels. I felt like a child in comparison, all dressed up in my blue, star-covered dress and bun, staring at Owen and willing him to look at me, *me*, his girlfriend.

But his eyes were suctioned to Kara, and I recognised that look on his face, in his eyes. It was one of desperation, hunger, and of pride, pride in Kara, for whatever reason.

And that was when I knew.

He hadn't been visiting his mum's body for all these weeks, taking trips into the woods to stand by her and weep. The false eyelash in my bed wasn't Judy Sharpley's – why did I ever think it could have been? That night in the garage, when I caught him kissing Kara, wasn't a one off.

He'd been shagging her all along.

is lilz coming tonight?

yeh

why

just kinda hoping we don't have to pretend

it'll be fine

she's lilz

she won't catch on

don't worry x

THE REALISATION

There are certain moments in your life when everything becomes crystal clear, and suddenly you wonder why you ever believed anything in the first place.

Everyone lies. No one can be trusted.

And even your boyfriend of five years, virtual best friend and soulmate, can betray you in the worst way possible.

I stared at Owen as he wandered over to talk to Kara, smiling at her and letting her hands brush his chest as she reached for a can of beer. I watched them talking, laughing, trying to connect the dots in my head. Trying to figure out the truth, the whole truth, and make sense of this all, inside me.

I didn't like or trust Kara, but how could she do this? How could she do this to Loz? And Owen…

It had all been a lie. Kara and Gethin weren't dating; I thought that was too strange to be true. And all those nights when Owen would disappear off to see Gethin, or to visit his mum's "body", he was no doubt seeing *her*. That day when I went to Leeds with Zoe, and Mum and Dizzy left Owen in charge of the house… I swallowed back the lump in my throat, picturing the rumpled sheets of *my* bed, the smell of Chanel perfume around *my* room, the glitzy false eyelash falling out of *my* duvet.

Fuck him.

FUCK HIM.

I was holding a can of cider, which I squeezed so tight that liquid spurted out of the top. Gethin stared at me, frowning. He reached out to grab the can and said, "Lilz? You good?"

His voice sounded like it was coming from a million miles away.

Through the kitchen I floated, desperate to get away from Kara and my boyfriend. Through the hallway, the living room, into the little back garden surrounded by rotting fence panels and a blow-up paddling pool turned green with algae and disuse. Gethin's ancient dog, Devil, was resting in the corner, watching the party. The party. The fun-filled, friendly party of our teenage dreams, the party where memories were made and everything – *everything* – changed.

I sat on one of the patio chairs, feet off the floor, dress sagging around me. It was chillier out than in, but I didn't feel the cold. Some boys were blowing up balloons in front of me, laughing at the fart noises they made. The moon blinked in the sky above.

And I couldn't stop wondering why.

Why? Why had Owen cheated on me? Was I not enough for him? Did I not fulfil him enough? Was everything I'd been taught not to worry about actually... true?

My scrawny frame, skinny body, flat chest. My zero sense of style, thin blonde hair, pale skin. My old clothes, lots of baggy jeans and hoodies and t-shirts, and sport socks under my trainers. The ancient underwear I'd owned since I was a kid, saggy grey knickers and faded bras.

All the things I thought Owen loved me for, accepted.

All the things Kara Faulkner was not.

I tried not to picture the specifics of the cheating, but I couldn't help it. I'd seen it once before, in the garage, though this was ten times sharper. Kara's naked body, on the bed, Owen's arched and covered in glistening balls of sweat. The freckle by his nipple, the wiry hairs beneath his armpit, the crescent-shaped mole on his shoulder… all the little details only *I* should know. The things I'd found out about Owen, the things I'd noticed, things I thought I'd hold onto forever.

I was going to be sick.

I'm not religious, but I understood, in that moment, the value of waiting until marriage, the way it creates a whole new bond between a couple, elevates them as one. Because thinking about Owen sleeping with another girl – and *Kara*, of all people – felt like the ultimate betrayal. How could I touch him again, knowing I was no longer the only one? How could I feel special to him when I knew he'd looked at someone else, our friend, with the same level of desire, and not been completely turned off by the fact she wasn't me?

It was too much. It was *all* too much for me. I was shaking, and had the most horrific goosebumps, and the boys were still making fart noises and snorting as the balloons went whizzing into the air with a crack. I watched a blue balloon, the perfect shape and size, deflate in one of the boy's hands in a matter of seconds, go from being perfectly formed to a sagging lump of plastic.

And then there was Judy Sharpley, of course.

How could Owen do that to me, knowing I held his greatest secret in his hands? That I'd seen him standing over his mother's body and watched him mop the bloodstains from their council flat's grimy floor, licked the splatters clean off his face. That I'd helped him carry the body, wrapped in my clothes and those big black bin bags, to the Forest of Death on the outskirts of Vibbington, and held him tight as he sobbed.

How could he do that, knowing I had the power to ruin him?

Then it all came flooding back to me.

Owen, looking me dead in the eye as he laid down his threats all those weeks ago... *I could take you down in a minute, you know. Frame you for the murder. And your mum, even Dizzy. There's no evidence in my car, and you have a key for my flat; you could've killed Mum in the bath, gotten your mum and Dizzy to help cover it up. Or blackmailed me into doing so.* Owen, saying all this with the coolest, most calm expression, morphing into someone I no longer knew and loved.

In hindsight, I should've realised that the police are too clever to have believed any of that. But sat in Gethin's garden, tossing this over in my mind, I couldn't help but freak out. What if Owen really did have the power to take down Mum, and Dizzy, and even Loz? What if he really could frame me for Judy Sharpley's murder? After all, there was no evidence of the bodily fluids in his car, and we'd cleaned the garage thoroughly, right? As for the flat... I had a key. Everyone knew I had a key, that I was round there just as much as Owen.

These thoughts were stupid, of course. I clearly hadn't been watching enough crime shows. That doesn't help the fact that Lilz, at the start of August, really, truly believed she was trapped. She'd just found out her boyfriend was cheating on her, but she couldn't do anything about it for fear of ruining her life, and her family's.

She couldn't tell anyone, either. Because as she sat there, on that garden chair, watching the boys make their way inside, Lilz Dart realised something. Something Lily Dart – me – now knows isn't true, was never true.

Could she really trust anyone? Could she really trust Loz, enough to tell her that she'd covered up a murder and carried a sawn-in-half dead body to the middle of the woods? Or Zoe, as nice as she may be, enough to confess to the scrubbing of bloodstains, the bleaching of the bath, and trust that she wouldn't go straight to the police? Could she trust her mum, even, or Dizzy? But Dizzy was pure and innocent, just a twelve-year-old girl. She couldn't cope with such a burden. It wouldn't be fair.

An hour previous, Lilz Dart thought she could trust Owen. But she couldn't trust Owen. He'd completely betrayed her trust by sleeping with Kara behind her back, in her own bloody *bed*. And if she couldn't trust Owen, who could she trust? He was her *person*. Except he wasn't. Not anymore.

And with that, Lilz Dart started to cry.

THE TEARS

Zoe Forlani found me sat outside a half hour later, tear-stained and choked up and bawling into my hands. The lap of my starry dress was soaked with tears and I was shivering so badly I thought my arms might fall off.

"Lilz!" she exclaimed, rushing forwards to hug me. "What's wrong?"

She was with her three friends, of course. Kezia was funny and loud and obnoxious, whereas Maz was quieter, more sensible, with big brown eyes and a welcoming smile. Nadia was the most like Zoe, pretty and tall and perfectly proportioned, yet still ridiculously smart and kind and brilliant. They were the kind of girls I would have hated in school, yet here they were now, smiling at me and offering to go fetch some water; did I want to wear their jacket?

Which is how I ended up wearing Maz's woolly cardigan on a summer's night in Gethin's back garden, Zoe's arm round my shoulders, Nadia holding out a glass of cold water and Kezia holding a rather grim-looking tissue she'd pulled from somewhere. I was grateful, though. I took both and proceeded to take long sips as I wiped at my face. My eyeliner was no doubt smudged beyond repair.

"Where's Owen?" Zoe asked, rubbing my shoulder with her hands. "Shall I go and find him?"

"Please don't," I snuffled, to which she shrugged and nodded. "I just... I'm tired, and overwhelmed. I don't know why I'm crying."

Which was the biggest understatement of the year.

Owen was inside somewhere. And as sad as it sounds, I was even *more* sad that we'd come to this party together and he hadn't even noticed I was sat *outside*, in the cold, completely by myself, sobbing into this stupid dress. He was probably too busy having fun with Kara and Gethin to even notice I was missing.

"We all get like that sometimes," Maz said, smiling. I felt bad then, because her arms were goosebumped and her lips were turning blue, but it was August, so I figured she'd survive. "When I'm on my period, I sob for the entire week. Like, everything sets me off. Mum forgot to buy cow's milk for my cornflakes? Sobbing. Character dies in my favourite show? Sobbing. I decide to rewatch *Stranger Things* for the fiftieth time that year? Sobbing."

"What's your favourite show, Lilz?" Nadia queried, trying to distract me. "We're all big *Stranger Things* gals. We even had a party for Kezia's sixteenth which was Eleven themed…"

"*How I Met Your Mother.*" Even the thought of it was comforting, and I was suddenly ridiculously glad that these girls were here, asking me questions and caring and bringing me water and not digging too much into why I was crying, why I was so obviously devastated.

"Oh my gosh, same!" Zoe exclaimed, eyes lighting up. "I connect so much to Robin, honestly. I mean, apart from the fact I'm a lesbian…"

Kezia rolled her eyes then, but it was in a jokey way, like she would've laughed no matter what Zoe said, they were that kind of close, a Loz-and-Lilz kind of close.

My tears soon dried up as I sat there on the patio with Zoe and her friends, chatting about nothing, mainly just listening until I was asked a question or someone wanted to know something about me, about sixth form, how to prepare for their impending GCSE results, etc... and it helped, in a weird way, to be distracted from what was going on inside, from thinking about where Owen was and what he was doing.

It helped, but it didn't make me feel any better.

All my internal organs still flipped just thinking about Owen and Kara, together, doing that, behind my back.

Thinking about Owen looking at her, naked, comparing her to me, thinking about her in that way, maybe even thinking about Kara *while* he was with me.

Thinking about Kara touching my boyfriend, tainting him with those inky fake-tanned fingers of hers, her Chanel-scented body, the smell he had to shower to remove when he returned home each night after seeing her, wherever they met up.

Thinking about the fact he clearly didn't love me, not like I loved him. Because if he did, he wouldn't have *done* that. If he did, I would have been enough for him. Because as Owen Sharpley's girlfriend, I didn't have the ability to look at any other guy in that way. As his girlfriend, I wanted him and only him. The thought of him even *kissing* somebody else made me feel squeamish, sick to my stomach.

Zoe and her friends had no idea what emotional turmoil I was going through inside, but I appreciated them being there, trying to help me, even though they didn't know why. I appreciated the way Zoe kept squeezing me in reassurance and saying things about boys being jerks, because she knew, she could tell. She knew the problem was something to do with Owen, which brought me back to the conversation we'd had on the train coming home from Leeds, and all the conversations before that about long-term relationships and my boyfriend and being young, too young to know.

Which got me thinking.

Was I really so naïve that everyone around me saw that me and Owen weren't destined to last, and I'd just been too blind to see it?

Did everybody else see him as disloyal and imperfect, a typical boy?

I thought I knew Owen better than anybody… but was it the other way round?

***

Zoe offered me a ride home, but I told her I'd be okay. I needed to go inside and find Owen, talk to him about all of this. There was no other choice, not when I would never get to the bottom of the matter otherwise.

"Are you sure?" she asked, worried I'd try and walk it in the dark. "Maz only lives down the road, so we'll have an empty seat in the car. Mira's taking us on a late night trip to KFC because she's bored and stressed about her A-level results, so it'll be heaps of fun…"

I did, in fact, need food – and KFC sounded really, really good right about now – but I shook my head, because I didn't need to go and sit in a car full of giggling girls while Owen went back to Kara's, not knowing where I'd gone. I needed to do this, as hard as that would be. I needed to talk to him.

"I'll see you at work, yeah?" Zoe asked, leaning in to hug me. I nodded. I only had a few more days left until I took time off to go on our family holiday to Dorset, which Owen was supposed to be attending too. That's when it really hit me how up in the air everything was now, how fast everything had changed. My boyfriend – my Owen – had cheated on me. We might be over. He might not be a part of our family for much longer.

I felt the lump come back to my throat as Zoe squeezed tight, pulling back to look at me.

"Whatever you're going through, you know you can talk to me, right?"

I could, but I didn't want to.

And maybe that was my downfall from the beginning.

More tears leaked from the corners of my eyes as I waved away the car containing Zoe and her sister, Nadia and Kezia squashed into the back. Maz's cheerful body was disappearing in the opposite direction.

It was fine.

It was all going to be fine.

the 12k gc :p 72 participants

---

kev | head boy @everyone
guys we need first aid out front
eva just smashed her head on the pavement

eva | head girl @kevjones.com
kev i'm literally fine?? it was a tumble.
have you had too much to drink?
and can someone open this bottle for us :)

nora @everyone
can confirm kev has had too much to drink,
and will be dealt with accordingly.
anyone wanna come play twister?

lish @everyone
can confirm nora has ALSO had too much to
drink and will be dealt with when i beat her at
twister. anyone know why lilz dart is crying?

owen @aliciamcknightxo
we're all good, i'm taking her home.
enjoy your night, everyone!
class party, gethin x

THE CONFRONTING

I sent Owen a text at ten to one, after I'd been sat on the pavement outside Gethin's house for a good half hour with no joy. He was still in there, though the music had died down and most people had already left, leaving the core of our sixth form – Ethan Morgan's group, the head girl and head boy, and a few others – sat around in the living room, drinking and talking and probably totally clocking onto however Owen and Kara were acting in there. The thought made me burn with humiliation, though I knew it wasn't my place to feel embarrassed.

are you coming out soon? ready to go home x

He replied quickly, a short and sweet message which almost brought a smile to my face.

aw where have you been, we missed you. coming out now :)

I checked the group chat briefly as I waited, only to see that Alicia McKnight had put something about me crying. What a *bitch*.

As much as Loz used to like the hockey team, I couldn't stand them in that moment, sat there on the curb, pale and shivering, trying to cover my face and hoping, praying, that their group weren't still sat in the window staring at me as I cried.

I was still sat there, on the curb, hugging my arms tight to my chest, as Owen Sharpley waltzed outside in his white t-shirt and jeans, smiling at me, holding out his arms for a hug.

I was too weak and tired to object.

We didn't speak on the way home, just held hands and wandered, slowly, back to Owen's flat. The door was locked but he'd remembered a key in his pocket, so we let ourselves into the cold space, the same space which had once been filled with the stench of flesh and blood, and now sagged in the middle, sad and unlived in, hardly a home. It may have been cleaner than it ever was when Judy was alive, but that didn't mean it felt like home.

Owen pulled me towards the sofa, where he sat, me between his open legs, staring at him, and tried to kiss me. I didn't kiss him back. And I think that was what did it.

"God, Lilz," he said, rolling his eyes. He'd clearly had a bit to drunk, but not enough that I'd discard anything he next said as the alcohol talking. "Why do you always have to be so uptight?"

I winced, which he noticed. Of course he did.

"What's wrong?" my boyfriend asked, after a pause. "You look… different. Have you been crying?"

The fact it had taken him half an hour to notice almost set me off again.

"Lilz?" he echoed. "What's happened?"

"You."

One word was enough to cause realisation to dawn on his face, for those big dark eyes to turn sour.

He knew.

He knew that I knew.

And everything fell apart.

"You've been sleeping with Kara," I continued, to which

his mouth fell open wide and he tried to shake his head, but it was pointless, so pointless. "Don't try to deny it, Owen, please. I saw the way she looked at you tonight, and how you looked at her. And... that night in the garage. It wasn't a one-off, was it? You've been sneaking off with her most nights, and you even brought her round here last week. You slept with her in *my* bed, Owen. *My bed!*"

My voice was an octave too high now and Owen's cheeks were pink, but he still had the nerve to say, "I couldn't bring her round here, could I? She'd have seen the bloodstains in the bath."

I sprung off the sofa, body practically vibrating with rage.

"How dare you? How dare you do that to me, after everything we've been through, everything I've sacrificed for you! How *dare* you –"

"Lilz, let me explain –"

"No! What is there to explain? You've cheated on me, Owen. You've slept with Kara!"

"It's not as simple as that! I've always said –"

"It's not as simple as that? As what, Owen? As the fact you've lied to me? The fact you say you love me, but if you really loved me, you wouldn't *do* that. You wouldn't... you wouldn't..."

"Lilz." Owen leapt up, rushing to put his arms around me, but I was unresponsive, like I could hardly feel him. Because I couldn't. Something had switched in me, these last few minutes, staring at him try to explain away the fact that he'd cheated on me with Kara Faulkner, somebody we weren't supposed to even *like*. I didn't know him, this version of Owen, the one stood before me. I didn't know him at all.

"You can't make this better. Nothing you say will –"

"I love you, Lilz. You know I do. I love you more than

anything in the world. You taught me how to love, how to… feel. But I'm broken, Lilz, and this whole thing with my mum has just made things worse…"

I'm broken, Lilz.

A line. A line, like one from a movie or book. An excuse, and an embarrassing one at that.

"I needed Kara to feel something, and to give me a release. I've been with you since we were twelve, Lilz. I just wanted… I wanted…"

"How long has this been going on for?"

"Just… since that night in the garage."

I pressed my fingers in my ears, repeating all these la-la-las just to block out the sound of his voice. He needed Kara, because I wasn't enough for him. He needed Kara, because he was a selfish prick and I deserved so much more, so much more. But all I felt in that moment was pain, red hot pain –

"Surely you understand how I feel, Lilz," he continued, trying to tug my hands from the sides of my head. "You must sometimes get the urge to do something you can't do with me. I can't fulfil you fully, not anymore. It's been five years, Lilz. I want to be with you forever, I just… I just…"

I couldn't believe it. Couldn't believe that after everything we'd been through together – everything I'd done for him – he could still be such a *dick*.

"So you're saying you still expect me to stay with you, and just accept that neither of us can fulfil the other?"

I still remember saying that, shouting it at his stupid face and watching a glob of spit land on his nose. He wiped it away with his finger as he stared back, trying so desperately to get me to believe him that I realised then just how much he didn't mean it, didn't mean any of it. He was just saying what he wanted in an attempt to get me to weaken, and forgive him. He was manipulating me, pure and simple; there was no other way to go about saying that.

We were seventeen. This all might seem quite dramatic from a couple of teenagers, talking about sexual fulfilment like we had any real grasp of the *meaning* of the phrase.

But although we were seventeen, we felt so much older, so much more experienced than our years. Because no matter how old you are when it starts, five years down the line is a long time for two people to have learnt a lot about their relationship, about how to act, how to make it last, how to satisfy the other. Some couples are *married* for less time than we had been together, at that point, which basically gave us all authority to make big assumptions and punch and kick where it hurts.

And here we were, Owen shaking his head at me like I was in the wrong, not him, having a conversation no seventeen-year-old should ever have to have with their boyfriend, the kind of conversation they only show on the soaps. The kind of conversation which stings and aches, cuts so deep it leaves a scar, the permanent kind, the kind which never fully heals.

"You have to understand my needs, Lilz," Owen continued, trying to put a hand on my waist. "Because we can't break up, you do realise that. We're in this for the long-run, and if that means I have to sleep with Kara from time to time, then…"

"But I'm not okay with that, Owen?" I posed it as a question because I had no idea how else I was supposed to make it sound.

I didn't understand what he meant, how he how be treating this like his actions were excusable.

Like he didn't care.

Like he really, really didn't care.

Not that I was angry, or hurt, or upset.

Like *he* wasn't even angry that I'd found him out.

Like he wasn't going to apologise.

But he needed to. He needed to, right? He couldn't just get away with this. He couldn't just breeze through the next stage in our life as if everything was fine and he hadn't been cheating on me all along, with one of our best friends at that...

"You'll have to be okay with it, Lilz." He put his other hand on my waist, tried to look me in the eye. "I need this. And we need each other."

I opened and closed my mouth, flabbergasted, as Owen continued to gaze at me.

"But... what if I want out? What if I don't need you anymore?"

Owen frowned, like that wasn't even a possibility he could comprehend. "You know what would happen then, Lilz. You'd be in danger, because I know the truth about what we did that night, and that ties us together for life. You can't just... want out. That's not how it works."

You can probably sense the unfairness of this situation, but Lilz of August genuinely couldn't see it. I remember just staring at him, feeling like my whole world was ending, and I was completely and utterly trapped by this web of intricate lies.

"Owen..."

"I love you, Lilz. This is difficult, I know. But we've got this. We're doing fine." Then he smiled a weird, twisted smile, and added, "Besides... I'm not the only one who can have fun, you know. What about that Zoe girl?"

I wanted to smack him.

I wanted to smack him so, so hard that I shocked the

smirk off his gloating face and knocked even just a shred of sense into his thick head.

But I didn't.

I didn't, because I didn't think I *could*.

And that fear was ruining everything.

close your eyes
and wish for
the best...

THE TRIP

Mum drove us to Dorset. She'd booked a little caravan in a field full of other middle-aged holiday makers and families, and the journey was a good six or seven hours, especially with summer holiday traffic. It was mid-August, and everything was hot, sticky, the leather seats sticking to my bum. At one point, Owen offered to take over and drive.

"Not a chance!" Mum objected. "You're our guest."

Our guest. I wonder what Mum would have said at the time if she knew Owen had been cheating on me the whole summer so far, bringing Kara round to our house when she and Dizzy were out. She wasn't comfortable with Owen and I sleeping together round at our place anyway, but inviting Kara, *Kara*, to get into bed with him…

I suppose I'll have to tell Mum now, though. Tell her about Kara, and Owen, the cheating, the night in the garage, all that weed they consumed. Because the story isn't a whole story without context, background.

Her face when I told the police about Owen was an absolute picture. Mouth open wide, crow's feet spread right around her eyes. She reached out to grab my hand and just held it like that as I spoke, told them everything, all of it, about how Owen killed his mum and singlehandedly wrapped up her body, using jumpers and clothing from Dizzy's wardrobe, clothing which still had my name written into the labels in Sharpie. She didn't want to believe it, but she did. Because Owen wasn't perfect. And everything just made too much sense.

Anyway.

Back to the trip.

It was mostly fun, I think. Hazy and relaxed, just the four of us eating ice cream straight from the tub and walking through endless fields and country lanes. The beautiful scenery almost made the long drive worth it. We watched the first three *Harry Potter* movies that night, Owen's legs splayed casually over mine. I rubbed his ankles, stroked his big toe. He still had the audacity to text on his phone the entire time, but what could I do?

The caravan was teeny, but Owen and I slept on the sofa bed, Mum and Dizzy on the big double at the back, just a thin ply plank separating us. You could've heard every word the two of us spoke in there, and so we didn't, not even a little. Owen turned the light off the minute he got under the covers, then arched his body to cuddle me, hold me close. My own limbs were stiff. I didn't want to hug him back, whisper, "I love you." I didn't want him to even be here, not really. But admitting that made my chest ache.

I won't lie and say it was a bad trip. I also won't lie and say that knowing my boyfriend had slept with another girl and chopped up his dead mother ruined the fun, because it didn't. But maybe that was because I knew my time was running out, that this was all too ludicrous to remain under wraps for much longer. That every time Owen Sharpley touched me, it felt like a sin.

And so we carried on enjoying ourselves, lounging in the sunshine and drinking pints at the local pub, giving Dizzy a little beer in her lemonade and picking out sundresses from the local charity shops, oversized t-shirts and crappy touristy flip-flops. We laughed and snapped photos and smiled,

smiled, smiled, until our faces ached and my brain hurt and I wanted to scream so loud the whole campsite could hear me.

On the third day, Owen and I wandered out over the fields, his hand in mine. The world was green, very green, like the new background of my phone and the teeny tree which had recently joined the peace lily in my room. It was calming, peaceful, breathing in and closing my eyes as Owen's fingers squeezed mine, just a little. It was drizzling, too. Warm, lazy drizzle, half-arsed and petrol-tinted.

"This is lovely, isn't it?" Owen said, out of nowhere. He was still holding my hand, but his grip loosened as he turned to me, hair flattened by the rain. "Like… really, really lovely."

I nodded. There were sheep in the next field, dotting the landscape. The sun was shading them yellow, golden, like tiny stars lighting up a night sky with their glow. Dorset was nice, much nicer than home. Yet it was so far detached that none of this – not the walk, Owen's rained-on face, his hopeful expression – seemed real. Maybe it wasn't. Maybe I really was living in a fantasy land, one I escaped the minute the police knocked on my door that day, lemony shower gel oozing over the floorboards –

"What happened, Lilz?"

I turned to Owen, frowning, as he fixed me with the most earnest of expressions. I didn't know what he meant, at first. What happened, Lilz? What happened?

"We were so happy. Life used to be simple."

"Your mum happened."

Owen nodded, falling silent. The air around us buzzed, a bee zipping past my ear at lightning speed. My boyfriend's grip refastened on my hand. "I… I know. But she'd been happening for as long as I can remember, Lilz. Sometimes I wonder why I couldn't have just waited a few more months, until I turn eighteen, move out... I could've left her behind. She wouldn't have followed me."

There were a lot of things Owen and I could have done differently, which is what still grates on me now. Such a long list that makes everything – everything, everything we went through – feel redundant, pointless, a waste of my precious time and heart.

He could've told me. Confided in me, his girlfriend, about Judy's lifelong abuse, the teasing and taunting and constant jibes.

He could've asked for my help, or talked to my mum, Loz's dad, an adult who knew what to do about all of this.

But he didn't. He let it bubble up inside of him, until it was too much. Until it was *all* too much for both of us.

"We can't dwell on the past." My voice was flat, emotionless, which was exactly how I felt.

"I know," Owen continued. "I just... I feel so guilty, Lilz. About all of it. Because it's my fault, I caused this, and now everything's ruined and I –"

"Breathe, just *breathe*."

But Owen couldn't breathe, wouldn't breathe, dropping to his knees and making all these raspy gaspy noises. His legs were smeared with mud and grass and his eyes were glassy, red, nostrils flared as he clutched my arm so tight he left finger-marks.

"I killed my mum, Lilz." Owen was getting more and more frantic, shaking his head over and over, over and over, as I tried to calm him down, to get him to chill, to focus on the sheep and the fields and the view and something concrete, anything concrete, something he could... "I killed my mum!"

Owen killed his mum. Held her head under the water, watched her legs kick and bubbles fly from her mouth. He killed his mum, and sawed her body in half with a bread knife.

I suddenly felt sick. Very, very sick.

"You can't tell anyone," he said, eyes fiery, mouth quavering. "Lilz, you can't tell anyone!"

"I'm not going to," I told him, but that wasn't enough, not now. "Owen, please breathe, I'm not going to tell, I –"

"I'll go to jail! I'll go to jail, and I'll – I'll –"

"Owen, I'm not going to tell, I promise, I *promise* –"

Owen Sharpley was convulsing on the floor, knees embedded in the muddy grass of the path as sheep baaed and rain fell all around us, drip-drip-dripping onto the ground and forming puddles, big puddles, lake-sized puddles. The sky was now a nasty grey and there was Owen Sharpley, bawling into the mud, making the most horrible of sounds, like his heart would break.

I felt sorry for him, of course. I felt so, so sorry for him. Because despite everything, Owen was traumatised. Truly traumatised, in a way he must've been holding inside of him for so long, unable to express how he really felt about this whole thing. The twelve-year-old Lilz who had stood in Tesco car park as she had her first kiss would have felt bad, terrible even, would've reached out to give this boy a big hug.

But we weren't twelve anymore.

Owen was a grown man. A fully-grown man, almost an adult. He had armpit hair and GCSEs and a job and a car, and he'd killed his mother. He'd allowed those emotions to get so strong, so overwhelming, that he'd cheated on me, repeatedly slept with a girl we were both supposed to be friends with. He was a grown man with the mentality of a little boy, and that wasn't okay. It just wasn't.

And standing there, in that field in Dorset, looking at

Owen's tear-stained face and freckled, splotchy cheeks, I realised that for what felt like the first time ever. I saw Owen Sharpley for what he really was, not what I'd always thought he was, and that sucked. It really, actually *sucked*.

And although I still love him now, and probably always will, it was in that very moment I think I began to… stop.

***

We spent the next few days holed up in the caravan as it rained on-and-off, before heading home at the weekend. We watched so many movies my brain hurt, and play excessive amounts of *Mario Kart* on the old Wii (we'd bought more controllers since I was a kid). Mum made us a big roast on Friday night in the crappy caravan kitchen, and Owen joined in by boiling the broccoli and making me separate gravy because I didn't like the chicken flavouring.

I took a lot of photos, too. Nice photos, the kind Zoe would approve of. She'd been posting summer selfies and beach snaps all week, freckled skin glistening and brown eyes fluttering at the camera, and left a dozen funny comments on my Dorset dump, commenting on the sky and the view and my blonde hair, blowing in the wind as Dizzy snapped a photo from behind, bikini top and baggy jeans and sunshine, the whole shebang.

I omitted all photos of Owen from the post. I took a few for my own memories, of course, silly pictures of him curled up on our sofa bed, laughing at Dizzy for falling in a stream. There was even a photo of him sat in a beer garden, beaming and waving, freckles dark from the sun and hair the perfect shade of floppy dark blonde from a week of highlights and sun-bleached scandal. He looked good in that photo. Good, and not at all like a murderer.

Because that's what he was, really. A murderer.

And whether Judy Sharpley deserved it or not suddenly not enough to excuse that fact.

Now, I'm not saying that seeing Owen break down in that silly Dorset field changed my mind just like that. But… it contributed, at least. It helped me to see him as a human, nothing more. A human, a flawed human, who'd made a series of mistakes and needed to be punished.

I still couldn't tell on him though. I just… couldn't. He was my boyfriend, my person. And I was trapped. Scared. I hadn't yet even considered the kinds of traps I could lay, plans I could set into motion. I thought I was stuck, and that this was how it was going to be from now on. Wrong, stilted, heartless. Kissing Owen and thinking how much I wished it would end, picturing him with Kara so often I drove myself mad. The crying, the tentative touches which no longer made my insides fizz up and nerve ends tingle.

All I could focus on, as the week drew to a close, was the green. The green hills, the grass, the trees and bushes and grass. And it gave me hope. Constant hope. Hope that there really was more to life than Owen Sharpley and the love we'd once had, the love I had no idea how to replicate.

I bought a teeny succulent on the last day, from a shop in the village. A smiley little green plant, which I held in the back of the car the entire drive home, stroking its jelly-like leaves and smiling to myself.

It was called Georgia, I decided. It was gorgeous, too. It would grow and grow, no matter what else was going on the world. She would grow, grow free, even if I didn't.

dizzy's birthday

21 august 2024 at 2.30pm

sparrow heights, vibbington

wear your dancing shoes!

THE BIRTHDAY

Dizzy's birthday always falls in the late summer holidays, which isn't an ideal time. A little less than two weeks ago, Dizzy had friends – a lot of friends, good friends – but she was also turning thirteen, and stubborn, and had spent most of August in bed with a romance novel in one hand and popcorn in the other, ignoring her blowing-up phone and posting a trillion photos to Instagram to bask in the attention.

So when Mum suggested she had a birthday party to mark my little sister becoming a teenager, Dizzy pouted and shrugged and said, in a very year eight kind of voice, "Erm... I mean, sure. But who would I invite?"

"Marcie?" Mum said thoughtfully. "And Ellie, and Mia..."

We were all in the living room, the three of us, my crappy laptop open on the table. Mum was scrolling through the party décor section of Etsy, like we could feasibly afford any of the handmade bunting and wooden "Dizzy" signs on offer there. But she felt bad about working so much this past year, and wanted to make Dizzy's thirteenth special.

"True." Dizzy frowned. "I mean, I'm gonna have to be nice to them all again when we go back to school. They're just so boring, you know?"

I rolled my eyes at Mum, who smiled back at me. She clicked on a seller from Shropshire who made all this lilac décor, tablecloths and bunting and boxes full of goodies, and I nodded when her mouse hovered over the teen bundle. Because as much as Dizzy liked to act all tough, I knew that she'd love a pretty party for her closest friends, a raucous bunch of year eights who'd each had sucky sleepovers and bowling parties this year, who loved everything pastel and aesthetic and Instagrammable.

Besides... Dizzy's party gave me something else to think about. Something that wasn't Owen, or Judy Sharpley's rotting body, or the image of him shagging Kara. Something neutral, positive. Something *fun*.

"Will Loz come?" Dizzy piped up suddenly, and I shrugged in surprise. Loz. Dizzy loved Loz; she always had done. Who wouldn't love their older sister's prettier, cooler best friend and blossoming influencer? But I hadn't heard from Loz in at least two or three days now, since we got back from Dorset. And she hadn't been to visit yet, not once this entire summer.

"I don't know," I said. "She'll probably still be in Nottingham..."

"Owen will come," Mum reassured Dizzy. "And what about that new friend of yours, Lilz? The one you went to Leeds with?"

"Zoe!" Dizzy exclaimed. "I follow her on Instagram. She's so *cool*."

I glanced at Mum, hesitant. "You want me to invite Zoe?"

"It'd be nice to have a mix of people here. Right, Diz?"

"Erm, definitely. Marcie, Ellie, Mia, Owen, Zoe..."

"I'll invite some of the people in my phonebook, get on the blower to Aunty Kym and Uncle Mark." Mum checked the screen again, finalising the purchase of the lilac teen party box, a small smile on her face. "Are you okay with all this, Lilz? Me and you are on cake duties."

I smiled and nodded and leaned across to hug Dizzy. Because although having Owen and Zoe in the same room at

Dizzy's little party was my worst nightmare, it was my sister's thirteenth birthday.

What else could I do?

***

Our building had a small patch of grass round the back, just big enough to place the occasional marquee or bouncy castle. A week and a half before the police came knocking on our door, Mum and I set to carrying down every piece of movable furniture we owned and placing it on that communal stretch of garden, chairs and tables and even my bedroom desk, the beanbag I'd had since I was a kid.

"I really hope Dizzy loves this," Mum said wistfully, pulling her blonde hair back into a loose pony. "Do you think we've made it cool enough?"

"Dizzy's above all that," I said, though I wasn't really sure if she was.

I'd invited a whole bunch of people in the end. Zoe and her best friends, Kezia, Maz and Nadia, who were cool and chilled and would definitely make the party a whole lot more fun. Owen, of course, though I'd neglected to mention anything to Kara and Gethin, who I hadn't seen since the party. Zoe's sister Mira was driving, and said she'd come in for a drink in the garden if the weather was nice. Aunty Kym and Uncle Mark were stopping by with our cousins Matt and Leo, who were more than five years older than me, now graduated from uni and living with their respective girlfriends.

I'd invited Loz, of course. She was probably busy shopping with Sofia or something, because she hadn't replied.

Dizzy had invited quite a few girls from her class, as well

as some of the boys. I knew she fancied one of them, but I wasn't sure which. And honestly? I was trying not to think about it. Because the more I remembered that I was Dizzy's age when I got with Owen, the more I wanted to ship the party decorations all the way back to Shropshire.

"These are wonderful," Mum said now, pulling out a string of lilac stars. "Look at this, Lilz! A bargain or what?"

Inside a cardboard box was a whole feast of lilac treats; party rings and purple gummy shrimps, glazed doughnuts and beetroot crisps, colourful grape Fanta cans and syringes filled with Vimto. I stole a party ring before Mum could tell me off, and busied myself with laying the lilac tablecloth across my desk for the food and drink to go on.

The sun was shining, high and bright in the sky. It felt like an omen, somehow. That this was a great day for a party, and that Dizzy was going to *love* it.

Aunty Kym and Uncle Mark came first, with Leo, who was now twenty-four and teaching at one of the local primary schools. His little brother Matt, twenty-two, came with his girlfriend – coincidentally also called Lily. They'd graduated from uni last year, and were both grinning as they hugged me and started showing pictures of their new flat together, their dog Luigi. In tow was their old schoolfriend Remy, who worked part-time at a fruit and veg shop and had brought us all these different jams and chutneys, beaming as he spread them out across the table.

"And how are you doing, Lilz?" Matt asked, smiling at me. He'd always had a kind face, ocean-blue eyes and messy brown hair, arm slung casually around his girlfriend's waist. "Sixth form treating you well?"

"Not bad," I replied politely. "I'm passing everything, now, which is something."

"Are you considering uni?" Lily asked me, beaming. She'd just graduated from Oxford, apparently. With a *first*. "Or maybe an apprenticeship?"

"I've… been looking at Leeds," I said honestly, which of course elicited a squeal from Lily and a nod of approval from Matt, as the conversation dived into a territory I was finally comfortable with. I'd researched enough over summer that I felt confident enough to tell them the courses I'd been looking at, the grade requirements, how I wanted my life to pan out…

I didn't even notice that Owen wasn't here yet.

Zoe was late, but it didn't matter as she waltzed round the side of the building with Kezia, Maz and Nadia on her heel. They hugged me and giggled and chatted away about something which went over my head, Mira standing back to help Mum string purple stars all around the back of the building. Mrs Carlos lived on the bottom floor, and gave permission for us to use her oven for pizzas and dough balls, to put fairy lights on her porch.

"It's a lovely block," Zoe said, grinning at me. "It must be so fun to have neighbours who live, like… *in* your building. Like, a constant sleepover, or uni halls, or boarding school or something!"

Zoe didn't really get it. She couldn't see what a privilege it would be to have a *detached house*, to not be conscious of every move you made in case you stepped too loud on the creaky floorboard and woke up Mrs Carlos below, or play your music so loud that the family above started shouting down at you out of the window. She couldn't see how nice it would be to have more than one living space, a garden all to yourself, one you could plant things in and sunbathe on the grass without anybody overlooking…

But I nodded and laughed and said it was fun, *kinda*, you know.

When Dizzy and her friends finally showed up, running down the road and landing with a crash at the gate, we all broke into song. A cheery rendition of 'Haaappy Birthday' which dissolved Dizzy into tears and got her friends way too hyped, a problem only made worse when the gate opened and they charged straight for the party rings.

I thought thirteen-year-olds were supposed to be somewhat sophisticated nowadays, in their bodycon dresses and expensive trainers and claw clips. But Dizzy was ecstatic at the sight of the treat box and lilac décor and all her favourite people in the same place at the same time, so much so that she tackled me to the ground and squeezed me so tight that I shrieked.

"Thank you, big sister," she wasn't, sugary breath warm on my cheek. "You're the best."

"You're the best, little sister," I retorted, to which she blew a raspberry in my face and bounded off to test out the Vimto syringes and funny little shrimps.

Pretty soon we were all so caught up in the party, bopping to music and chatting amicably and enjoying the sunshine, that I didn't even notice who was here yet and who wasn't. I was just having fun, drinking and eating and laughing, flicking Dizzy's blonde hair out of her eyes as the earth spun slowly round, round, round...

Until a car door was heard outside, a loud bang which shuddered the talking to a stop. Taylor Swift was still blasting from Matt's speakers, loud and cheery, her old stuff... *1989*, *Lover*, the summer of love and –

There was Loz, standing at the gate, blue eyes wide and filled with tears, as she opened her arms out so wide I thought she was trying to pull herself apart.

"You… came."

"Of course I came." My best friend rolled her eyes as I launched myself at her, almost knocking the wind out of both of us. "Did you really think I'd miss Dizzy's party?"

dizzy's party is on weds

if you can make it

no worries if not, she wanted me to ask

hope everything is going well with you :)

i love you

xxx

THE GATECRASHER

I spent so long hugging Loz that I genuinely think I could've squeezed all the life out of her. But I didn't, because even when I let her go, she bounced back to her regular Loz-shaped self and grinned at me, all tanned skin and blonder-than-blonde hair, cleavage and white teeth. My best friend, gorgeous as ever, standing right before my eyes.

"You look different," she said at once, pulling at my t-shirt. It was oversized and lilac, very on-theme, and I had one of Dizzy's claw clips in my hair, black cycling shorts hidden beneath my shirt. "You're actually semi-brown for once. What is this witchcraft?"

"I stayed outside long enough that I surpassed getting burnt," I told her, grinning. "And you look different, too, my dear friend. You're all dewy and youthful, like a nymph!"

"Post-breakup glow," Loz explained. "I'm a whole new woman."

"I need to hear *all* about it."

I grabbed her hand and pulled her through the party, up the back stairs and into the kitchen, which was quiet and cold, awaiting the party's aftermath. And then I turned to look at her, look at her *properly*, take in her blonde hair and freckled nose and expression that just seemed so openly, genuinely happy to see me.

Because I couldn't believe she was here. I just… couldn't. It seemed crazy that Loz should have travelled all the way from Notts to see me here, to come to Dizzy's thirteenth birthday party, and that she was sat in my kitchen now, my best friend, reaching out to take my hand across the counter.

"So," she said, immediately reaching for a banana. "What's going on with you and Owen?"

I opened my mouth to speak, then stopped. Because of all the things I'd been expecting her to say, asking about Owen was nowhere on the cards.

"What do you mean?" I asked, cheeks pink. "Owen and I are… fine."

"No you're not."

"What?"

"Liz, something's going on. You don't mention him when you call me, and you went on your first holiday together without letting Instagram know he was even *there*. I mean, cute scenery pics, but what's with all the grass and sheep?"

"I like grass and sheep," I said feebly, but Loz's eyebrows were raised. "Did I show you my new plants yet? They're in my room, they all have names and –"

"What's happening, Lilz?" Loz was looking at me. Properly looking at me, like she could see straight through every word I was saying. "Are you and Owen breaking up?"

"What? No!"

"Then what's going on? Are you having troubles?"

"Troubles?"

"You know, arguing, growing apart, that sort of thing." Loz paused, frowning, before she said, "Is this about his mum?"

My heart stopped, just for a second. I opened my mouth and let it hang, then said, "His… mum?"

"Yeah, his mum. You know, Judy upping and leaving like that, going south to stay with a friend."

Relief rushed through my body, quenched quickly with an

overbearing sense of dread. "Why would you think that?"

"Because Owen's mum left him, Lilz. And that's kind of a major life event."

"He's doing okay." Was I supposed to go along with this, or pretend the reason for Owen's change was the trauma he felt about his mum leaving? I didn't know, couldn't tell. It was all happening too fast. I wasn't expecting Loz to come here today, let alone start asking me questions about –

"Gethin says he's struggling," Loz continued, "that he's not himself, that he's acting odd." Then she lowered her voice, and I could see in her eyes what she was going to say next. "He... he told me about Kara, Lilz. What's been happening since that night in the garage. And... he told me you know."

I felt every morsel of blood in my body rush to my face, taint it red, bright red.

Because they knew.

They *all* knew.

Gethin, Loz... all of them knew that Kara and Owen were shagging behind my back, and none of them had the courtesy, the *care*, to do anything about it.

"Why didn't you tell me, Lilz?" Loz asked, still munching on her banana. "I would've gotten the first train up here to come and knock his lights out, you know that! And Kara... I mean, she's just a conniving, back-stabbing bitch, and I'm planning to never speak to her again, but you know."

"How... I don't get it. How did Gethin find out?"

Loz flushed, looking down. "I think... Owen told him. After that party you all had at Gethin's, or something. Owen told him you found out, and so Gethin told me, assuming you would've already let me know what was happening. I've been waiting for you to bring it up, but when you didn't, I – I

_"

I didn't know what to say.

Because they knew. All my friends, the entire group. They all knew that Owen had been cheating on me, that I knew about it and had stayed with him throughout. They all knew I was weak and pathetic and so completely in love with my boyfriend that I couldn't leave the person who'd been *sleeping with somebody else* behind my back.

They knew, and it made me feel like the most stupid person in the world.

Because I was, wasn't I? It didn't matter what chokehold Owen had over me, what trauma he'd been through this summer to lead him to Kara's side.

He was cheating on me, cheating on me with *Kara*.

Yet we were still together, and I was still very much loyal to his side.

"Why didn't you tell me, Lilz?" Loz said, voice softer now. "You don't deserve this. Owen doesn't deserve someone as wonderful as you, either. He's treating you like shit."

"I know." You could barely hear my whisper, two syllables just audible in the silent kitchen.

"Do you want me to whack him in the balls?"

I shook my head, giving a little snort of laughter, as Loz smiled at took a last bite of her banana. And then she grabbed my hands across the table and squeezed, big eyes staring into mine.

"Why are you still with him, Lilz?"

I shook my head, vision blurred, lump in my throat so big I could've choked on it.

"You need to break up with him. This isn't right."

"But I love him."

Loz sighed, clearly feeling sorry for me, *poor little Lilz*, too weak to break up with her cheating boyfriend and admit to the world that her relationship was flawed, so flawed.

But that wasn't the only reason, was it?

And I couldn't tell her the other.

21/08/2024 16:28:57

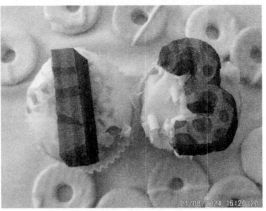

21/08/2024 16:20:20

THE TENSION

When Loz and I ventured back down to the party to find Owen, Kara and Gethin stood around the food table, snacking and syringing Vimto into each other's mouths, the tension was so thick it almost swallowed us. Dizzy and the others were all dancing and singing by the speaker, hyped up on sugar and candy and grape Fanta. Mum had long disappeared to the shop to get alcohol for all of the adults, and Loz had a tight grip of my arm.

"Loz!" Kara squealed, rushing to give her a hug. "You came!"

"You weren't invited," I said at once. Because she wasn't. Maybe if she hadn't left a bloody *eyelash* in my bed, sure, but she had, so she wasn't.

"That was very rude of you, Lilz," Owen said. I felt his arm slide around my waist, hand latching across my stomach. And I couldn't do anything but breathe in and nod, knowing that if I looked sideways, I'd see his dark blue eyes and every piece of love and regret would surge through me once again, taking the courage I needed to say this.

"You weren't invited," I repeated, keeping my gaze level with Kara's. "Could you go, please?"

Kara frowned. "Go? But I like Dizzy. And it's her party, not yours."

"And Dizzy is my sister," I said. "And if I don't like you, she doesn't, either."

"Oh, don't be a bitch, Lilz," Owen started to say, but Loz

fixed him with such a glare that he was forced to roll his eyes and back off. "Oh, fine. Come on, Kaz, let's go."

"Kaz?" Loz spat. "*Kaz?*"

"It's a nickname," Kara retorted. "Bit like Loz... but less short for lozenge."

"Are we leaving?" Gethin asked, narrowing his eyes. "Your mum hasn't even brought the drinks yet, Lilz!"

"They're not for you anyway. They're for her, and for Aunty Kym and Uncle Mark."

"Spoilsport." I felt Owen's fingers slip under the fabric of my t-shirt dress, play with the waistline of my shorts. They were like worms. Worms, slimy worms, trying to bed their way into my skin. "Are you sure you want us to leave?"

"I want Kara to leave," I said, but my voice sounded so pathetically broken and forlorn that a flash of guilt struck Owen's face, so stark I almost thought I imagined it.

"Okay. We're going." He pulled away, straightening up.

Then he took Kara's hand.

Bold as brass, in the garden, at my little sister's thirteenth birthday party.

"You do realise that the minute you walk out of this garden with her, you and Lilz are over?" Loz was staring at him incredulously, her big heart spilling over her face.

But Owen just smiled and shook his head, and blew me a kiss. "No. We're not."

And then he sauntered out of the garden, Kara and Gethin in tow, and disappeared down the side of the building.

Nobody had seen. They were all too busy dancing, having the time of their lives. It took a solid minute for me to process what was happening. For me to turn to Loz, eyes wide, and make some sort of explanatory noise which caused her to shake her head, gobsmacked, and say, "What the hell?"

"I…"

"How can he treat you like that, Lilz? What has happened since I left to turn you into such a wet blanket?"

"Loz, it's complicated."

"Complicated? How can it be *complicated*? He's cheating on you, Lilz! He's cheating on you, and you're letting him walk all over you!"

"I don't want to talk about it."

Loz stared at me for a second, taking it in, then nodded, twice, and turned on her heel to go.

"Okay. Fine." She turned to face me one last time, before sighing and saying, in her most defeatist tone, "I need to go, too."

***

The party lasted well into the evening. I brought some of my summer work down to do after a while, scribbling away making flashcards on some of last year's content, as Zoe twirled around me with a big grin on her face.

"Our GCSE results came out on Thursday!" she said, grinning ecstatically. I knew that, of course. She'd sent me a photo of her string of eights and nines, and of the new custom Doc Martens her parents had bought her as a well-done present.

When I got my GCSE results, Mum bought Domino's and we ate it watching shitty TV in the living room as I tried not to cry. I remember her ringing Mr Roberts, the head of sixth form, to make sure my handful of fours and fives were enough to get me onto three A-level courses. They were – just.

"So, like, we're having a little get-together on Wednesday night, round at mine. A few friends, snacks, a hot tub…"

It sounded awful, but I smiled anyway, trying to look enthusiastic.

"You wanna come? It'll literally just be Kezia, Maz and Nadia, and a few girls from school, no boys. Oh, do say yes, Lilz! We really want to get to know you now that we're definitely gonna be at sixth form in September."

"I don't know," I said, shrugging. "Hot tubs aren't really my thing."

"We're only doing that later, and we won't all fit anyway. You can sit on the side, if you want, enjoy the free drinks and crisps?"

I knew she meant well. And GCSE results were a big deal to Zoe, to her friends. So I nodded at last, and her face broke into the biggest, most ecstatic beam.

"That's amazing! Oh, wonderful, I'll go tell the others…"

That was when my phone started ringing. Buzzing, insistently, on my lap, against my thigh.

"Sorry, can I take this?"

Zoe nodded and skipped away, as I turned my phone over to reveal the name there.

Owen.

"Hi." His voice was muffled, like he was trying to be quiet. He didn't sound like Owen. He sounded like Judy Sharpley, for a second. Shrill and northern and blunt, that "hi" holding more than a string of sentences ever could.

"What do you want?"

"To apologise for earlier."

"Why?"

"Why? Because I had to leave with Kara, and clearly Loz was in a tizz about that. Why does she care, anyway? It's our business. Why's she even back?"

"Let me see…" I paused, pretending to think. "Maybe

because she found out about you and Kara, and wanted to see if I was okay?"

I checked to see if there was anyone listening before moving away from the garden and down the side of the house. Mum would be back soon. And I didn't want anyone else to hear this; Loz knowing was bad enough, but I didn't know what I'd do if Mum or Dizzy found out that Owen had been cheating on me all summer.

"You're fine," Owen said. I could hear the eye roll in his voice. "I'm coming round later, anyway. I just wanted to let you know I only left with Kara because she would've gotten all funny otherwise, you know what she's like."

I wanted to hang up.

In that moment, stood on the phone to the boy who was deconstructing my heart and putting it back together all wrong, I wanted to *hang up*.

But I couldn't.

I *couldn't.*

"I love you." That was how he always ended his phonecalls. By saying he loved me. That he loved me always, for better or for worse, no matter what was happening in the world.

And I was left standing down the side of my house, screen black, wondering how we got from this to that, to back to this.

🔍 **what to do if your bf**

... cheats on you

... is racist

... is a misogynist

... slaps you

THE SLAP

"Hi." My boyfriend stood on my doorstep, leaned closer for a hug, a kiss. I wrapped my arms around him tentatively as Owen stroked my hair, wet from the shower, and added, "Mmm, Lilz, new shampoo? You smell like coconut."

"It's shower gel," I said, before stepping back to let him into the house.

Mum and Dizzy were watching TV in the living room, all partied out. We'd dumped most of the decorations in Mrs Carlos' flat downstairs, on her porch beneath the overhang, in case it rained. I could hear *How I Met Your Mother* playing now, and it hit me, for the first time, that I might no longer be the subject of Owen's very own how-I-met-your-mother saga. That it might be... Kara, or somebody else.

Because I knew how tonight was going to go, the ultimatum I was going to pull.

If I had the confidence, anyway.

I led Owen up to my room, which was colder than the rest of the apartment. I'd had the windows open all day because of the heat, and a draft had chilled my room now that it was evening, breeze drifting in from outside and spelling the end of August, September now imminent.

Owen lay down on my bed and frowned. He was staring at the bookshelf, trying to figure out why it looked different.

"You don't read," he said. "And you don't like plants."

"I literally bought one in Dorset." I sat at the end of the bed, folding my legs beneath me. Georgia the succulent was smiling at us, bashful beneath her plump leaves. She looked pretty, had grown healthily since we returned from our holiday. She seemed to like the indirect sunlight and the few sprays of water I'd given her, using a plastic bottle I'd saved from some of mum's room spray.

The books were all Dizzy's, shitty, second-hand romances written ten years ago when mobiles were hardly a thing and talking about sex in a teen novel was all kinds of blasphemous. And no, I didn't really like reading. But it was a nice, calming distraction, now that Owen was out all the time and there was so much on my mind. And I'd have to get used to reading – even if it was just simplistic, clichéd stuff – if I wanted to get better at writing essays, a personal statement. All this would come in handy eventually, right?

The one at the top was about a girl who moved to boarding school in Paris. I was about halfway through, reading a few chapters before bed each night. It was soppy, and cringey, but I wasn't hating it. That was a miracle in itself.

"Is this all because of that Zoe girl?" Owen continued, wrinkling his nose. "Because if she's turning you into some Pinterest girl... I swear, next thing you know, you'll be going to pride parades and eating acai bowls."

"Not likely," I said, settling back into my pillow. Because this was good. Owen being Owen, talking shit and being generally ignorant...

This was what I needed. It would relax him, before I brought it up again. It being Kara.

Oh, God.

"What even is acai?" Owen asked. "Like, some sort of protein supplement or some shit?"

"I think it's a berry," I told him.

"A berry? I've never seen an acai berry in the supermarket. Imagine that. Blueberries, strawberries, raspberries... acai."

I once would've laughed, but the joke fell flat.

"Are you okay?" Owen sat up then, squinting at me. "You're being very... quiet."

"I'm fine."

"You sure?" An arm snaked around me, pulling me closer. But I scooted backwards and gave him a crooked smile from across the bed. "Lilz?"

"I want to talk about Kara."

Owen just rolled his eyes, like he was sick of talking about it. Which he probably was, but still.

"Owen…"

"Lilz, there's nothing to talk about. It's just a bit of fun, which I think I'm entitled to. And if you can't understand that, tough."

"I *can't* understand it. And I shouldn't have to, Owen. You're making me into a laughingstock."

"What do you mean?"

I blinked at him gormlessly.

What did I mean?

I think that was what hurt me the most, and still does. The fact he couldn't see why him sleeping with another girl while we'd kept alive the image of Lilz and Owen for so long would be harmful, painful. The fact he wasn't bothered how many people knew we weren't perfect. It was our thing, our Lilz and Owen thing.

Or so I thought.

"Owen, everyone thinks I'm pathetic for staying with you. You're cheating on me, and I can't do anything about it because… because… because I helped you bury your mother. And it's humiliating, actually humiliating, because I can't tell anyone, not even Loz, why I'm still with you."

"Why you're still with me?" Owen echoed. "Why you're *still with me?*"

You see, unless you know Owen Sharpley in real life, you won't understand what I mean when I try describe his face in that moment. No words can do it justice.

Because Owen Sharpley is – *was* – a relatively mild man, on the outside. Calm and contemplative, scary in his silence. It's why for the last however many years, my boyfriend was treated with mild fear and scepticism from most, apprehensively viewed as a bit of a monster. Too cool for school, and too cool for everybody else.

But in that moment, he wasn't calm.

His eyes were dark. So dark they almost looked black, glaring at me in the stark light of my bedroom, the sky outside a lighter shade than blue, even though it was past nine. His eyebrows were knitted and his lips were so tightly pursed they could've split open and spewed white blood all over his face.

"Why you're still with me?" he repeated for a third time. "What's the alternative, Lilz? That you break up with me?"

"What – I – I – yes."

The slap came out of nowhere.

Hard and cold and right across my cheek, so sudden I'm sure it must've left a mark. And I just… sat there. Reeling from his touch, his fingers thwacking my white face, the surge of blood I felt rush to tend the spot.

He slapped me.

Owen – the love of my life, my best friend and soulmate – *slapped me.*

"You can't break up with me, Lilz. Not now, not ever." His voice was so still it was almost startling. Startling, and scary. Scary, because he seemed so... blasé. As though what was happening was normal, and he could control me by hitting me, hitting me in the face like some sort of animal.

Owen never got into fights, ever. He never hit back when the boys at school taunted him, didn't have a violent bone in his body. Apart from the one which had pushed Judy's shoulders under the bathwater, watched her kick and scream until her voice was hoarse and her eyes went white, white, white, like panna cotta.

"We're in this together, whether you like it or not."

"I know. I know."

I know.

"Have you got that?"

I nodded meekly, staring back at him, at that furious expression and slightly trembling hand, flaccid and pink by his side.

But I didn't have it. I didn't have it *at all*.

I couldn't say it to Owen's face, but I knew, in that moment, that what he'd done wasn't right. He'd hit me. Hit me, his *girlfriend*. I might have had a dozen excuses for him murdering his mother, but now, sat in my bedroom as he looked at me like I was evil, pure evil, I didn't feel safe. I wonder if Owen ever felt like that, too.

And that was the moment I knew.

I knew what I needed to do.

I just didn't know *how*.

THE CONFESSION

Zoe's party was on Wednesday. I wore a swimming costume beneath my baggy t-shirt in case I felt like getting into the hot tub, but I wasn't anticipating it. Because this whole last week, I hadn't felt like... having fun. Not with Owen, not with Mum and Dizzy. Not with Loz, who hadn't messaged me since she found out I was a weakling with no backbone who couldn't leave her cheating boyfriend.

And I still hadn't done anything about The Owen Issue.

Because what was I supposed to do? I had no plan, no backup. I couldn't even remember the spot in the woods where we had hidden the body, or... or... anything. If I went to the police now, I'd have no evidence, nothing.

And I didn't want to go to the police.

I wanted to leave Owen, but I didn't want him to go to prison. Owen was soft, liked gaming and daytime TV and old movies, hoodies and buttered toast and cheese-and-broccoli packet pasta. He wouldn't last two seconds behind bars.

And if I left Owen, he'd frame me for the murder.

That, I didn't doubt.

So by the time I arrived on Zoe Forlani's road, Mira's car in the drive, I still had no idea what I was going to do, that's the honest truth. All I knew was that I was there, in my swimming costume and baggy t-shirt, flip-flops on my feet and phone dead in my bag.

Zoe's house was huge. Properly huge. She let me in via the side door, talking and laughing about nothing in particular as she led me back to where the party was. Maz was wearing a big tie-dye t-shirt over her bikini, but Kezia and Nadia were lounging in just their skimpy costumes, laughing and welcoming me into the circle. There were a few other girls scattered around, all year eleven and clearly intelligent and beautiful, and I didn't half feel out of place. But none of them could make me feel as inadequate as Owen had done, so it didn't really matter. None of it did.

We were strictly on mocktails that night, by Mr Forlani's instruction. He was nice enough, coming out to check on us but not dawdling around a group of bikini-clad teens for it to become weird. Mrs Forlani brought out snacks, breadsticks and hummus and olives with garlic, and Mira stopped for a quick chat, clearly on good terms with most of Zoe's friends. It must be nice to have a close age-gap, I remember thinking. Maybe if Dizzy was older, we could be more like friends than sisters. One day...

The music was good, too. Not my taste, but chilled, laid-back. Ed Sheeran, then a random block of George Ezra which went on for far too long and hurt every brain cell left inside me. And there I was, Lilz Dart, sat in the circle, talking amicably to a girl by my side as Maz complimented my hair and green nail polish and laughed along to all my jokes, and Kezia asked how psychology A-level was, and Nadia yapped on about my latest Instagram post, the photos of Dorset.

I felt normal.

More normal than I'd felt in a long time.

We got into the hot tub at around ten, when the sky was dark and fairy lights lit up the garden, and all eight of us crammed into the tiny box, splashing water over the sides.

I'd never been in a hot tub before. It was nice. Weird, but nice. A bit like an extra bubbly bath, but I didn't exactly want to associate the experience with being in a bathtub. The water was hot and steamy and we took a billion photos, and somewhere, lost amongst the steam and the bubbles and conversation, all thoughts about Owen and Judy and the orange-stained bathroom tiles finally started to evaporate…

Or so I thought.

Zoe kept looking at me. That whole night, no matter who I was speaking to, what I was doing. Even when I braved an olive, took a bite of hummus and breadstick, Zoe's eyes were on me, narrowed, like she was trying to figure out what I was saying, why I wasn't acting like… well, Lilz.

It took until eleven for her to say something. To stand up in the hot tub in her lime-green bikini, sopping wet and bright against her dark skin, and hold out a hand to me.

"Lilz? Come with me. I wanna show you something."

And so I took her hand. I took her hand in a completely innocent and friendly way, because yes, we were just friends, and I had a feeling that was the way it was always going to be between us.

But it felt nice. Warm, and comforting.

She led me inside, passed me a spare towel from the sofa as we made our way upstairs. She tied it round her body while I wrapped mine over my shoulders and huddled, like it was a blanket. Her room was empty and quiet, so she flicked on the light and shut the door behind us.

And then she gestured for me to sit.

It felt weird, in that moment. The silence was too silent and Zoe looked serious, very serious, as she leaned back against her pillow and said, deadly serious, "What's going on?"

I feigned a frown, teeth gritted. "What do you mean?"

"With you. What's going on?"

I opened my mouth to speak, but Zoe was too smart for that. She shook her head and hold up a finger to my lips, shaking her head.

"You haven't been yourself tonight, but you've been distant for weeks. And all that crying at the party... it wasn't you. It's like you've got the weight of the world on your shoulders, and you don't think anyone else will notice."

"No one else *has* noticed." I said that quietly, under my breath. But Zoe still heard.

"I've noticed."

Her brown eyes bore into mine as I tried to search for some sort of explanation. An explanation to why she cared, to why she would ever care. But all I could find was sympathy, and interest, genuine interest. Like she really did just want to help.

"Lilz, you can trust me. I'm your friend. Whatever you're going through, I just want to help."

I nodded.

"Lilz..." Zoe took my hands. They were still warm and moist from the hot tub, but mine were cold, ice cold, and heavy, like lead. I could feel my eyes drooping, mouth falling slack. Because after all these months of holding it in, I finally felt I could tell someone the truth, the real truth. Or... some variant of it, anyway.

I took a deep breath, shuddered.

Was I really about to do this?

What did I have to lose?

Nothing. Nothing at all. I'd already lost everything that mattered to me, and if I carried on like this, things would only get worse. I needed to start being honest – at least in some ways.

I sighed, squeezing her hands. They were running as cold

as mine now, the blood all squeezed away, tainted by my ice.

Then I said, "Owen killed his mum. Drowned her, in the bath. And... I helped him hide the body."

hope you're having fun!

i am :)

thank you x

don't do anything i wouldn't do x

that doesn't sound too difficult, does it?

THE GRAVE

The streets of Vibbington were silent, but I was warm and dry in one of Zoe's oversized hoodies and Mira's trainers. The others had long gone home and it was past one in the morning, but I reached out to grab Zoe's hand in the street, feeling her skin warm against mine.

We were doing this.

We were really, truly doing this.

The walk to the Forest of Death wasn't too far. Nothing in Vibbington was. It was a teeny town, which is why I loved it so much. But now, walking towards the forest with Zoe's hand in mine, it felt so small I could feel it suffocating me. Drawing in, hands around my neck, strangling –

"Almost at the entrance," Zoe said, voice soft, and I nodded. We were. We were so close now, and I wasn't ready. But would I ever be? Probably not.

The path was rough and wet, slick with mud and gravel and weeds. The forest was luscious, fruitful, the perfect August night. It was muggy, but there was still an element of cold in the air, hidden behind the heat. Zoe's hand was the only warm thing there in the woods, and even that was clammier than anything.

We made our way down the central path, Zoe and I, into the forest and beyond. There was no moon out, but blueish clouds were visible in the sky above, like a dark sheet of marble. The trees waved and hissed and crackled as we walked, no doubt getting Mira's perfect trainers muddy and the threads of Zoe's hoodie snagged on thorns and branches.

"You lead the way," she whispered suddenly, approaching a narrow section of the path. I had the torch, so I didn't mind going first, creeping along on our mission. It cast a golden glow all over the gravel, warm yellow and pretty, like the light of a bonfire.

I couldn't remember where we'd hidden the body. But I knew the general area. In the part of the woods which was so overgrown not even a dog could run away and find poor Judy, where rabbits and foxes would hopefully keep away from our two sections of bin-bag-clad flesh.

We were approaching the area now. It was darker, trunks growing close together, stream rushing faster and faster in the distance. We didn't cross the bridge, instead veering off the path into the woods by its side. A proper forest, unlit and unventured, so thick with nettles and undergrowth we could barely walk in a straight line. Neither of us were wearing trousers, which was our first mistake. The thorny branches scratched our calves and nettles stung our knees, and after a minute I felt so weary and battered that I just wanted to turn around and go home.

But we couldn't do that.

We had to go on, on, on, into the forest.

We had to find the body.

It was the smell that hit us first. So deep into the woods you never would've expected such a foul, pungent aroma, not even from the carcass of a deer or rabbit, or a bigger animal, a runaway dog or cat.

No, this was more than that. It was horrible, bloody, but in a completely different way from the bathroom that day. Rotting flesh, soggy fingernails and blood-soaked skin. I could practically smell Judy's sunken eyeballs and all that optic fluid, leaking over her newly hollowed cheeks and clavicle, muscle and fat melting away, into the clothes we'd wrapped her in.

Clearly the black plastic wasn't doing much to mask the smell. I could only be glad that no one had wandered this far into the forest for months, clearly, that no one was poaching here, that the land here was public and not owned by that menace Giles, who was known for laying fox traps and trying to catch vermin. Because Judy Sharpley would definitely count as vermin, pollution. Years of takeaways and microwave meals had built up under her skin and were now seeping into the forest floor, the branches and leaves and ground waiting to be revived by spring, hidden under bracken and decay.

I carried on, hoping Zoe was stuck somewhere behind me. There was no point even trying to be quiet now, given how quiet and hidden away this part of the forest was. And Judy's body was somewhere nearby, I knew it. I could smell it, but more than that, I could sense it. I could sense the evil in the air, both belonging to her and her killer, thick and gloopy and… filled with something more. Something darker. Something only I could feel.

"Are we nearly there?" Zoe asked, though the question was redundant; you could've smelled Judy Sharpley anywhere within a five minute radius.

Clearly she was here, in this section of the forest, rotting away.

The smell was getting stronger, however. More pungent, like it was filling the air with particles of decaying flesh. I imagined, in that moment, how terrible multiple dead bodies must reek, let alone one. How did serial killers do it?

All I wanted was my green back. My beautiful, calm green.

So much that I could bask in it, take a bath in luscious lime, deep emerald.

In that moment, I made the decision to paint my bedroom green. It had been blue for long enough.

In contrast, the forest was black, yellow beneath the torch's glare, but it smelled... brown.

Brown, like blood staining a sanitary pad, repugnant, left to linger for far too long. Brown, like meat left out in the sun, a nice steak growing a horrid, long-lasting stench, one which could turn the air a whole new shade of umber.

And then I saw it.

A flash of white, of a torch hitting shiny plastic.

Two black lumps on the forest floor, embedded under a million years of bracken and fallen leaves, so it felt.

"We've found it." My voice cut through the silent, Zoe stopped dead behind me. She was barely breathing. And there it was. Judy Sharpley, still wrapped up away from the heat, perhaps well-preserved, we'll never know for sure. I grabbed Zoe's hand again and squeezed. There were a thousand words trapped in that squeeze, but she understood.

Of course she did.

"It's still here," she said, more reassuring than anything. "Are you okay, Lilz?"

I nodded.

Was I okay? This was what I was expecting, right? For the body to still be there, exactly where we left it... and for Owen to have not moved it, because why would he? He wasn't a freak. We'd hidden it well.

But seeing the body here, showing it to Zoe...

It signified the start of something, the start of something more. the start of the truth, the cold truth, my version of such.

The start of the end.

We knew where it was. I had to report him, now. Zoe knew, too. We had to. We had to

we had to

       we

        had

          to –

Reminder — Report
phonecall to pudrow
and make sure
they have it on log

THE TIP-OFF

We found Judy Sharpley's makeshift grave in the early hours of Thursday, but September third fell on a Tuesday that year. So how did those next five days go, I hear you ask? How?

I slept over at Zoe's the night we found the body – or morning, I suppose. It made the most sense. We slept in late, and I called in sick at the diner. Then we went into Vibbington for lunch at one of the cafés there, ate our body weight in quesadillas and mango smoothies, ordered a ton of delicious ice cream and nutty chocolate brownies for afters. Zoe kept talking, talking, talking, trying to take my mind off things, which I guess helped. It was enough to know she was trying to help me, even if she wasn't having much success.

Then we wandered through Vibbington onto Keel Road, which is where we made the phonecall.

Keel Road is known in Vibbington for being the perfect place to leave anonymous calls. It's a dodgy area, and the local boys are always taping up the CCTV cameras, covering the lenses with sticky goo so many times that the council have stopped offering up funds to replace them. Like our estate, the crime rates are kind of shitty, and there's a huge drug problem; one gang was busted a couple of years ago for having a whole plantation of marijuana in someone's back garden.

But there's also a telephone box there.

So here we were, wandering onto the road and looking left and right for suspicious individuals, ready to empty our pockets. It took coins, so Zoe was careful in wiping them first before slipping her sleeves over her fingers and punching the numbers into the machine. She didn't ring the normal number. She had a little card in her pocket for a certain Officer Joy, and frowned as she squinted at the digits.

"She dealt with my sister last year when the whole Poppy thing happened." Poppy was the girl who had an affair with a teacher at the sixth form, one of Mira's best friends. "She's really nice. She used to bring my parents chocolates – Quality Streets, the real deal – because they were so cooperative in the investigation."

She scowled again as she tapped in the last few digits, then looked at me expectantly.

"What?"

"You'll have to speak," Zoe said. "Joy recognises my voice, I've spoken to her a hundred million times. Either that or she'll think I'm Mira, and we'll dig my sister into a huge pile of shit."

I sighed as I took the telephone, swallowing. I'd have to put on an accent. What accent? The only thing I was really good at was my Irish impression, from when Loz went through a huge Niall Horan phase. It wasn't that bad. But having a random Irish teenager tip the police off about Owen's mum lying dead in the forest might be a bit suspicious, and too far from the truth for Joy to take us seriously.

"Just speak more broadly, like a proper Northerner," Zoe suggested. "Go! Don't overthink it."

And before I could do anything else, she'd already pressed dial.

The phone was cold against my cheek. We were squashed into the phone box so tight I could hardly move, Zoe's breath hot on the back of my neck. The phone rang and rang and rang, until there was a sudden snuffling sound and a woman's voice was heard at the other end.

"Hello, PC Joy speaking. How can I help?"

She must have separate numbers for work and for home, I remember thinking. *Imagine being that rich.*

"Ha-hallo," I said, trying to make my voice sound as Yorkshire as possible. If I looked at Zoe, I'd either laugh or cry, and I wasn't sure either would really be appropriate. "I'm calling to report a murder."

Officer Joy paused down the line. I swallowed.

Suddenly, none of this felt like a good idea.

"A murder?" she echoed. "How did you get this number?"

"A… friend."

"You need to ring 999, or –"

"No, you don't get it. I need to tell *you*."

I could tell Joy must be panicking somewhat, because there was a rustling noise as she tried to find her paper, a pen, flapping to write this down.

"Okay, okay, I'm listening."

"I'm in Vibbington. Have you… have you heard of the Forest of Death?"

"The Forest of Death?" Officer Joy's voice was slightly pained as she hesitated, then said, "Yes, yes I have. Why do you ask? Is that where the murder occurred?"

Of *course* she'd heard of the Forest of Death; it had that name for a reason.

To my side, Zoe was nodding and egging me on, eyes wide.

"Tell her," she mouthed, "Tell her now, then hang up!"

"Yes," I continued, "I was walking my dog there when I found… found two bin bags, big black ones. They looked like… well. You know. And the smell. The smell was foul."

"You didn't actually see the body?"

"I mean… I didn't, but you could see the outline, you know. And the smell. Rotting flesh, morning breath. It couldn't have been anything else."

I should've just said yes. Instead of telling the truth, I should've said I'd seen a body, seen the arms and legs and flailing body parts.

But I didn't, and now she didn't believe me.

"Okay," she continued, but I could hear the disbelief in her voice. "You're saying you saw a black bag, and there was a foul smell, and so you *think* it could've been a body?"

"I'm sure of it."

"How sure?"

I glanced at Zoe for help, but she was shaking her head as though at a loss for words.

"I mean… I don't know what else it could've been. It looked like a body. It was a body. Please just get somebody out here to check on it, or I'll… I'll… I don't know what will happen to it. A child might stumble across it, or an animal, or somebody vulnerable. You need to check it out."

"Okay, okay, we'll get someone to go over the forest over the next few days, but we're a bit thin on the ground right now, you see. It might be difficult to get there before Monday…"

"Monday is fine. Monday. Monday."

Monday gave me time to prepare. To fully accept what was happening, and to say goodbye, to enjoy normality, whatever that might look like, before it was stolen from me forever.

"Can I have some more details about your location?" Joy continued. "Where abouts in the forest was this bag located?"

And so I told her. I told her about the path, the bracken, the way you veer sidewards once you reach the bridge, careering into the most overgrown parts of the woods, the parts you'd never usually dare venture. But my dog ran off through the trees, I had to follow him. That was how I smelled it. The pungent, reeking mass of flesh.

"Okay," Joy said, and I could hear her nodding, nodding, writing this down. "We'll certainly get some people to check it out this weekend, Monday at the latest."

"Thank you," I said. "Thank you, honestly."

"Can I get your name?"

Zoe shook her head, pulling the phone from my hand.

And then we hung up.

***

Part of me was scared the validity of our report would be seriously jeopardised by us hanging up on Joy. Clearly it wasn't, but that was what I was most scared of. This internal fear started eating me alive as I swum through Thursday, like I was doing breaststroke in treacle, heart thudding and thudding and thudding as the day progressed into night.

I watched TV with Dizzy, cuddling my little sister close on the sofa. And I tried to imagine how tomorrow would go down, or the day after, or the weekend, whenever they found Judy's body...

Dizzy would be heartbroken, spooked, crushed. Owen had slept in our house on and off since she was old enough to properly register my boyfriend's existence. He was just as much her friend as my boyfriend, an older brother or cousin, given our lack of close family members and the absence of those we did have.

And Mum... Mum loved Owen. She knew he wasn't perfect, but he was like a son to her, a son she'd never had. Since Judy was so awful, she'd taken care of Owen, taken care of him in a way she maybe shouldn't have. My mum was loving and caring and liked to look after people, and she'd taken Owen in for as long as I could remember, showering him in the love and support she thought he deserved,

Owen had been my best friend my entire life. I'd known him longer than Loz, Kara, Gethin, now Zoe, and he knew me inside out, both physically and metaphorically. There wasn't an inch of my body his fingers hadn't touched, a slice of my skin he'd failed to caress.

He was my boyfriend, and he loved me.

He loved me.

He did.

But now we were here.

Owen was going to be arrested. Which sucked. It made me feel sick with fear and guilt, and regret, regret so heavy it weighed on my stomach. When you love someone, you'll feel guilty leaving them, even if you know it's the right thing to do. It's human nature, as silly as that might sound.

Zoe had convinced me this was the right thing, but I wasn't so sure now. I trusted her, but still. I'd known her such a small amount of time compared to Owen. Owen was Owen, and Zoe was just a lovely, bubbly mess who made me feel somewhat alive, in all the ways Owen killed me. She'd injected colour into my dull life, turned black to green and blonde to the sun...

But Owen had given me his whole life, his body, his mind, soul.

And I'd just grassed him up to the police.

Grassed up my boyfriend, my boyfriend of five years, to

the police.

There was no coming back from this.

Not now.

dan's household supplies   55877
22 main street vibbington   aug 30 2024
east yorkshire ---- ---

item(s)   value

brush...........................£2.50
english sage....................£6.10
roller..........................£1.25

SUBTOTAL........................£9.85

total amount paid in cash

PLEASE RETAIN FOR YOUR RECORDS

THE GOODBYE

I painted by room green on Friday. Two coats of pretty sage, on each wall. I tore down my posters had Mum draw some leaves above the skirting board, which I filled in with a teeny tester pot of dark, glowing green.

And then I rang Loz.

"Yes?" she replied, voice sceptical. "I'm packing for Notts right now, Lilz. Can this wait?"

"You're going?"

"Yes, I'm going home tomorrow. I start college next Wednesday, and I need to be prepared –"

"I only need an hour or so. Please, Loz."

My best friend sighed, and I heard the familiar beep of her hanging up.

I was just filling in the last few leaves when there was a knock on the door. It was Loz, of course, holding two cans of Venom and a big smile, and she kicked her shoes off as I let her in.

"Peace offering," she said with a shrug. "For not even *trying* to understand."

"You're not to blame," I told her, taking one of the cans. It was cold and delicious and refreshing, the tropical flavour slipping down my throat.

"Have you been decorating?" Loz asked, frowning as she sniffed the air. "I can smell paint."

"Wait and see."

My bedroom door was closed, so I nudged it open with

my toe to show Loz. My best friend stopped. Mouth open and eyes wide, she stared around my new green paradise like she couldn't believe her eyes, then she took one step forward and entered the glen.

"It's green," is all she said.

My plants were drooping significantly and clearly didn't get on with the paint fumes, so I opened the window, aware of how stifling the room felt. But Loz didn't even notice. She just kept gazing round, eyes wide, as she took in the colour I'd picked. It was one of vintage furniture and rose gardens, of the grass in renaissance paintings. It was labelled "English sage" but had a touch of Scotland about it, of the highlands and dusty, dying grass, beautiful and endless and calm.

"When I said it was complicated," I told Loz, leading her to sit on my dustsheet-covered bed, "I really meant that."

"You've painted your bedroom green," she continued. "That's not very Lilz Dart of you."

"Because Lilz Dart is changing," I said. "*Lily* Dart is changing."

"Lily." Loz nodded, wrinkling her nose. "Gosh. You haven't been Lily in all the years I've known you."

Because I hadn't changed in all those years. Since meeting Loz, two little girls sat next to each other in a stuffy primary school classroom, I hadn't morphed into anything other than what I thought I was supposed to be. I'd been so afraid of becoming a better version of myself that along the way, I'd… failed. I'd failed myself in letting everything go, in watching my personality zoom out of control, stay safe in black clothes and loud music and a fear of anything not manmade.

It upset me, only because I didn't know how much of that was *me*. How much of Lilz Dart was Owen's girlfriend, not a real person.

It upset me, because I felt like I ruined my life just to stay that person, to stay Owen's, forever. I'd made one petty mistake after the other, each leading here, here, to now.

"I like the green," Loz added. "It's beautiful. And I like the plants. They do feel very Lilz, actually. Very *Lily*."

"I miss you," I said. "I miss you so much, Loz."

My best friend wrapped her arms around me and squeezed, planting a kiss on the side of my face as she hugged me.

"How can you miss me, Lilz? I'm right here. And I'm not going *anywhere*."

***

I tried to spend as much time with Mum and Dizzy as I could over the weekend, trying to maintain some level of normality for as long as was possible. They helped me redecorate my room, the three of us going into town on Saturday for new bed throws and cushions and funny little succulents to hang above my bed. Mum splashed out, which wasn't like her, but I think she was enjoying the fact I finally wanted my room to look nice, to match the rest of the house. I didn't blame her.

It looked wonderful, in the end. Peaceful. I bought a whole host of new books to read from the little shop in town, choosing stuff I'd never heard of but which the girl working there said would be right up my street. Books about teens my age, about to turn eighteen, entering pivotal stages in their lives. Books with gay characters, bi characters, books about racism and bullying and all kinds of other topics. They were all brightly coloured and the text didn't look too small, and I thought I'd be okay reading them. Probably.

We ordered Indian food and ate it on the sofa on Saturday

night, finally relaxing. Because if the police hadn't found Judy's body yet, surely they wouldn't until Monday, now? And if that was the case, there was no point dwelling on it.

Chicken korma, plain white rice, delicious poppadoms, hot and crunchy and salty. I lay back after to enjoy the telly and the gentle buzz of Mum testing Dizzy on her French vocab, as the room spun and my belly felt full and delicious and satisfied. And life was good. Life was very, very good.

On Sunday, Owen came round. Mum decided to do a makeshift roast, so I rang him in the morning, asked if he'd like to join us. He was out with Gethin and the boys; I could hear them jeering and laughing in the background, but there was no Kara to be heard, unless she was keeping her horrid, scratchy laugh under wraps for once. Owen said yes, he'd love to come round for the roast. What time?

Which is how he ended up on my bed in my new green room for the very last time, smiling as he edged closer to me. I kissed him. I kissed him hard, so hard that his eyes opened wide as he leaned back and smiled into me, both our hearts beating fit to burst.

"Wow," he said, eyebrows raised. "Okay, Lilz."

We continued kissing well into the afternoon, following our familiar pattern, the ritual we knew so well. Soon the clothes were off, and I was lying against my new green throw, the terracotta cushions by my head, staring into Owen's dark eyes as his body pressed into mine and a skyful of stars erupted above our heads.

The last time.

The last time for Lilz and Owen, and he had no idea, no idea at all. Unlike our first, there was a wall between us only I could see, feel. A wall built on lies and trust, or a lack thereof, a wall impossible to tear down. A wall Owen would soon be made aware of, when the police came knock-knock-knocking on his door, *let us in, let us in!*

It was bittersweet, though. Because this was *Owen*, and I loved Owen. But it was over. I think I should've realised that way back in June, when our relationship crossed a line nobody should ever have to cross. Nothing I could say or do would change that now.

When we redressed and made our way downstairs to Mum and Dizzy, the table was set and Dizzy was proudly taking photos of her big dish of stuffing. Mum had made chicken and roast potatoes from a packet, boiled some broccoli and made a jugful of Bisto gravy. But it was delicious, and warm, and homely. And sat here, with all the people I loved most gathered round me, I felt happy. So, so happy.

Until I remembered that we'd never have this again, and reached to clutch Owen's hand under the table.

I think he could tell something was wrong, because his jaw locked and he couldn't take his eyes off me, and they were searching, searching, looking for an answer.

But I couldn't provide one.

And when I kissed him goodbye that night, I knew, for sure, that it was the last time we'd ever be *us*.

Vibbington Community

geoff sharpe
does anywon no why theres police gone into the forest???

elvin carter
probably some hippy drugged out of their mind stuck up a tree #britishhumour

geoff sharpe
looks serrios, they have got dogs. i reckon murrder

jenna collins
maybe you should all stop speculating and consider those inolved?? *eye roll*

THE THIRD

Monday passed without a flutter. I was on edge, of course, but there was nothing, not a sound, from the internet or the local grapevine, not from Owen or Kara or Gethin, not from Loz all the way in Notts. And when Zoe popped round to check on me, we both concluded that us hanging up must have given the police the hump, that they were no longer interested in investigating the forest.

I was all for leaving another, slightly more urgent tip-off, but Zoe told me we should wait a few days to see if anything came of all this. And so I did.

The third of September dawned bright and early, a Tuesday, sun streaming through my window. Whether the sun lasted is another matter, but eight hours ago, there I was, waking up and stretching and yawning.

I clicked onto Facebook first.

There were a few posts from the Vibbington community group, but one in particular caught my eye.

does anywon no why theres police gone into the forest???

The comments were all pretty similar. Confusion and worry, given the forest's past record of suicide and overdosing and drugs. But nobody seemed to know why a grainy picture of two fluorescent figures had been captured at dawn creeping into the forest with torches and worried expressions, or why they'd returned two hours later with a van and a stretcher and a whole load of other officers.

They'd found Judy Sharpley's body. That had to be it.

I got up and dressed around nine, after lounging about in bed scrolling through my phone. I was still on sick leave from the diner, and would be for as long as I could pull it off. Zoe said she'd tell me once they started to get frustrated, but for now, the thought of going back to work made me feel queasy. There were much more important things at stake than burgers and fried eggs.

Mum went to work in the morning, but was back by lunch, making the most of Dizzy's last day off school. We all went back tomorrow, though God knows what will happen now, with the whole town in an uproar. But that's not important. Mum dropped Diz off to go see a friend at one; they were heading into town to refresh their school wardrobes for year nine, to buy accessories and bags and pencil cases, nice new shoes.

I decided to have a bath at two. I filled it full of hot, soapy water and lay there, basking in it, the first bath I'd had since Judy. It was warm and cosy and lovely, the window ajar and letting in a nice, fresh breeze. I used bodywash, of course. It was on the edge of the bath when I heard the knock on the door.

You know the rest.

How Mum started shouting up the stairs for me to come down, and how I tried to clamber out of the bath and knocked my bodywash onto the floor. It was lemon, and yellow goo oozed over the floorboards as I wrapped myself in a towel. I pulled on the crusty clothes I usually wore for work because I'd barely had the effort to put anything in the wash recently, and everything was a little fusty and crusty and grim, reeking of burger fat.

Down the stairs I went, stepping over Dizzy's crap. Owen's messages were urgent, freaked, but what could he do? It was too late now. The police were here, and they knew what happened.

Or so I thought.

wtf is happening???
why are there police outside your block?

You tell me, I wanted to say. *Isn't this all your fault?*

Puck and Barker, they were the officers. Nice guys, friendly, smiling at me as I took my seat and nodded at them bleakly. At least they were nice when they proceeded to turn my life around, to strip it from good to bad in a matter of seconds. At least they did it well.

"Lily Dart?" Puck – or maybe Barker – asked, trying to smile but falling into a grimace. "We have some… questions for you."

I nodded, trying to act calm, collected, like I didn't know what they were talking about and didn't really care.

"Okay," I said. "Okay."

"We found a body in the woods this morning, on the other side of Vibbington," Barker told me, but the words, the specifics of them, fell on deaf ears. I already knew what he was going to say, what he was trying to tell me. I thought they had it all figured out. "An adult female, presumed to be in her early forties. We're still trying to identify her, but given the state of the body and how long it's been there, it might take some time."

Wait.

The body hadn't yet been identified?

I froze, trying to keep my expression neutral, but my heart was racing and my mind was whirring.

If the body hadn't been identified, why were they here?

Why had they come to speak to me?

This wasn't part of the plan. The plan was that the police would come to me *after* they identified the body, after they spoke to those close to her. That they'd figure out my connection to the deceased and call on our flat on the off-chance I might have information, that they could call me a suspect.

Puck took over, frowning at me. "The reason we're here, Lily, is because a jumper was left tied round her body, a school jumper, with a Vibbington Secondary School and Sixth Form logo. Your name was written in the label. Lily Dart."

My name was written in the label.

Of *course*.

I glanced at Mum, face turning more and more crimson by the moment. She was staring back, eyes wide. Every school year, since I first started at Vibbington Secondary almost six years ago, Mum had written my name in the label of all our school jumpers, of which there had been a whole jumble piled into Dizzy's drawer that night. She wore mine now – they were too expensive to buy new. I grabbed one because I assumed a school jumper would be impossible to identify; all the other kids wear the same. I completely forgot they were *labelled*.

"Do you have any way to explain this?"

I turned back to the officers, mouth gaping.

"I…"

"I think we need to continue this conversation down the station," Puck said, turning to Mum. "Ms Dart, if you could find someone to supervise your youngest daughter while you both –"

"No."

Puck and Barker turned to stare at me, startled by my outburst, the certainty in my voice. Barker stood first, taking a step towards me.

"If you're refusing to cooperate…"

"No, I'm not refusing to cooperate." I glanced at Mum, who looked completely bewildered, frown lines on her forehead more evident than ever. "I know who the body is. And I know who killed her, and how."

Puck and Barker were serious now, poised to grab me – or do *something* to me, should I be having them on – and stood, hands on their belts, as I stared back.

"It was Owen Sharpley." My voice was cool, level.

I didn't feel cool, or level.

I wanted to cry, to crumble, but I couldn't. I *wouldn't*.

"Owen Sharpley?" Barker echoed. "Is that someone you know?"

"He's my boyfriend." I took a deep breath. "The body you found is his mum."

I knew from Mum's expression that she understood, then. That she knew I was telling the truth. Owen's mum had been missing for months, and maybe my own mother was naïve in thinking she really would just run off like that. Judy Sharpley was mean, but she wasn't a monster without reason. She had a life here, once upon a time. A life she'd supposedly rejected to run off with a random old college friend, disappearing from Vibbington's face.

"His mum?" Puck echoed. "And what's her name?"

"Judy," I said. "Judy Sharpley. She… she used to live across the road."

Puck nodded, exchanging a glance with Barker, who immediately tapped something into the tablet he was holding. "Okay, okay. Judy Sharpley. And how do you know the body we found is hers?"

"Because my boyfriend... blackmailed me into helping him hide it," I said, voice still calm, flat. "After he killed her."

The gasp from Mum was involuntary, because she quickly clapped a hand over her mouth. But she was staring at me as though she needed at answer, shaking her head, not wanting to believe it. Because I didn't want to believe it, either.

But I had to.

"You're saying Owen Sharpley, you boyfriend, killed his mother?" Barker said now. "And that he made you help him hide the body, and that that's why your name was on the label?"

I nodded. "Yes. He drowned her in the bath, then he... he... sawed her up, with a bread knife. You know, one of those serrated ones. He chopped her in half."

If I looked at Mum, I knew I'd cry. Her face would be green and her eyes would be full of tears, and I wouldn't have been able to stop myself.

"Your boyfriend drowned his mother, then chopped up her body for disposal?"

I nodded again, and Puck and Barker exchanged glances. The four of us rose, knowing instinctively what was going to happen next.

"We're going to have to ask you both to come down to the station," Puck said. "Barker, get backup round to Owen Sharpley's place. We can't let him get away. What was the address, Miss Dart?"

And so I told him. I told him where Owen lived, because I was telling them the truth, telling them where they'd find my boyfriend, my Owen, and what had happened that day in June.

Only I wasn't telling the truth.

Not even a little bit.

Are you surprised?

Because Owen hadn't drowned Judy that day. Of *course* he hadn't. Owen didn't have a violent bone in his body. He was meek and mild and, no matter how much hurt Judy had caused him, he didn't have the strength to kill her, the conviction.

When he'd come to me on June second, whimpering and deathly pale, he hadn't explicitly said what he wanted to happen next.

But I knew. Of *course* I knew.

Owen had chopped her up, that's for sure. In a moment of blind panic, no doubt, caused by worry that we were harbouring a dead body, panic when he stared into the bath at his mother's body, lifeless and limp.

But he hadn't killed her. Oh, no.

That was all me.

lilz???

lilz wtf is going on

they're making me go
to the police station ilz

lilz what did you tell
them???

answer me!

THE STATEMENT

I was sat in the interview room for about two minutes before Puck came back, weary and clutching a notebook. And now here I am, sat across from him, Mum to one side and Barker guarding the door.

I'm cold. It's cold in here. Because there's no sun, obviously. The window is tiny and covered in bars, and the only furniture in the room is a table and chairs.

I wanted that nice Officer Joy to come and sit in on the interview, because from what Zoe said, she was ten times more likely to listen to my side of the story. She'd be sympathetic to the female cause, or something; male officers are much more likely to simply blame the girl.

"Hello, Lilz." Puck smiles at me, nods at Mum. "We need to ask you a few questions before we let you write your statement."

"Okay."

I've seen people write statements on TV, in documentaries. It's an important part of putting somebody behind bars; to set the record straight. And if that's what has to happen, I'll do it. I'll blame Owen, write lies all over that silly sheet. I'll sign my signature and grit my teeth and stare Owen Sharpley in the eyes as he tries to defame me in the courtroom, trembling with rage, hand ready to fly out by his side.

"Can I ask a question first?" Mum asks, frowning. "Is it definitely Judy Sharpley? I mean, has there been a formal identification?"

"There has." Puck looks haunted, then, clearly brought back to the image of unwrapping Judy's body in the woods to reveal – "It's definitely Judith Sharpley."

Judith.

She never looked like a Judith.

Mum nods, sinking back into her chair, and for a moment I think she's going to cry.

But she doesn't, of course.

And the interview picks up from there.

"So, Lilz," Puck says, readdressing me. "I want you to tell me exactly how you know Judith, and how you know her son, Owen. You say the two of you are dating?"

I nod. *Dating* doesn't quite feel like the right term for what Owen and I have – had – but I suppose it's the most accurate descriptor. "Yes. I've been with Owen since we were twelve, so almost five years. But... before that we were best friends, for literally years and years, ever since we were kids. My family is basically his, and vice versa."

"And you two spent a lot of time together?"

"I see Owen almost every day."

Puck grunts, but averts his gaze to Barker. "Okay, okay. So the two of you were close?"

"Closer than close."

When his eyes meet mine again, they're sceptical. "Five years, eh? That's a long time for a teen relationship. I think when I was that age, my most serious girlfriend stuck around about two months before she gave me the elbow."

I want to say that Owen and I are different, that we aren't like the other couples we know, but that seems stupid now. I shrug instead, like I don't have a clue how Owen and I managed to keep our relationship alive for so many years.

"Moving on," Puck continues. "I want you to take me back to the last year. We estimate Judith's body has been outside in those woods for about three months. What do you have to say about that?"

Exactly three months, actually, I want to say, but instead I just shrug. "It... it was June, yes, I'm pretty sure."

"June." Puck appears to agree with me. "And what was your relationship like in June, Lilz?"

"It was good. Normal."

"And how was Owen?"

How *was* Owen?

"He was good, too. Normal. I... I had no indication that he'd do anything like that."

Puck sighs, adding, "That's often the case, isn't it?"

I nod, like I'm supposed to understand what that means.

"Can you remember what happened the day Judith died, Lilz? If you can, I'd like you to talk us through it. It would really help to get a timeline straight, figure out the sequence of events which led to Owen's alleged strangulation."

Alleged. I almost snigger at that.

I look at Mum. Her lips are pressed tight together and are white with effort, and she looks like she's still in shock. She should be picking up Dizzy from town right about now, but instead she's here, nodding along to everything this man is saying, acting like everything's absolutely fine.

"I... I mean, yeah. Yeah, I can."

"Okay, great. Just take a minute, collect your thoughts, and start where you want."

But I don't need to collect my thoughts. I've had the last three months to think about what happened on June third, to construct a story in my mind. Over time, it became so real I almost started to believe it was true. But in those first few days, all the effort came from convincing *myself* that Owen was a murderer. From repeating over and over and over in my mind that it was *Owen* who drowned his mother, imagining him pressing her shoulders down into the water and watching her struggle for air...

The image in my head is crystal-clear now, but not because it's a reality. It's a reconstruction. Owen's hands have overtaken mine, my slender white fingers morphing into his bigger, broader ones. I can remember the way Judy's naked body writhed and rippled in the water because I *saw* it, watched it. I remember the noises she made that night because I heard them –

And yes, you read that correctly. *That night*. Not that *morning*, the morning of June third, when Owen rang me to tell me Judy was dead, *his mum was dead*. Although Owen wasn't certain of it, Judy Sharpley had been dead all night. He stood outside the door as I drowned her, tears running down his face in silent relief. And then we'd gone to sleep in our separate beds, him promising to dispose of the body, promising I wouldn't have to think about it again. Only he hadn't. Worried that she might still be breathing, that he had to dispose of her quickly, he'd *chopped her up*.

Tears are running down my own face freely now as I glance back up at Puck, Mum placing a hand on my back and indicating for me to go on. I know what I need to say. I've got this practised. I can do it, *I can do it*.

And so I do. I tell Puck all about Owen, his hands digging into Judy's flesh as he pushed her below the water. I tell him that Owen rang me the next morning to say he needed my help, and told me I had to help him get rid of the body, because if I didn't, he'd find a way to frame me, send me to jail. It's weak reason, but what else am I supposed to say? Puck nods and nods and nods, looking so sympathetic, and Mum chokes on a sob.

They feel so bad for me. Of course they do.

And if I'm being completely honest…

I do, too.

@thereallilzdart

this is just
the beginning

THE TRUTH

I was round at Owen's when I heard the commotion. Sat on his bed as he chatted to his mum through the bathroom door. I'd gone round after Mum and Dizzy were asleep, bored and fed up of my psych homework. Judy was in the bath. Soaking away the woes of being a large, sad woman, skin grey, face filled with weariness.

"What do you *want* me to do?" Owen asked. I remember hearing a hard edge to his voice, something sharp, nasty. He wasn't happy with his mother, that was for sure.

I don't even know what happened next. All I do know is that a screaming match erupted out of nowhere, and suddenly Owen and his mum were throwing things and shouting, shouting, furious at one another, bath bombs and Judy's large jar of bath salts landing with an electric smash on the tiles above the bath.

It's horrible to think about now, but that's what was happening. A fight. Until it wasn't. And Judy said, in cold blood, voice as serious as I'd ever heard her, "You should never have been born, Owen Sharpley."

I think that's what did it.

Owen's face was white as he came back into the room, body trembling with anger. I took one look at him and wanted to burst into tears. I loved this man. I loved him so much, and he was being treated like *shit* by his own mother.

"I want her dead, Lilz." His voice was flat and his eyes were dull, but I knew, in that moment, that he really meant it. His relationship with Judy had always been fraught, but this was different. It was serious. Owen had had enough.

He wasn't asking for an assassination, but it was near enough. I didn't need to think twice before springing up and racing to the bathroom.

It all happened so fast.

The scream, me crying, "How could you *do* such a thing?"

My hands, grabbing Judy Sharpley's shoulders and pushing down, down, down.

Her head, her bulbous head, disappearing below the water. Her eyes were terrified as they stared up at me through the murky liquid, grimy with her own bodily fluids and the amount of bath products she'd used. Her hair spread around her head as she kicked her fat legs and the rolls on her stomach blub-blubbered, slapping against one another like pigs playing in the mud.

Until she stopped.

Just… stopped.

Stopped moving, stopped blowing bubbles beneath the water.

Her body was still as I stepped back into the bathroom, feet on the bathmat.

"Lilz?" Owen was standing at the door, staring at me with wide, terrified eyes.

"She's sleeping," I said, half to convince myself, half to convince him. "She's asleep."

"Lilz," he echoed, the fear in his voice so abject I could've ripped it away and wrapped it round my neck. "Lilz, what did we do?"

What did we do…

Not what did *you* do.

It was both of us. Both of us had done this, had caused

this.

"I need to go," I said to Owen, but only because I felt sick, so sick, like I was about to spew everywhere. "Owen, I –"

"She's sleeping," Owen repeated, as Judy's body bobbed above the water, head unsubmerged and eyes staring blankly forward. "She's just taking a nap."

And maybe she was. How would we ever know? Because the next day, Owen had chopped her in half. Severed her body, right down the middle.

And there isn't really any coming back from that.

oli @everyone
has everyone heard the rumours?? mental
isn't it *mind blown*

eva | head girl @bigmanoli
with all due respect, i don't think we should
speculate until we know hard fact. this is such
a tragic event. rip judy.

gethin @everyone
yeah come on, let's not shit on owen when
he's down
but they were always a weird couple...

loz @everyone
whatever owen's done, do NOT bring lilz into
this. he's a shithead and whatever happened
was entirely his fault.

gethin @laurenaccorn
we don't know that yet, do we?
pizzas at mine later? i think we all need to
discuss this big time

THE END

I write my statement. I write my lies. I give it to Puck, who nods and says we can leave.

And there, in the waiting room, is Owen.

Sat, all by himself, on a little plastic chair. He looks so small. Small and pale and fragile, all dark eyes and floppy hair and frown as he stares at me, stares like he's never seen me before, and says, "Thanks. Thanks a lot."

I'm scared Mum will retaliate for me, but she just shakes her head sadly and begins to walk away.

"I'll wait outside," she says, and I nod.

I know there must be CCTV in here, so I don't want to say too much. And yet I know what I'm doing as I sit down next to Owen, far enough away that we're not touching, and turn my head to look at him. He does the same, and we simply stare for a few seconds before one of us breaks.

"Why?" he says eventually. "I assume it was you who gave them the tip-off. Just… why?"

"Because of Kara." Is that why? Maybe, maybe not. I don't think I'll ever know for sure.

"You grassed me up to the police because I cheated on you?"

I start to nod, but Owen shakes his head in disgust.

"No, Lilz. No. Surely there's more to this than… that."

"It just felt like the right thing to do."

"The right thing?"

"The right… outcome. The only way to make you see

sense."

"See sense?"

"Face up to it. Accept what happened that day, instead of running from it, ruining my life in the process."

"Lilz. What the fuck?"

But I'm already standing up again, because I'm scared that if I stay for much longer, I'll never want to leave. And I need to. I've done my duty. I've settled the score. *Owen* killed his mother that day, not me. Even if he didn't technically hold her head under the water, wasn't the one to watch the last puffs of air escape through bubbles from her nose, he's the murderer, not me. Never me.

"I gave you the best years of my life, Lilz." His voice sounds like it's going to crack in half, so I take that as my cue to leave.

"And you took mine."

And then I walk out of the station to Mum's waiting arms, without a backwards glance.

thanks a lot, lilz.

thanks a lot.

this contact is now blocked

acknowledgements

As I write these acknowledgements just months before release day, I think 'Dead Fine' might be my favourite book I've written so far.

My third self-published book, and third addition to the Emma Literary Universe. A book I poured my heart and soul into, but still managed to write through so much happiness and laughter, inspired by long East Yorkshire summers and days at "Maythorpe Beach", enjoying the sun; and inspired by ketchup stains on a white plate, blood from a razor on the edge of the bath, sunlight streaming through the window and staining everything orange, like a bleached bloodstain.

I wrote this book because I love summer, and I love murder mysteries, and I love UKYA. Combine the three, and you have something hot and sticky and saturated, energy drinks going warm in the sun, corner shops open too late, ice cream dripping down a clean-shaven leg. I wrote this for anyone who has ever romanticised the idea of summer love, or a childhood crush turned to something more; for anyone who doesn't understand how bittersweet supposed perfection can be. I wrote this book for you, Sana, my writing partner-in-crime and blood-splattered author friend. And for you, Martha-May... you who romanticises everything, and loves love more than it deserves.

So firstly, I want to say thank you to you two, and for our whole group chat. Bridget, Hannah, Christina, Isobel... I'm so grateful for the support and genuine interest you've shown my works over the last few years. It means so much to know that there's a body of young writers out there encouraging each other to succeed, and to write more, always. Our community is so special, and I can't wait to see your own works flourish as we grow and change, and write a million more characters into our world.

Thank you to the UKYA community, which has been such a supportive space since I first embarked on my publishing journey. Thank you to the self-publishing community across the internet, and to Haley Brown, Katherine Gray and Cheryl van Gent in particular for your mutual advice and support – you're going to do great things!

Thank you to my mum, for helping me edit my stories and letting me know when things don't make much sense. Thank you to the rest of my family, and for everyone who ever thought I could possibly release my books into the world like this.

Thank you to Driffield Secondary School and Sixth Form, who influenced this book more than any other. To the head of sixth form for being much better than Mr Roberts, and everyone else who made my time there so special, something to treasure.

Thank you to my friends, for the photos and daytrips and memories made. Thank you to Hannah for sitting in Costa for hours on end while I made the title pages for each chapter, and for making one caramel iced latte last a whole afternoon.

Thank you. Thank you for buying, and for reading, and for giving my books a chance. Whether this is your first trip to the ELU, or your last... I hope you stick around, because I'm very, very happy to have you here.

NOBODY KNOWS...

GUIDED

BOOK ONE

EMMA SMITH

NOBODY KNOWS WHAT HAPPENED
THAT NIGHT... NOBODY BUT MACEY.

NORMAL, RIGHT?

MID-
NIGHT
SHER
-BET

EMMA SMITH

YOUNG LOVE NEVER LASTS...
BUT FRIENDSHIP MEANS FOREVER.

EMMA SMITH

is a young adult author from Yorkshire, England. She wrote and illustrated her first "book" when she was seven years old and hasn't stopped writing since. When she's not walking on the beach or drinking an iced coffee with a crumpet and some chocolate, you'll probably find her reading something dark and mysterious… and most certainly YA.

@themmasmith on Instagram

emmasmithbooks.com

Printed in Great Britain
by Amazon

34870984R00199